# Spirit
# Within
# Her

John and Anne Spencer are active researchers in many fields of the paranormal. John is the author of several books including *Perspectives* published by MacDonalds and *The Paranormal* published by Hamlyn. John and Anne together compiled and edited *The Encyclopedia of Ghosts and Spirits* published by Headline. They are both personal friends of Heather Woods and her family.

# Spirit Within Her

## THE STORY OF HEATHER WOODS AND THE STIGMATA

as told to
John and Anne Spencer

B🌿XTREE

First published in Great Britain in 1994 by Boxtree Limited

Text © John and Anne Spencer 1994

The right of John and Anne Spencer to be identified as Authors of this Work has been asserted by them in accordance with the Copyright, Designs and Patents Act 1988.

1 3 5 7 9 10 8 6 4 2

Designed by Robert Updegraff
Printed and bound in Finland by WSOY for

Boxtree Limited
Broadwall House
21 Broadwall
London  SE1 9PL

A CIP catalogue entry for this book is available from the British Library.

ISBN  1 85283 496 X

Picture Acknowledgements

Front cover photographs:
top and bottom right © The Press Association
middle left: ©The Estate of Heather Woods
Back cover photograph © Dave Cooper

Plate Section:
© Betty Eades 5 (top right and bottom left); © The Press Association 6 (bottom), 7 (top); © Hazel Spencer 1 (top and bottom); © John and Anne Spencer 6 (top), 7 (bottom left and right), 8; © The Estate of Heather Woods 1 (middle), 2–3 (photograph by Matt White), 4, 5 (top left and bottom right)

# CONTENTS

Behold, I have graven you on the palms of my hands

ISAIAH 49:16

# FOREWORD

*This story is told largely by Heather in her own words. It is compiled by us from over twelve hours of video-taped interview, over 130,000 words of dictated memories, access to all of Heather's private diaries, and access to the 60,000 or so words of writings that Heather believed were channelled guidance from God. Included in our many interviews with Heather was a period of three days when she lived with us both and allowed us – even encouraged us – to 'drive her hard' to get her story out. It is her belief that part of her mission for Jesus Christ is to tell her story as widely as possible. We are both privileged to have been able to share this experience at so personal a level, and to have found in Heather a friend – far more important to us than the none the less undeniable fact that she is a remarkable woman, with a truly remarkable story.*

*Heather's memories cannot be 100 per cent accurate – we believe that no-one's can be – particularly given the length of time which has elapsed since some of the events she recalls. We have verified as much as possible with other people involved in the various stages of her life, and her memories bear up very well. There are times when it appears that minor details are confused, and times when her memories have been romanticized or exaggerated. Her childhood memories of course sometimes fall into this category. However, these memories are what she sincerely believes happened; they form the basis of the person that she is in her own mind. In order to appreciate the real Heather, the reader must understand that it is her beliefs – rather than some objective set of facts – that are important.*

*Where her memories perhaps do injustice to others, we have tried to present their alternative viewpoint; in some cases we have changed names to avoid embarrassing those we could not locate or interview.*

*Understanding the suffering she has triumphed over, understanding her religious mission, and certainly understanding such exceptional claims as the stigmata, requires a deep understanding of the person that is the real Heather. This book aims to provide that understanding.*

J S and A S

*Note: Heather's own words are indicated by the use of standard typeface; our own comments or interviews with others are indicated by the use of italics.*

# ACKNOWLEDGEMENTS

In researching this book we have had considerable help from many people, and we extend our thanks to them for their time and trouble in giving us interviews, and for the additional efforts many have made in doing further research on our behalf.

We extend particular thanks to:

Heather's sisters, Dawn and Angela. Heather's son, Lindsay. Heather's daughter, Barbara. Heather's father, George. Heather's aunt, May Bull, and her husband, Roy.

Father (Bishop) Eric Eades' wife, Betty. Helen Whatton. Bishop Marcus of Heather's church.

Doctor Bhanja, Heather's doctor for over two decades. Mr Lupton. Dr Nigel Chapman.

From the Homes and care institutions: Gill Clapson, Ann Espin, Nora Baines. Thanks also to Jane Heaney of Lincolnshire County Council for her own research into the Children's Homes and for putting us in contact with former staff and children from the Homes. May we stress that at no time was confidentiality breached by her actions: she always contacted our intervie-wees and gave them the opportunity of contacting us; never did she supply names without the person's knowledge or consent.

We would like to extend a very special thanks to Hazel – Heather's eldest sister – and her husband, Warwick. They both gave up a good deal of their time, and went to a great deal of trouble, to ensure that we had as wide a range of supporting material for the book as was available. Our thanks also for their hospitality, and for their friendliness when they stayed with us, during the closing weeks of drafting the manuscript.

We also thank those who have provided photographic material for inclusion in the book; apart from Heather herself that includes Hazel and Warwick, Lindsay, and Betty Eades.

# INTRODUCTION

*At the age of nine Heather Woods came home to find her suitcases packed. Before she could ask why, she and her sisters were uprooted from their happy home. For the rest of her life until adulthood, Heather was shunted from one institutional Home to another. She endured sexual abuse, bone-aching physical violence and mind-numbing mental cruelty at the hands of a variety of her 'benefactors'. She ran away over thirty times, to be punished whenever she was caught.*

*While other children drifted off to 'dreamland' to the sound of lullabies sung by their parents, Heather often fell asleep to the sound of her own sobbing. An aching memory of her childhood was of sitting in the 'best' room of the care Home, dressed in her best clothes, waiting for a promised visit from her parents, knowing that they wouldn't turn up – just as they hadn't turned up the week before. No caring parent of loved children can read her description of straining her neck up to see a car outside – hoping it meant a visit for her – without pulling their own children closer into their arms and thanking God for a life with love.*

*In her formative years the abuse was coupled with tragedies, including her mother's breakdown, imprisonment and eventual suicide, and her own attempted 'suicide', or at least cry for help. In later years she would endure the birth of a brain-damaged son, the death of a husband she loved dearly, and separation from her daughter.*

*By the age of forty-four, when we spoke to her, her body was racked by breakdown; it had endured cancers and other illnesses that had required many visits to hospitals, eight major operations, and most of her major organs operated on or removed.*

*The story of her triumph over all this is spiritually uplifting, and peopled with wonderful souls: 'Pop', who took her in from 'care' when she was eighteen years old and gave her her first real home; her priest, Father Eric, who was to share in her most extraordinary religious and spiritual moments; and Ray, her husband. Heather's description of their joint combat with their own histories – Ray was also an abused child – is soul-lifting. It was two years before they really made love, and then they clung together gently for hours – two human beings touching each other without violence – feeling pleasure in physical contact for the first time in their lives.*

9

*Then in 1989 she took steps on the path to a religious mission, though she hardly knew it at the time. She has channelled messages from the spirit world, and was part of a healing group using psychic healing with enormous success. She became an ordained deacon.*

*But a miracle was yet to come. In 1992 she underwent an extraordinary phenomenon: the stigmata – marks representing the bleeding wounds of Christ on her hands, feet and side and the appearance of crosses on her forehead. These were shared as they happened with her congregation and, of course, the medical profession. Hers was filmed and photographed probably more than any other equivalent case in history.*

*She is sure it is all part of God's mission for her – a mission that she believes is the reason why her body has mystified her doctors in its ability to keep going. Heather knows it is for His purpose.*

*Hers is a story of triumph over a tortured mind and an abused body by an unyielding spirit; it embraces human resolve, the paranormal, miracles and religious vision. It will transform your life as you read it.*

# CHAPTER ONE

# Spirit Rebellious

## Formative years

HEATHER WOODS WAS BORN *Heather Bradley in Lincoln on 6th June 1949, the third of five girls: Carol, Hazel, Heather, Dawn and Angela. The family lived in that city at St Giles, and soon moved to a house in Carlton Grove. Her parents, George and Winifred Bradley, had married young. Heather always believed that her father had felt pressured into marriage by her mother; that her mother probably threatened suicide to get her own way. (George denied this in an interview given to us, but acknowledged that such a belief must have coloured Heather's thinking about her early years. He did point out that his first real shock was in discovering that his wife was only sixteen when he first met her – she had told him she was older.)*

*The eldest daughter, Carol, died of cancer at the age of three; the first of many pressures and strains on Winifred that would soon prove too much for her. Not long after Carol's death George left the RAF under pressure from his wife, who had become somewhat neurotic about his flying, and who was already being treated for mental illnesses.*

*Heather's recollection of these years is that her father embarked on a series of enterprises, some less legal than others, that occasionally resulted in what Heather refers to as 'moonlight flits' – leaving in the dead of night to avoid detection. Other members of the family seem to have had the same impression but George told us this was not the case; he denied any wrongdoing or illegal activities. He believes that his various jobs as a sales rep may have given the impression that he was moving around a lot. Again, though, he acknowledged that Heather's beliefs must have influenced her thinking towards her childhood years.*

*A third difference between George and his daughters was that both Heather and Hazel recalled their father's many liaisons with other women, describing him, perhaps fairly generously, as a 'bit of a devil'. George insists these claims are untrue, that it was his wife's liaisons with men that strained their marriage.*

11

*Heather's recall of the first years of her life is basically warm, a home and a family and the games and joys of childhood. She doesn't, she admits, remember all that much of it. Given what was to follow in the next four decades, this is hardly surprising. The background was almost surely one of strain between her parents; certainly theirs was a turbulent relationship.*

*The first horror of Heather's world was all too painful, and all too terrible. She was seven years old when 'Steven' – someone well known to her – found her alone in the house. (Heather asked for this man not to be identified, but her sister Hazel confirmed to us that Heather had told other members of her family about these events.)*

He forced me to kiss him, at least he kissed me and I could feel him forcing his tongue into my mouth. I didn't like it but he was threatening me with his strength and telling me at the same time not to tell anyone else. It was to be our secret. He kept telling me that it was fun, it was a game. Then he started pushing his hands into my clothing and touching me. I was really frightened; he kept telling me it was nice, it was a game and it was fun. But he was using all his strength to force me at the same time.

He worked himself up too much and I remember he forced me onto my back and pulled my underwear off. His arm was stretched above mine, holding my arms down on the floor and I could feel him undoing his own clothes. I was really scared. He penetrated me, I could feel him pushing himself inside me, but all the time he was telling me not to tell anyone, and telling me it was fun, it was a game, our special secret.

*Hazel recalls that the same person once took her aside while the family were playing in the woods near their home and 'tried to get up my skirt'. Dawn remembers him kissing her on the lips. Their father, George, also confirmed to us that he 'had been suspicious' of this person and suggested he had caused other family disturbances of a similar nature.*

*Heather's early life was all too often one of intrusion upon her; in care Homes and institutions there was little in the way of privacy or self-value. But even before the institutions imposed their will over her, Heather was having to face this man oppressing her, intruding her, violating her. It must have been an awful experience, and yet to Heather what was to follow was at least as bad – not least because it would be in the places where she was supposed to be cared for and protected. It is significant that Heather has few memories of her life before the rape; it seems that this violation cut her off from her own early – and possibly largely pleasant – memories.*

*Heather was unable to share this rape and abuse with her mother until later in life, but she thinks perhaps something of this person's attitude or actions became known to her parents. It was after this episode that her father announced they were moving to a farm. Whether the move was connected to her father's work or to do with the abuse she was never sure. But she remembers that she came home from school one day, and there was a removal lorry waiting to take her and the family away. No opportunity to say goodbye to friends; just cases packed and away. It was a pattern that would typify much of the remainder of her life as a teenager and as an adult.*

# On the farm

*If the child in Heather suffered in being forced to move from her first home, she quickly found solace in the tranquillity and beauty of the farm that was her next home. Her father worked for a company selling farm supplies and he rented the farm through a contact he met in his job. George was out or away most of the day. Heather doesn't remember seeing her father much during their time there.*

*The late 1950s was a time of social and political upheaval: the EEC was formed; King Feisal of Iraq was murdered in a coup; General De Gaulle became President of France; and Britain reverberated to the slogans of the Campaign for Nuclear Disarmament and the Aldermaston march. Elvis Presley was drafted into the US army and Buddy Holly died in a plane crash.*

*In the Vatican they were laying to rest Pope Pius XII. The white smoke announced that Cardinal Roncalli had been elected to the Papacy, taking the name Pope John XXIII.*

*In the hot summer days of the Lincolnshire fens Heather knew little or nothing of all this. Her world was fields and grass, haystacks and sunshine, and coming down to breakfast to her mother standing in front of the range and the smells of bacon sizzling and eggs frying.*

*Heather thought the farm enchanting in so many ways. The house itself had a character that endeared itself to Heather and her sisters. They were voyagers to a new world, exploring and discovering in a new and exciting environment as alien to them as, say, Jules Verne's undersea world had been to his readers.*

The first thing I remember about the farm was mud. As we drove in with the lorry there was mud everywhere, but then we saw this lovely house. We ran here and there, opening doors and peering here, there and everywhere. We found this lovely spiral staircase right in the middle of the house – beautiful grainy wood. And my bedroom smelt so sweet; it was scented by apples from trees right outside the windows. I could lean out of my window and pick the fruit, hardly needing to stretch. Orchards surrounded the house.

The farmyard was a playground of bales of straw and lowing cows for all of us. We used to play in the bales of hay, looking for little red weasels.

One of Dad's jobs was to milk the cows: I loved to watch. 'Can I do it?' I asked. And together we laughed – one of few joyous times we shared – as I milked my first cow. Another time Dad taught me to pluck chickens.

We were messing around in the garden one day, exploring our new world as kids do – Dad was with us, which he rarely was – and we discovered The Well. I first found a circular 'lid', lifted it and looked down into the dark depths below.

'What's down there, Daddy?' I asked. Dad told us it was a well, and pointed to steps leading down inside the hole. We all looked in and could see green weeds in the clear water below. Many times I, and at other times my sisters, went down the well-steps and drank from the crystal clear water.

Many hot, balmy days were spent playing 'two-ball' on the wall. You bounced the ball against the wall and caught it on the rebound. There were so many flies that, as we played, we would squash them. The ball came back covered in the bodies of the victims; we'd count how many we'd swatted.

Even school was a pleasure. We would walk out to catch the bus to Louth; the school was an army of brown. I remember the farm as a host of golden yellows of summer, and school is a memory of rich autumn brown. Brown socks, brown knickers, brown uniform. We spent happy days at the school, and tranquil and playful ones at the farm.

Once home from school, I would get changed into my rough clothes, get out the bike and ride around collecting the eggs from the little chicken-huts. The eggs went into buckets strapped either side of the bike. Once these buckets were filled with their fragile cargo we had to walk the bike back. In the fields we had to ride and walk through, there were wooden planks every ten feet or so bridging the drainage dykes.

One day, after a night of heavy rain, Angela and I were doing the round together. We were laughing and joking, and playfully running about each other, but we were taking care to protect the eggs. We'd collected all the eggs, we were walking back, and we'd already crossed all but one of the slippery wooden bridge-planks. On this last one Angela went first. I shouted to her, running ahead of me, 'This is a bit slippery.' I couldn't have been more right. I slipped, and before I knew it I'd fallen in the dyke. The bike fell in on top of me, the eggs and the buckets crashed in all around me. I remember I was laughing and spluttering even as I bobbed up through the scattered chickweed on the water; I came up through the middle of the frame of the bicycle.

As I dragged myself out Angela laughed her head off. I was laughing too. I was wet through; I left the bike and eggs there in the dyke and splodged into the house.

'I fell in the dyke and dropped the eggs and the bike. I'm all wet,' I told them all, somewhat unnecessarily I suppose.

We never did go back to get the bike out; perhaps the bike and the buckets are still down in the dyke somewhere.

One day that was really magical and enchanting I was playing with my sisters and we discovered what we came to call our Secret Garden. We were playing round the back of the house and we found a tight bundle of weeds. We had to really fight them and pull them apart and behind them we found a sliding door. It was paint-peeled and decayed and we talked up a story – which I suppose we came to believe – that the door hadn't been opened for centuries. We managed to slide it open; and inside we found an overrun, walled garden; a private and closed world that belonged to us alone.

In the times we played in our Secret World we developed a little graveyard for birds and mice that we found dead around the farm. We would dig a suitable sized hole, place the deceased within, bury them and say a little prayer. We then made little crosses out of lollipop sticks.

All of us made a pact together. 'We must never tell Mum and Dad about this place. This is our place, and only ours.'

For a while we were living like Enid Blyton's Famous Five. One day, pulling aside weeds and bushes and nettles, we found a large round stone. It was about four feet across, and it had a handle on it that you could sit on and spin round on. It was a grinding stone that grinders used to use to sharpen knives and garden tools for householders. We cleaned it up and played a game, running round the garden 'selling' sharpening services to each other. 'Any knives, scissors to sharpen?'

*Heather's parents probably knew full well about the garden, and the games the sisters played in it, but for the children it was their first sanctum sanctorum.*

To children, summer days go on forever. If Heather's summer days on the farm could have gone on forever she would have been a happy child. Sizzling bacon, drinking from the well, collecting the eggs, the brown army marching off to school, and laughing home, and reigning in the Secret Garden.

But one sudden, brain-numbing day, Heather came home to find her bags were again packed and already standing outside the house. Her father's car was there, and the girls were taken away. Just as before they never even had a chance to say goodbye to their friends. For Heather it was the end of a golden period; the only time she was really happy for any length of time during her childhood was at an end.

And Heather embarked on a journey that left the Secret Garden behind forever. Just as Captain Nemo, the hero of Jules Verne's novel 20,000 Leagues Under the Sea, committed the bodies of his submariners to graves in growing coral to keep them – and his secrets – safe from human, prying eyes so the paint-peeled door of the sanctum of the Secret Garden closed forever over the animal graveyard and the children's secrets. The 'Famous Five' – like childhood – was quickly forced to an end.

## Mablethorpe

The girls were taken to Mablethorpe, a seaside town north of the Wash, on the East Coast of England. The earlier move from Lincoln to the farm had already transported the family forty miles across the Wolds to the farm at Saltfleetby. This was, by comparison, a short hop to the nearby coast. Even so, it was a giant leap for the girls; it was a tender age to be separated from their parents, even though they had not yet been told just how long they would be away. At the time Heather was ten years old.

The situation was a forced one; their mother was 'ill in hospital' – a euphemism for her deteriorating mental state. At that time she was in the process of a breakdown; eventually it would lead to alcoholism, drug abuse, institutionalization, operations on her brain, and finally suicide.

Given the social pressures of the time – 1959, into 1960 – it was not likely that their father could easily bring the children up; he had been advised to seek help. Sadly, Heather believed that her father didn't want to bring them up, though he told us that if he could have, he would have done so. Their father told them they would be 'staying with friends'. It was another polite euphemism; they were going to a foster home.

Dad took us in the car and introduced us to this lady. I can't remember her name. She and her husband had an adopted son, Michael, the same age as me.

It was a railway house; a house connected to the gate house of the crossing between the railway and the road. The husband's job was to open and shut the gates. Of course, he was tied to the train timetables. Even in the middle of a meal he would have to get up from the table, go outside and get the gates open for the trains if one was due. I remember that as the trains went past the walls used to shake. The house would rumble, and the ornaments would rattle. There was a strong smell of smoke in the air after a train passed; I don't know if we enjoyed it then – nowadays I look back on it with a feeling of nostalgia.

At night our beds would rattle and shake. We would look out of the windows at night and see the trains screaming through.

*In the dark nights, Heather and her sisters leaned on the window panes, looking out into the blackness, and they would watch as the trains rushed past them, unstopping, going from wherever to wherever. The girls would see the lighted fires of the steam-train boilers and catch a glimpse of the passengers in the carriages. Heather must many times have seen the symbolism of her life unfolding – unknown destinations.*

We were told that we'd be there for just a few weeks, and perhaps that was the intention. In fact we were at Mablethorpe for a year.

We saw Dad maybe three or four times in that year, and always for very short periods. We were beginning to understand how life was going to be, I think.

Our foster mother would tell us that our father was coming to see us and we'd get really worked up and excited. Sometimes he wouldn't turn up and we would be so disappointed. But there were those few times when he did.

'How's Mum now?' we would ask when he arrived. All I ever remember being told is that she was no better. We kept asking when we would be coming home and Dad would tell us that it would be a while because, 'Mummy isn't well enough yet'.

He would bring us a big bag of sweets. We would ask if we were going to go out for the day with him, but we never did. Before we really knew that he'd arrived we'd be standing on the drive holding our big bag of sweets and waving goodbye to his car as it drove off.

But despite all that it was a happy time. We weren't far from the beach, and we used to go down there to play on the sands with Michael.

*Buckets and spades in hand the sisters and Michael would troop off down to the beach. Under a warm sun and cool breezes they would frolic about, build sandcastles, jump on each other's castles and chase each other in near-anger/ near-playfulness. But there was already a sense of 'making do' with what you got in life coming into Heather's thinking.*

I remember Bonfire Night. I asked if we could go guying. 'Oh no, no, you mustn't do that,' their foster parents told them,

'That's begging.' But I was determined to do it; I suggested to Michael and the others that we go out, and say that we were going to the beach. They all agreed.

We got hold of some coffee, wetted it and dirtied our faces with it to make ourselves up as guys. Then off we went guying. A troop of us marching along the road singing and shouting 'Guy, guy, guy, stick him in the eye.' And of course we had to ask, 'A penny for the guy, please.'

We got loads of pennies and I think we spent them on sweeties and things. After the guying we did go down to the beach; we paddled for a while and then came home. We never did tell our foster parents about it.

*Whatever the arrangements, which Heather was not of course privy to, they came to an end presumably when it was realized by all concerned that the family was broken up for a period that – if not permanent – would certainly be going on for some time.*

We came home from school one day and Dad was there. The cases were packed already. Dad said we had to go into a children's Home because Mum was still poorly. She wasn't able to take care of us. I didn't want to go. Our foster mother told us that she could take two of us, but not all four. Dad didn't want to split us up, I suppose, so we had to leave. I was really upset.

*The romance of the night-trains, sunny days on the beach and guying in the streets; they were all abruptly coming to an end.*

*Heather and her sisters were to exchange these enchantments for the darker recesses of an orphan-like existence that owed less to Enid Blyton and more to the mind of Edgar Allen Poe. They were moving into the grimness of institutional Homes so vividly described by Charles Dickens.*

## Clarence House

You let the children play outside,
    when darkness falls, do you?
It makes things quieter indoors,
    but is it wise to do?
Suppose you read to them a bit,
    play a game or simply sit?
How nice if home's the kind of spot
    where children know they're loved a lot.

*(from the 60,000 words or more of channelled and other writings Heather
recorded during her years of the stigmata)*

*The first of the care Homes Heather was sent to she described as Dickens'
Bleak House; large iron gates creaking open over a long drive that led to the
old mansion. The front door was shadowed behind huge white pillars. The
sisters had been taken to Clarence House, Horncastle, some twenty miles
from Lincoln.*

*The Bradley girls were ushered into the Home and shown their rooms.
Heather remembers a generally good atmosphere even though she was frightened by the upheaval in her life. She was at school with her sisters and
friends, and enjoyed her school life. Indeed, throughout all the problems the
care Homes would produce, school was always a pleasure for the young
Heather.*

*The Home was under the matronship of Miss Scott, with much of the
day-to-day running by staff called 'Aunties'.*

There was a lovely warm family atmosphere. We all huddled round a
big wooden table. There was a jug of hot cocoa and a plate of biscuits.
I often sat next to Aunty Shirley as she read us a story. One time, she
was reading a story and I was leaning against her. She was quite a big
lady. She lifted me up and I just put my head on her chest, and felt so
happy and warm and drowsy, sitting on her lap, feeling the warmth
and softness of her body. She held me, and cuddled me, just briefly; it
was so lovely.

Not every Aunty was like Shirley though; there was also Aunty
Patricia. It seemed to me that Aunty Patricia always zoomed in on me.
She was very rough, too rough for a children's Home. She was obvi-
ously very ill, or something.

*Hazel, describing her own memories of Aunty Patricia, said 'she was like a Gestapo agent', and that she put a lot of fear into children.*

She ran baths with cold water. There would be two or three of us and Aunty Patricia would strip us off. She seemed to get joy in tugging the clothes off us; being so young we'd just whimper, 'Oh please, I don't want to do that.' But we were physically put into the freezing water. And she would use on us the brush that we scrubbed the outside steps with. She really seemed to enjoy this; she would let out this twisted laugh. 'Please, no. What have we done?' we would be crying out. 'No more.'

Then she would seem to change; she'd get us out and dry us. Suddenly she'd be really nice and lovely, though she never apologized.

*The threat and fear of what could happen to you, what could be done to you, in those Homes was often worse than the beatings or the deprivations. When you were beaten you could go to bed aching and sore and crying; but any night Heather and the other children could lie in bed not knowing if footsteps heading their way could result in some irrational beating or verbal abuse. In the early years of Heather's institutionalization the people chosen to run Homes were not caring; they believed in authority, in power, and in keeping order with a fist of iron and a rod of steel. Some of the housemothers that we interviewed, from a later Home, confirmed that as soon as they saw what was happening in the Homes they determined to make changes. One said: 'When I went for an interview ... I was horrified, I couldn't believe it. I decided I was going to have a really good try to change things.'*

*Nor was the horror of the Homes entirely – or even predominantly – one of violence. The most compelling memory of Home life was the lack of love. The children were the 'stock in trade'; the rules and regulations were more important to the staff than caring and loving. If one thing categorizes Home life in those early years more than anything, it was that children were deprived of their childhood fun and laughter. Most children have the capacity for endurance and resilience; there would have been playtime and laughing and fun – but always with a shadow of uncertainty and fear hovering over them.*

We'd be playing in the day room and the door would open; we knew without looking up whether it was Miss Scott or Aunty Shirley, they were lovely. We also knew if it was Aunty Patricia; it was just a different feeling.

Sometimes Aunty Patricia would choose two or three children for her 'games', though not always the same ones. At the bottom of the garden there was a stream, a nice big tree and a little shed. She'd take us in with her and just say, 'Sit down. No need to be frightened.' It was her niceness that was more terrifying than the shouting at us because we knew it was a cover.

She would stroke your hair, then grab two or three hairs and yank them out. One minute she'd be nice, then suddenly she'd just yank at your hair to hurt you. She would come from behind saying, 'This won't hurt,' and then grab your neck and squeeze it for no obvious reason. She would lean in and whisper 'Don't tell anybody because I can do worse than this.' So we daren't say anything.

I sometimes wet my bed. Around that time I was obviously wetting the bed because I was frightened. Patricia seemed to get joy out of this; she would come up and shake me. She called me 'a dirty little girl' and made me change the bed and take the sheets and wash them.

One weekend Miss Scott was away. All of us sisters had, by then, been moved from the bedroom to the dormitory which had about eighteen beds. We had all gone to bed. It was late, lights were out. There was no talking.

I called out, 'Why don't we jump from bed to bed, just go round jumping.' So we all leapt around the room, from bed to bed, and suddenly I'd call out, 'Right'. It was like musical chairs; when I called out 'Right' everyone would get into the bed they were on at that moment. Suddenly we heard somebody coming up the stairs. I was on Brenda's bed and I leapt under the covers. The light went on. I was snuggled under the covers hiding.

Brenda was on medication for something. I heard Aunty Patricia right next to me say, 'Come on, Brenda, take your medicine,' and she shook me. The next thing she pulled back the covers and there was I looking up at her. 'What are you doing?' she shouted. If it had been Shirley she would have said, 'Oh, come on you lot, stop messing about,' but Patricia was quite angry with me.

One day Aunty Patricia called to me, Brenda and others. 'Upstairs,' she called out, 'We're going to have a bit of fun.'

Clarence House had these beautiful, big, graceful, wide staircases. Under some of the stairs there was a little door, and inside were three steps leading down into a closet. Aunty Patricia said, 'Don't be frightened, we are going to have some fun. I am going to put you all in there. Come on, off you go.' Then she pushed us in. She started kicking and pushing us. 'Go on,' she demanded.

We were crying, begging her not to do it. But she just pushed each of us down the steps. We were all frightened and sobbing. We all fell down into the darkness. She shut the door, and it was pitch black. Brenda was screaming. She had hurt her arm; we didn't know it at the time, but she had actually broken it. We all started shouting and banging on the door.

It seemed to be ages before she opened it. We came out and there was a horrible sight; Patricia was standing there laughing like a fiend.

The door bell rang. Aunty Patricia ignored Brenda's crying, saying, 'Right you lot, get up and go in the play room. Don't you say anything. This is our game.' We were frightened by that; we just scurried away from her.

Brenda kept telling Aunty Patricia her arm hurt. Aunty Patricia would hit her arm and say, 'Of course it doesn't hurt, let's have a look.' Then she would twist Brenda's arm until she screamed out, and then leave us.

I told Brenda that Miss Scott would be back that night and that we ought to tell her about her arm. But Brenda daren't, and I was scared too because of the threats from Patricia. But when Miss Scott came home somehow she found out about Brenda's arm. She called us to the office. 'Tell us what happened,' she said. Brenda told her that Aunty Patricia had put us in the cupboard. I was too frightened to speak, I just couldn't say anything. I feared she could come to our bedroom at night and get us.

*In a child's simple world there is one solution to fear and to threat...*

I had already decided to run away, and I was making my plans. There was a tree with a tree den. We were allowed to climb on this tree. Rather than playing I would deliberately practise my climbing. Just kind of climbing up so far until Miss Scott or someone would shout, 'Come on, Heather, get down, you'll hurt yourself.' But this tree was my climbing practice for my escape.

I knew exactly what I was going to do to escape and yet it all happened so quickly. I sneaked down the stairs. My sister Hazel had woken. She asked what I was doing. I whispered, 'I'm running away.'

I tiptoed down the stairs. I went through to the kitchen, took two Weetabix and some bread. I climbed out of the window, and instantly realized that it was freezing cold. It was snowing. All I had on was my slippers and maybe an extra skirt over my nightie.

My climbing practise worked; I got over the gate easily. But I was slipping all over the place on the sleet and snow. I kept looking back as I was walking.

It was snowing and dark. My feet were wet through. I was shivering and crying. I was walking, quickly – almost running – for half an hour or so. It was about half-four, maybe five o'clock in the morning. A house light just ahead of me went on. I was drawn towards this bungalow and before I knew where I was I knocked on the door and cried, 'I've run away from Clarence House.'

I was invited into the house, and I met the couple that lived there. They were, I guess, in their forties. A lovely couple. The man was dressed; I wondered if he was ready for work. I suppose that's why the light went on.

I felt their warmth. They seemed very friendly; it was homely and very caring. The room seemed big, but cosy and friendly. And I felt so small.

They sat me on the couch in front of the fire and the wife put her arm round me. 'Oh, you poor thing, why have you run away? What's the matter?'

The husband gave me a drink. He told me they were going to ring the Home to tell them I was there. I asked him not to, and asked if I could stay with them, but he told me that he had to telephone Clarence House.

The husband made the phone call, then he came back. The wife and I had been sitting there, talking, she with her arm round me. The husband came back from the telephone. 'Aunty Patricia is coming for you.' 'Oh, she's not, is she? Was she mad? Angry?' I asked.

He told me not to worry, that everything would be all right. I didn't say, 'I don't want to go'. I didn't say how frightened I was. I knew she was coming for me and I suppose I caved in at that point. Just gave up. I don't know why I didn't tell them about the things she did.

*In fact the staff at Clarence House already knew that Heather was gone. Dawn had been intending to run away with Heather, but had been too frightened when the time came; she told Hazel about it. Hazel, in turn, had woken Shirley and told her; Shirley had in turn woken Patricia. Hazel had had more fears for her younger sister in the 'big wide world' than she had for her in the Home. Back at the bungalow Heather was savouring her new-found freedom, not knowing how short-lived it was to be.*

In ten minutes or so the doorbell rang. The husband went to answer it to let Patricia in; but she wouldn't come in, she stayed on the doorstep.

'Aunty Patricia has come for you. She is going to take you back.'

The husband offered to run us back in the car. Patricia told him not to bother. She said that the walk would do me good. I'm surprised that that didn't make the couple think something was wrong, taking a small child back through the cold and snow in flimsy clothes.

We walked together to the door. They didn't notice, but Patricia looked at me with a face that said 'I've got you now'. There were no words of greeting, just that look I'd seen so many times before. I thanked the couple for the comfort they had given me. Patricia said, all sweetness, 'Silly little girl, I don't know.' Then the door was shut. Just as it banged shut she thumped me in the back, swearing at me, pushing me. 'I'll make you pay for this, you wait.' She pushed me all the way home. I slipped several times and she kind of held me, and pulled me up. But rough. Then she would push me down again, up and down again, saying 'Come on, I'll give you a hand.' She was squeezing my arm, hurting me. She was enjoying it.

'You wait, I'll sort you out once and for all,' she threatened. I was absolutely petrified and sobbing. But I didn't even bother saying, 'Please don't hit me' or 'What are you going to do?' I knew because of what had gone before that a beating was imminent.

We got back to Clarence House and Aunty Shirley, the nice aunty, was up waiting for me. She came over: 'What have you done, look you're wet through.' She started to rub me down, and make me feel warm and comfortable.

I said, 'I'm sorry.' I didn't say, 'Don't leave me with Patricia,' because it would have made matters worse when Patricia got me on my own.

Shirley told both me and Patricia that I should be given a bath and be tucked into bed. Patricia offered to give me my bath and dress me. I argued as forcefully as I could that I wanted Shirley to do it and pleaded with her not to leave me alone with Patricia. But Aunty Shirley just agreed that Patricia could bath me.

I never did get that bath. Patricia pushed me into the bathroom. It was a dark room, a wooden room. All these sinks, round tins of solid toothpaste, lockers with our towels and flannels. And there were wooden hairbrushes. Patricia stared at me: 'You have to pay for it now. I have got to hit you. You can't run away and not get punished.'

And she picked up my wooden hairbrush and kind of held me at her arm's length. This heavy wooden brush in one hand and holding me with the other. 'This will hurt. You have to be punished.'

And she showered hits all over me, though not on my head. She was hitting me on my arms, my bottom, all over. She started to swing me round towards the brush, hitting me harder, hitting me all over.

I was screaming, 'I won't do it again. Please don't hit me any more.' This went on for a long time. I was screaming and she was hitting me and I was screaming for her to stop.

The screaming must have been horrific; Dawn in her bedroom could hear it, and Aunty Shirley was alerted by it.

I was shouting so loud Shirley must have heard and she came down. But Patricia heard her coming, She said, 'That's Shirley. Don't you make any noise.' And she put the brush back. She pretended to be nice, 'There, there, that's it, let's get you up to bed.'

Shirley asked if I was all right; she could hear that I was sobbing. Patricia told her that she was just going to put me to bed, that I was just upset because of everything that had happened. So she got away with it without Shirley knowing. At least on that occasion.

Miss Scott was there in the morning when we came down. She called me into the office. 'I hear you ran away. Why have you been naughty?'

I told her that I was upset because 'I wanted my Mum', but then I blurted out the story that Aunty Patricia hit me with a brush.

But Aunty Patricia had told her I was hysterical, or very upset, and that she had just slapped me. So Patricia had already given her version. I told her that she did it to punish me, but Miss Scott kept saying that she was sure she wouldn't have done that.

'You won't run away again, will you?' Miss Scott asked. I told her I was sorry, but that I was unhappy. Miss Scott told me that she was going to have to telephone my father and let him know. I asked her not to tell my mother, because it would upset her. I looked her in the eyes, and added, 'If you tell my Mum that I've run away I promise you that I will run away from every Home. Everywhere I go I will run away.'

*It was a promise that Heather was to keep with a vengeance.*

Some little while after my running away my Father came to Clarence House. He was in the office with Miss Scott for a while, then he came through to me. He asked me why I ran away, and he told me that they had had to tell my mother and that she was very upset.

I cried, I told him I was sorry. Dad told me they were going to move me to another Home. Apparently no one had ever run away before and they didn't like it.

Dad said 'Cheerio' when he left that day. I asked when we'd see him again but he didn't say anything.

# Homeleigh

*In 1961, the suitcases, Heather, aged 12, and her sisters arrived at Homeleigh; it was to be home for the next two years. In this Home Heather was to make that vital step from childhood into her teenage years.*

*For many teenagers in the Western world, 1961 heralded the start of major social changes that – for the first time – would affect them directly. It was the birth of the Cold War; Khrushchev seemed to be everywhere in the world, Kennedy had just taken office as President of the US. He would shortly suffer humiliation in the Bay of Pigs fiasco, leading him to seek to regain his glory by initiating the 'Man on the Moon' project. Teenagers were watching Hitchcock's Psycho, listening to the Beatles, and rocking and rolling. By the end of the decade they would have exchanged their inno-cence for political marches, protests against Vietnam and – in England – the rioting outside the American Embassy in London.*

*As before, Heather seems to have been untouched by the wider world around her, perhaps unable to appreciate the things other teenagers were doing; not one of her recollections to us mentioned these kinds of events. For her, this stage of her life was totally dominated by the strictures of Home life.*

*Homeleigh consisted of a group of eleven cottages. Each cottage had a matron, called Mother, and other staff called Aunties. Heather remembers her cottage was run by a Miss Clapson; a Miss Ransom ran the cottage that Angela and Hazel were put into. In fact, in the time she was there, the cottages were run and supervised by several people, including relief staff. The differences in approach of these various people were to be significant.*

*Overall control was by the superintendent and his wife, Mr and Mrs Vardy. They had a house at the end of a long drive that wound through the scattered cottages. It was quite a community; it had its own hospital, its own cobblers, its own laundry. There was a nursery for the babies and little ones.*

When we arrived, we Bradley girls, as we were known, were split up. Dawn and I were put in one cottage; I heard that this was a special cottage for those children that had been identified as in need of loving care. Angela and Hazel were put in a different cottage – I think that was a special place for those seen as needing discipline. Considering that I was the rebellious spirit the choice wasn't obvious. I might well have needed love – are there children that don't? – but my sisters seem unlikely to have been the obvious candidates for discipline. But that was the rules. I asked if we would ever be put back together in the same cottage.

'We've just not got the room. It was a rush, you know, to get you here. We'll sort you out, put you together, later.'

But they never did put us together in all the time we were there. In the Homes, you learn about institutionalized lying at an early age.

The institution had its own uniform; I remember the black shiny lace-up shoes that squeaked every time you walked. Every child had jobs to do in their cottage. Angela and Hazel were strictly controlled and worked hard; their cottage had a hard regime. We Bradley girls would swap notes on each other's lives when we were together at the school in town during the day.

The institution demanded personal sacrifices partly for hygiene's sake and, more often than not, rules for the sake of rules. The Home had its own barber but his creativity was curtailed; all of us had our hair cut short to reduce the likelihood of nits. Every Friday we would all have to have our hair washed and a stinking concoction of 'yellow nit stuff' rubbed in it. Then the staff would comb through everyone's hair to check and rake out the nits.

And there was the queuing up for the mouthful of cod liver oil. Green, thick and hard to swallow. I can still remember the awful smell of the ritual. And the same spoon for everyone. A troop of children, mouths open, each having the same spoon rammed in their mouths in the name of health and hygiene.

*Short-cut hair and the uniform of black boots or shoes made the hundred to two hundred children in the eleven cottages stand out like an Orphan Army to the other children in the town. One of the housemothers we interviewed, who had herself been a child in Homeleigh, told us that there was a real stigma to being from the Homes; Home children were blamed when things went wrong or went missing, and they were viewed as steerage passengers in life. The Orphan Army was sneered at, looked down on, were seen to be the ones that 'were different'.*

*Life at the Homes consisted of the usual rule-breaking of no great seriousness. Each cottage was separately walled around and you weren't supposed to see into other cottage 'gardens' where the swings, sea-saws and playthings were. Heather – like so many others – would climb the walls and peek in, to be met, more often than not, by a ruler over the knuckles and a command 'Get back to your own cottage'. Heather sneaked over a lot, rebellious in that way. She did plenty of things that she knew she wasn't allowed to do. Mostly she got away with it.*

*Life was not bad, even quite happy a lot of the time. They were provided for within the confines of what was thought necessary in the early 1960s, in those days before a lot of black-and-white TV docu-dramas turned the tide of opinion from discipline to love, and changed institutions from putting rules first to putting people first.*

At school, I got friendly with one of the girls from the Home, and I think maybe I recognized there was something a little different about this Homeleigh girl. I had a chat with her. Andrea – as the girl was called – told me that her mum and dad ran one of the cottages – Mr and Mrs Crabbe. We got very pally. I would often sneak over to her cottage. Eventually we became 'blood sisters'; a little cut in the palms of the hands, shake hands, mingle the blood. 'Promise to be faithful. Promise to share.' And all that ...

My only contact with Andrea's mother, Mrs Crabbe, was when she shouted, 'Get back to your own cottage' at me.

*Later on Mr and Mrs Crabbe were to turn up as Heather's 'Mother' and 'Father' at another Home, with frightening consequences. But for now they were just distant figures.*

There were, of course, set meal times. Meals were taken at a long table; rows of nearly silent children itching to be boisterous. You had to hold your knife and fork properly. Angela was left-handed but in those days institutions frowned on such 'evil practices'; we were all disciplined to be right-handed. I used to eat with my fork in my right hand too; there was plenty of smacking and slapping for such sins. And you had to eat up all your food; otherwise you were not properly respectful and thankful for the food. But frankly much of the meat was fat and gristle. Everybody had to eat all their food, then they could leave the table. I can remember several times struggling – and I used to let them know I was struggling – but somebody would always stand behind me: 'You're not leaving the table until you have eaten it all,' they would say. I know I used to nibble little bits and nearly throw up. It would get to the point where I would just burst out crying or even sometimes I was actually sick or say 'I am going to be sick'. Then I got a special 'privilege'; I could leave the table knowing that I would have to eat it cold and congealed when I sat down to my next meal. You weren't allowed to get away in the end. At the next meal, sure enough the fat and gristle was back. Everybody had to finish what was on the plate.

*The Incident Of The Chocolates is burned deep in Heather's memory.*

There was a time when we were with children from another cottage; I can't remember if we were with them, or they were with us.

One evening, one of the staff left a box of chocolates on top of the piano but in reach of the children. Too much low-quality meat perhaps got the better of them and three of the sweets were eaten without permission. I had been away from the cottage during the day and evening when the chocolates had been taken. The next day all the twenty-four or so children were brought together in the sitting-room.

The housemother announced, 'I want to know who has taken these chocolates. If that child had asked she could have had one but she did not ask.'

Not for a minute was I stupid enough to believe that anyone could get hold of the chocolates just by asking but that was the way they would demoralize you from the start – by making you think you'd done the deed unnecessarily.

'Now come on,' the housemother continued, 'who is it? Let's get this sorted out.' For once I was relaxed and thought I could take a back seat on this one; not only had I been out during the time of the offence but what's more, everyone knew I had been out.

There were plenty of cries of 'No, no, it wasn't me.' Nobody admitted to it.

'Well, if you don't tell us who it is, we're going to take you upstairs one at a time until whoever it is admits to taking these chocolates.'

You could see that most of the kids were quite frightened. It was pretty obvious that 'being taken upstairs' was not going to be pleasant. The kids were kind of looking round as if to say, 'Come on, own up, who is it?'

Still nobody admitted it. So the two matrons of the two cottages said, 'Right, we are going upstairs. Aunty Myra, you send up two of them at a time.'

It was a nightmare. All the kids, hands wringing and toes crabbing would sit silently, accusing one another, as pairs of children were taken upstairs. The door up there would close and there would be that pause when everyone imagined the worst; we felt we knew what was happening. I visualized each kid one at a time told – or forced – to stretch over a chair, face down, ready for a beating. Downstairs all of us could hear the sound of slapping. We imagined it was a leather belt across their backsides. You could hear them screaming up there; almost hysterical crying. One child up there would be made to watch, and then as the sobbing girl or boy was finished with and stood aside another would replace him or her.

Downstairs the others waiting for their time were getting knots in their stomachs. The military tactics were sound enough of course; divide and conquer. The children waiting to be punished were all calling to each other 'Come on, admit it. Just say who's done it.' No-one owned up.

Two crying, shaking children would be brought downstairs, two more chosen from those assembled would be led away upstairs, already crying.

'Leave Heather till last', they shouted. They were, I suppose, recognizing that I couldn't have taken the sweets because I was out at the time. But I got the meaning clear enough; my time for a beating would come. Being innocent wasn't going to be any defence. Perhaps that was then almost the worst torture – waiting for what seemed inevitable. I suppose I had in any case already worked out that it didn't matter that I hadn't been there. It didn't even matter that they knew I hadn't been there. In the cottage that had been singled out because the children there needed love I was standing in the sitting room with my toes crunched up and my hands clenched knuckle-white, waiting to be leathered by people who made you call them 'Mother' and who knew I was innocent.

For once luck was on my side. Before each new pair of children was taken upstairs Myra would ask: 'Come on, who's done it?' It was getting close to my turn when one girl with ginger hair, Eileen, owned up. As they took her hand to march her away she cried out, 'It was me. Oh, I don't want you to hit me. It was me. I took them. I took the chocolates.' With that Myra shouted upstairs that the offender had been found.

Myra told her off for letting the other children get leathered, but the Mothers upstairs only seemed concerned about which of them had been in charge of the offending girl. They passed all of us frightened and beaten kids without any real feeling; as far as they were concerned the job was done. They apologized for hitting those of us who had been innocent, but it was an apology that made clear they'd do it again if they felt they had to.

*Dawn also remembered the incident very clearly. The children may have been taken out of the room in pairs but they were 'frog-marched' upstairs individually. Dawn was unlucky; she had the beating that Heather missed. As she described it, 'The Aunty took off her leather shoe, or slipper, took down your pants and gave you a good whelping.'*

*Heather's character was unquestionably formed in those Homes; that is clear from the way in which she recollects incidents. She recalls both mental* and physical cruelty with sorrow. Understanding what happened in those Homes is the key to understanding how Heather, in later years, took on the suffering of others, and ultimately of Christ.

We spoke to several of the staff who had been at Homeleigh at the time that Heather was there; Miss Clapson, whom Heather remembered with warmth and affection, Miss Espin who had been housemother before Miss Clapson and Aunty Nora of whom, again, Heather held good memories.

They confirmed that Heather's view was neither distorted, nor isolated.

Miss Clapson described the institutionalization: 'It was awful. I think I was the first one that looked for (the children) to be dressed differently, as individuals. The institutionalization was horrendous, like walking in 'crocodile' to church and school – long lines of two-by-two with no freedom for play or self-expression ... and not being allowed out on a Sunday. I was the first one that took them out on a Sunday, for picnics and playing on the field, and I was told off for it by the superintendent. I was even punished for doing these things; one of my punishments was being made to paint the staircase.

'When I went for an interview [to be a housemother] I saw a very young child peeling a bucketful of potatoes, another child was black-leading, and another was scrubbing. I was horrified, I couldn't believe it. I decided I was going to have a really good try to change things.'

Ann Espin was not just a housemother in the Homes, but had been in care herself and had been a child in Homeleigh. She described her impression of those years: 'No warmth. And there was some bad stuff going on. There was no latitude for personal development; that wasn't the flavour of the time then. You either sank or you swam; it had to do with your own coping skills. But [these Homes] took your identity away, and it took your confidence away because you were herded about in groups, not as individuals.'

If this mental oppression was not bad enough, there was physical cruelty as well.

Ann Espin recalls, 'It was the older, elderly housemothers who were there from wartime; that was when the harsh discipline was around. As younger people took over it definitely changed. There was even forced feeding in Homeleigh during that era but I helped to stop all that. I got a bit unpopular at times for what they saw as interfering.'

Things may have changed but the old habits still arose at times. Miss Clapson made clear to us that she abhorred violence, and would not tolerate it. But she acknowledged it. 'I'm not saying that there wasn't a possibility ... I know that some of the housemothers were very, very strict; how they would have dealt with situations I don't know ... There were things going on that were very, very wrong, and very unpleasant ... I can remember reporting an incident to the Superintendent and Matron (Mr and Mrs Vardy) because I felt that the children were being treated quite badly. I was most concerned. In one cottage there was a beating and I reported it. And it wasn't just one occasion, I reported incidents of beatings by a housemother on three or four occasions. There was one housemother who was so strict it was unbelievable. The least little thing and she was quite physical. She was extremely authoritarian, and got very angry with the children. I can certainly remember the hand – not a belt – being used on a group of children; on their bottoms. This happened in what was called the playroom. I went to see Mr and Mrs Vardy about it. They supported me on that. Shortly afterwards the lady concerned retired. There was an incident which occurred with [a girl called] Eileen and I reported it. Eileen was hit very badly by the housemother of her cottage, and I reported it. I had to separate Eileen and the housemother.'

Ann Espin also did not believe that punishments were always restricted to using 'the hand': 'They have used things to hit with in the past. Certainly when I was there as a child. Prior to when I was staff there was a lot of physical punishment. It could have been subtle though; when there were only two members of staff, and if one was off, things could happen. It was only the child's word against the staff then. I have heard that Mrs Crabbe used physical violence on girls at times; but I've not seen it. I've heard it from several different children.'

In an echo of Clarence House, Aunty Patricia and Brenda with a broken arm, Ann Espin told us, 'One of the biggest things for punishment was the cupboard under the stairs.'

One housemother seemed to be particularly bad, and unfortunately it was the housemother of Hazel and Angela, and one that Heather had a few 'run-ins' with: Miss Ransom.

Miss Clapson commented, 'Miss Ransom and I were not the same sort of person, absolutely not. I would not want to be named in the same category.'

Ann Espin commented, 'I was in care under Miss Ransom. She was awful, very authoritarian. Locked children in outside cupboards and under the stairs. My brothers also have horrific memories of her.'

Against this kind of background, Heather was struggling to find herself, and her meaning in life. In opposition to the chances of success were problems both internally and externally. Ann Espin commented that there was a permanent stigma to being from a Home; 'Homes kids always got blamed for anything, no matter what. And you couldn't defend yourself, you were brought up not to say anything out of order, out of line.'

Internally, Heather had never been given the chance to trust herself, to test herself, to stand on her own feet. And with the background of punishments in the Homes it would have been hard to 'spread her wings'; hence her *need to express her freedom naturally, by escaping. She was in the Homes during a time of change, and with plenty of harsh punishments going on. They were the threat to her every thought. For example, she was never force-fed, perhaps never even saw it, but it had been a punishment only years before and it would still have been talked about, perhaps still threatened. The reality of punishment is sometimes not even as bad as the fear; and it was the fear that was Heather's daily diet.*

*Soon after the beatings Dawn suffered and Heather feared, Heather decided to run away with a group of kids. She was in the washroom and heard the 'Head Girl' – the oldest girl, Linda – announcing her own getaway plans.*

I asked her if it was true that she was planning to run away. Linda was cautious but nodded, and told me that she was running away with others from another Cottage. I asked to go with them; I was already making plans. Linda told me I couldn't, and protested adamantly. But under pressure I got her to change from 'No' to 'We'll see'.

With the permission of the two boys also involved in the escape, I was allowed to join in. Linda talked about provisions with the two boys, three other girls and me.

'We're getting food together; we'll need to eat'. We all discussed what food to secrete away, and how to do it. When the planning was done Linda said, 'We'll meet outside the school gates at ten to four.'

After school on the day we'd planned for, we all started to leave the school gates for the trek back to the cottages. We mooched along slowly, letting the rest of the kids get far enough away, then we broke off for the Great Escape.

We weren't, to be honest, sure where we were going or, for that matter, what we were doing. But for all that we got quite a distance. We went across country, across fields. After a while we stopped to share out the food: cheese, bread, sweeties, some drinks.

*The Orphan Army was on survival manoeuvres. But the pressure of oncoming night was adding to the pressure of Institutional Power; the two boys lost their nerve.*

'We're not going any further,' they announced. Linda, the others, and I, assumed that they literally didn't want to go on, that they wanted to stay where they were. We didn't realize that the boys' intention was to go back to the Home – with the obvious consequences for us.

*Four hours into the escape, at about eight o'clock at night, and the remain-
ing troops of the Orphan Army were marching some way away from their
personal Colditz. With the night settling in they needed landmarks; they
came across a railway line and settled for that as a guide. Railways took you
places; so if they followed this one they had to end up somewhere populated.
The march had become a mooch; the five ambled along chatting and walking,
running a little, stopping to discuss their bravery, the Home, a host of other
things. Partly they were trying to boost up their flagging morale.*

We were trooping through a ploughed field, mud-sticky, wet underfoot and now it was starting to rain. Heads were down, hands were
clenched in pockets, the cold was beginning to bite into us along with
the realization that it was going to be a long, cold and dark night in
the Wild World.

The blue light of a police car sped by in the distance; it was sound-
less so it was either running silently or it was too far away for us to
hear its bells. Linda shouted, 'Everybody get down'.

*Cold and mud-caked, the Orphan Army crashed into the ploughed
earth, some fell deep in the water laying at the bottom of the muddy
trenches.*

Linda was the first to put her head up to inspect the battlefield. 'OK,
they've gone,' she announced confidently.

'They're after us,' I realized, whispering. Linda agreed and told us
all that we would have to find shelter, and somewhere to hide.

We splodged through the ploughed field, absolutely wet through
and finding walking, let alone running, hard because of huge cakes of
mud clinging to our feet. A major road gave us the brief comfort of
feeling that we were near people. We crossed it. There was plenty of
traffic, lots of people around us; early evening people going home
from work, or going out for the evening. Normal, happy people for
whom the road was just a bit of scenery. People who wouldn't understand the anguish and fear of the impending night to the small figures
they passed.

We had gone through mere tiredness, now we were getting bone-
weary. 'I've got to rest, just stop a minute,' I said. We fell onto a bench
just outside a wood. Between us and the trees was a small dyke. 'We'll
have a breather and then we'll get in that wood. Then we're out of the
way'. The five of us silently sat and slouched on the bench or propped
ourselves up on it, sitting on the ground. I think we were just hud-

dling together so that we could sort of smell each other, be near each other's body heat. We were, I think, gradually collapsing.

All of a sudden a police car lurched to a halt right near us; God knows where it had come from so quietly and so suddenly. As a body we turned to look the other way, and another police car was just rolling to a halt. The game was up.

Linda belted forwards, not surrendering to the enemy yet. 'Oh no, they've found us! Run!'

I leapt to my feet, and I felt the others do the same. Linda was already disappearing into the gloom and the trees. I screamed and leapt forwards, jumping over the dyke and shouting, 'Don't leave me, Linda!' I jumped towards her fleeing shape as it disappeared into the gloom; I just wanted to be with her where I suppose I'd feel safe. But I landed in the middle of a water-filled dyke and went in straight up to the knees in sticky-mud. I knew I'd had it; I called, 'Linda wait for me, wait for me'.

I could hear the car doors opening, and a lot of frantic heavy feet running in all directions. It was over in seconds; even as I looked around to check out what our chances were I could see that the police had already caught the others. A pair of firm, but gentle, arms gripped mine tightly. 'Didn't get very far, did you?' A slow, deep and respectful voice questioned me gently.

All I could do was keep crying, 'Linda, Linda wait.' But the policeman gently laughed. 'She's gone, she's miles away by now,' he said. Then he stepped down and helped pull me out.

Most of me came out but my shoe stuck in the mud as he pulled me; I'll bet it's still buried in that field somewhere today. All the coppers were together now, each holding their captive firmly. 'No point struggling. Come on, let's get you in the car. Get you to the police station and cleaned up.' They also assured us troops there would be no winners. 'Don't worry, we'll catch your friend,' one of them told us. They were firm but gentle. Strangely nice.

'Is this your first ride in a Black Maria?' one asked, although it was just a police car and not one of the big black wire-window vans usually called Black Marias. 'First of many?' he added knowingly.

The drive back was mostly quiet; I think the police were giving us space to think through what we'd done. They asked a few questions with no anger: 'Why did you run away?' 'Why do you girls do it, because we always catch you in the end?'

At the police station we must have looked like four muddy, wet, cold ragamuffins being herded out of the car. We were very grateful to be taken into the warmth, and given some warm soapy water to wash our faces, legs and arms with. I think we were even smiling. The police seemed to have some admiration for us; after all we had made it twenty miles from the Home.

We were driven back to the Home and led back inside under the supervision of Mr and Mrs Vardy. They told us to go into the front room. That's when the whole thing really came to an end; I was really disappointed to see that Linda was already waiting for us. She had been caught and returned to the Home already.

Like most of the children I probably only saw Mr and Mrs Vardy on Sports Days and such. This was the closest I had ever been to the superintendent and his wife; usually we were dealt with by the women in charge of our cottage.

So we all lined up in the superintendent's office and as if on cue he walked through. He was a big man, maybe over six feet, and he carried with him the strength that comes with authority. I thought, 'What's going to happen, now?'

The superintendent started with Linda, prodding her in the belly. 'You should know better,' he shouted, clearly meaning that she had betrayed her seniority; she was about fifteen years old I think.

Linda just stood there in quiet defiance; she knew she had been identified as the ringleader and that hers was the punishment, or at least the lion's share. She asked how they had been caught, how they had known where to search for us. 'Your two other comrades in arms, the two boys you took with you. When they came back they were frightened for you. They told us where you were heading.'

One by one Mr Vardy inspected the troops, coming slowly down the line of girls. To each one of us he delivered a little warning, but not fiercely. 'I'm surprised at you,' to one. 'You won't do it again, will you?' to another, and so on.

When he got to me he looked quite kindly at me. 'Heather, I really am surprised at you. Why did you do it?' What could I say? I just muttered something like 'Because I wanted to'. Mr Vardy asked me if I was going to run away again, and I told him that I would not. I started to cry a little.

'If you do it again, do it on your own,' he advised somewhat dubiously. 'Don't go with anybody else. It's people like her' – he indicated Linda – 'that lead others astray.'

Good advice I thought; next time I would make sure I did just that!

Mr Vardy nodded, dismissing the whole incident.

*Before the troops were finally dismissed there had to be The Warning: The Lesson To Be Remembered. As usual it came in the form of a beating; Linda was taken into an adjacent room and the girls had to stand quietly while they heard her cry out as six of the best were leathered across her buttocks.*

*It was left to the individual Mothers of the cottages to punish their children if they wanted to. Miss Clapson from Heather's cottage chose a different path: 'Come on, Heather, I've saved you an apple dumpling. I bet you're hungry, aren't you?'*

*Heather ran away from even these two Homes several times in all, sometimes just minor excursions. By the time she left care at the age of eighteen she believed she had run away around sixty times; a figure supported by most of the people who knew her through that time. On one much later occasion she was set up with a member of her family and all was looking good for her, then on the basis of a whim she ruined all her own plans by running away from even that situation.*

*Unquestionably she was self-destructive. But why? There can be little doubt that hers was not the sort of spirit for cages; and that the Homes, rules, confinements, even minor regulations, represented to her a challenge to be defeated. Her life was a struggle, partly because she decided to make it so. But again we must ask why? The answer is almost certainly that the Homes failed in one important area; they constrained her, tried to educate her, tried to discipline her; but they forgot to try to find out where her own talents lay, what her ambitions were, how she wanted to be educated. They never asked her what path she wanted to take, and therefore she ran away to find out what it was out there in the world calling for her. In her much later years she would find new – even extraordinary ways – to follow that calling; in these early years all she could do was express her needs by 'going on the run'.*

*If getting caught running away, or being leathered for stealing chocolates you hadn't stolen, was unpleasant or even frightening, at least they had a kind of vicious normality about them. The incident most harrowing to Heather was the Visit By The Parents.*

I'd seen little of my parents in the time I'd been in the Homes, often being let down by them. Some of my earliest memories of Homeleigh are of Miss Clapson seeking Dawn and me out.

'Right, Heather and Dawn,' she would say, 'We are bringing Hazel and Angela over. Go upstairs and get in your best clothes. Your Mum and Dad are coming to see you.'

Words literally couldn't express our feelings. There was a whooping and laughing and smiling and we would just run around, hopelessly excited. We'd run upstairs to get our Sunday Best on. These dresses and special sandals never came out for school, only for visitors or for Sundays. They always felt starched and fresh and new and you always felt proud wearing them.

Downstairs we'd march, Dawn and me together, in gleeful anticipation. Miss Clapson would be at the foot of the stairs. It was a guess who was the more excited. Miss Clapson had a real feel for the emotions of her girls; I always felt warm towards her. 'Come on, let's have a look at you. Stand up nice and straight.'

Miss Clapson would comb our hair and lead us into the front sitting room. A Very Special Room for Very Important Occasions. Hazel and Angela would be there. Miss Clapson checked we were all right, had everything we needed, quickly inspected her pretty, cheery and rosy-cheeked foursome and turned to leave.

'They should be here soon,' she'd say, 'Just sit and be quiet.' We couldn't be quiet of course, we were far too excited, but it was as if our excitement was also pent-up, in anticipation. We were sort of boisterous and whispery-giggling at the same time. When we ran around playing games in the room it was almost on tip-toe. A lot of the time we spent sitting on the sofas and armchairs, just looking into each other's eyes and smiling.

We would show each other The Gifts. These gifts were little things we made for our parents; little things like hand-drawn cards with funny messages on them, little rag-dolls and rag-animals we had clumsily stitched together, or knitted, as presents. 'This is for Daddy, this is for Mummy,' we would say, and we would show off our presents and tell each other how we'd made them. My favourite gift was a little knitted mouse. There was a bit of rivalry, of course, but it was friendly; 'Mine's better than yours' sort of stuff. We always wanted to show them that we loved them and were thinking about them; I guess we were hoping that we would be loved, and be shown love, in return.

People would pass the window; we would have to crane our necks up to see if it was our parents. We would laugh and shake our heads as each person passing by turned out to be someone else. Each time a car drove past all the necks would stretch up again.

Miss Clapson would look in occasionally and we'd ask her what the time was. She would jolly us along and then we'd get back to talking and running and laughing and craning our necks. All the time we were torn between playing and frolicking and trying to keep our best clothes clean and tidy.

After a half hour or so there was a feeling of mounting excitement; that it was getting so near the time that the very next car must be the one ... or the one after that. After an hour frustration began to set it; the knowledge that when they did arrive the visit would be curtailed by lack of time. But something was better than nothing.

There would come a point when The Truth would dawn; when we'd all suddenly realize that our parents weren't coming. It was Clarence House and Mablethorpe all over again. Sure enough, a quiet and consoling Miss Clapson would come back into the room.

'They just rang to say that they won't be coming now,' she would announce. No reason. Just 'won't be coming'. Perhaps our parents never even gave Miss Clapson a reason, or perhaps she decided not to pass it on.

What could we say? A few groans and 'ohs'.

*But that didn't reflect the anguish in the four pairs of slightly too-wide eyes; the four slightly tight, brave, smiles; and the four little hearts beating just a little too fast.*

*Hazel confirms Heather's memories exactly; 'There were many times when we were all brought together in a special room, we were dressed up to wait for our parents coming. There were many, many occasions when we waited for a long, long time and they never, ever turned up.'*

*Angela, when older, had the same memory of waiting for her father and him never turning up.*

*Dawn confirmed the general background but accepted her father's explanation (which he also gave us) that he never broke his promises. 'Quite possibly Winifred made promises. I went when I said I was coming.' Heather's father believed that perhaps he indicated he 'might try to get there' and that was passed on to the children more definitely than he had intended.*

*Whatever the reality, there is little doubt that these 'missed visits' – as they saw it – were traumatic for the children.*

These let-downs happened often. After a time we used to get a different message; it wasn't 'Your Mum and your Dad' or 'Your parents'; it was just 'Your Dad is coming to visit.' We didn't know what was going on with Mum at the time, though we were later to find out. The message may have changed but the effect was usually the same – no visit. We saw him very infrequently during those years. Even when he did turn up he usually killed the excitement. 'Can't stop long this time,' he would say, or something similar. Sometimes he would just give us a big bag of sweets and be gone again, just as he had done at

Mablethorpe. Often he stayed just ten minutes or so and then we would find ourselves – almost disbelieving it ourselves – standing at the window waving at his disappearing car going back down the drive.

After a while, when Miss Clapson told us to get changed into our Sunday best we would ask, 'Is there any point?' Angela and Hazel would come through equally despondent and the world-weary battle cry now was just 'So here we are again. Bet he doesn't turn up.'

Eventually we didn't even bother looking out of the windows any more. We didn't bother making presents. We didn't play and goof around; we just used to sit quietly in the room until Miss Clapson came to tell us we should go back and get changed.

*But miracles do happen sometimes. One day a surprise visit happened and both Mum and Dad turned up together. And far from staying just ten minutes they stayed a while and dropped the most beautiful bombshell; they had come to tell the children they had moved to a nearby house.*

It had been eight months since we'd seen either of our parents. I was outside playing on the swings and the see-saw when I suddenly saw Dad's car pull up outside. I ran in to 'Aunty' Nora crying: 'Aunty Nora, Aunty Nora. It's my Mum and Dad'; then I ran back out through the gate to the car and bundled all over them, hugging and kissing and whooping and jumping.

I asked if I could go and get Hazel. I got the nod and ran over to Hazel's cottage to spread the news.

Our parents told us they had moved into Horncastle. They were renting a big house just a mile or so away from Homeleigh. We would be able to visit. 'We're renting a house here in Horncastle and we're going to be able to see more of you. We're going to come and see you. You'll be able to come and stay.'

All us Bradley girls got really excited. After our parents had left we went inside to talk with Miss Clapson. Even at that age we were so institutionalized we didn't even ask if it meant we could go home to live with our parents; we just hoped we'd be able to visit them.

And visit we did. Dad told us he was going to come for us over the weekend and that we would be able to stay in the house with them for the weekend.

Even then we never expected to be able to stay permanently. We chatted and played and laughed with Mum and Dad; it was like one of those endless, time-stretched, wonderful weekends. Even going back to the Home seemed natural and acceptable. We just said, 'Goodbye Mum, goodbye Dad' and then returned to Homeleigh.

At the time none of us questioned why we couldn't return home. Looking back now I think there was probably a care order over us, and our parents had to 'prove' themselves as parents to the authorities before they could have us back.

*In fact Heather's father told us there was no formal care order.*

There were many visits and many very short 'droppings in' after school for a chat, a half hour here and there. 'Hi, sweetheart' would be Mum's standard greeting; a light voice and a warm smile. I would run breathless to see her after school, get a quick hug and a kiss and perhaps a drink and a sweet and then run back to the Home. I never told the people in the Home what I did, I was very protective of my time with my parents. I had to be careful never to be caught out; I sometimes had to run fit to bursting to get back in time.

*The Best News arrived one day. It had been a week or more since Heather had seen her parents. She came home from school, put her satchel down, and saw Aunty Nora heading towards her.*

'You're going home,' Aunty Nora said. I assumed the obvious; that I was going to the house to see Mum and Dad. But Aunty Nora's beaming face answered even before she opened her mouth. 'No, you're actually going home.'

In fact, 'home' was not the house I had been visiting. In the time since I had last seen them our parents had moved to another house in New Bolingbroke, towards Boston. It came with Dad's current job. Possibly it was approved by the authorities for the family to begin our life together.

After two years at Homeleigh all our bags and other stuff were packed. I hugged and held Aunty Nora and Miss Clapson and thanked them for everything. I told them 'Thanks for everything, I've been happy,' and of course I meant it at that time.

*There had been hard times but the human will is strong – often a child's will even more so. And when the future looks good, the bad times disappear like snow in the midday sun. Heather got into the car and they drove over to the other cottage to pick Angela up; they were all excited.*

When we were reunited at New Bolingbroke I was really delighted to see the change in Mum and Dad; they seemed so relaxed and happy. 'We're home at last. We've come home, we're home,' we all chanted as we hugged and kissed.

*The world suddenly looked good and the future looked promising. It was to last just a few months.*

## Home again

*For Heather, to be re-united with her parents was wonderful. On reflection, it was an unfortunate time for it to have happened; her mother was on a permanent downhill slide. She had been institutionalized herself; had had electric shock therapy, a cranial operation and an operation on the thyroid. The evidence of the brain-operation – a leucotomy to 'control her moods and temper' – was only just hidden where the hair had grown back over the surgery-scars. Either she convinced the authorities that all was well, or someone took a chance that didn't work out.*

*Both Heather's sister Hazel, and Heather's father, confirmed that her mother was never the same after the operation, and not for the better by any means.*

*Heather started at a new school nearby, and quickly made new friends. But home life was the special part of her life at this time. However, it was almost immediately fraught with tension caused by her mother's drink and drug problems.*

Hazel wasn't there a lot. Although Hazel was the oldest and in charge I still seemed to be the organizer. Mum and Dad didn't know about Hazel's boyfriend; once she even stayed out overnight and I don't think Dad and Mum missed her. When Dad eventually found out about Hazel and her boyfriend he laid into her.

*Hazel confirms that her father was waiting at the bus stop that night; he disapproved of her relationship with an older man and 'gave her a good hiding'.*

I think that, without realizing it at the time, I became Angela's and Dawn's 'mother', as Hazel wasn't there that often.

After school we would frequently come home to find our parents weren't there. We'd have no prior warning. We would just find the door locked, the car gone. The keys to the house would be left at the shop across the road and we would get into the house and make jam or peanut butter sandwiches for tea. There were an awful lot of peanut butter sandwiches at that time of my life.

There was a tyre shop nearby, with lots of tyres outside. I remember going over when it was raining. We'd been sitting outside and the lady over there said, 'Why don't you come over here until your parents are back. We feel really sorry for you, always on your own. Tell your sisters to come over and sit in here where it's warm and dry.' That happened quite a lot. We used to play in the tyres, running in and out of them.

*The children had suffered abuses from within their own immediate circle – Steven – and they had suffered several types of abuse in the Homes that were supposed to care for them. Now they were in the wider world, and many times left to care for themselves; precisely what the Homes had failed to train them for. They were in danger now from the world at large, and soon enough the danger was to materialize.*

One weekend Mum and Dad went out. They told us they were going for a drink, and that they would be back in an hour, then they just left us.

We were playing hopscotch when a neighbour, a man from a nearby bungalow, came out and invited us into his home. He and his wife were young, maybe nineteen, and they had a new baby.

'Would you like to come and see the baby?' he asked, and I went round there with one of my sisters, to their bungalow.

*That sister has confirmed the basis of this story to us; but has asked not to be specifically identified.*

I wanted to get back home after a while and said I was leaving, but my sister asked if she could stay for a while, and she did.

The next day my sister told me that the couple had invited her to go round to their home any time she liked. She asked me if I wanted to come. We both checked with Mum and Dad and they said it would be okay. Mum only made us promise not to be a nuisance.

Another time Mum and Dad had gone out and left us again, my sister again went round to visit the couple.

I suddenly realized that it had been an hour or so and she wasn't back. I decided to go and fetch her, I was a bit concerned that Mum and Dad would be home shortly. As I ran down the four steps of our house I could hear my sister running, although again I couldn't see her until I reached the bottom. She was crying and I called out, 'I'm just coming for you'.

She was very upset. 'What's the matter? What have you done? What's been going on?' I kept firing questions at her, but she wouldn't answer me. She was sobbing and crying. I took her into the house and she still wouldn't say anything. Our car drew up, Mum and Dad were back. I said, 'Now look, we are going to get into trouble. You're upset and crying and it might get Dad in a mood.' I suppose deep down I was frightened that if Mum and Dad thought they couldn't feel safe leaving us alone, if they had to stay with us all the time, that they'd probably put us back in a Home. 'We've got to let Mum and Dad see that we're okay.'

So nothing was really said for a couple of days; my sister didn't seem to be too distressed. Then the man came round again. He always seemed to know when we were alone; I don't think Mum and Dad ever met him or his wife.

He asked to see my sister. 'Would she like to come round?' She went round without protesting but very unenthusiastically. It was like she felt she had to, not that she wanted to.

After about ten minutes I got worried; something told me that something was wrong. I went round to their house to get her back, or at least see that she was all right.

*At this point Heather and the sister involved have different memories of the next incidents; those differences are quite revealing. Heather remembers reaching the house, no-one answering the front door and her going round the back to their french doors. Through the window Heather could see the woman of the couple holding her sister down while the man was sexually abusing her. Heather started kicking and knocking and shouting 'Leave her alone'. The couple jumped up suddenly when they heard her, then her sister jumped up and ran towards the front door of the house, and escaped back to their own home.*

*In fact the sister only told us of one incident, but Heather remembers it as two separate events.*

The man came after us but we got to our house first and I shut the door. He was shouting at us through the door. I told him to go away; he called back that he was sorry and didn't mean it.

'Don't tell your parents or the police.' Eventually I opened the door and he talked us round to not saying anything. We were young and frightened of course. Maybe we thought that somehow we'd done something wrong, and we were always afraid of being put back in the Homes. He promised he wouldn't come round any more, wouldn't bother us.

We got rid of him once he thought he was safe. My sister didn't really want to say a lot about what had happened; only that it hurt and that the woman did as much as he had. She said that she held her down and actually put her hand, not just over her mouth to keep her quiet, but also over her nose and mouth so she couldn't breathe. She was fighting for breath; that was the way they controlled her, made her docile.

*The sister involved confirmed that an attempted abuse took place, but she is quite adamant that the man took the chance of an attack because his wife had gone out, perhaps to the shops. She also does not remember Heather being involved until reaching the family home and getting on the safe side of the front door. The difference about the attack might suggest that there is a blocked memory in the abused sister; more likely that Heather actually did not witness it, but projected her concerns for her sisters by visualizing it so vividly she believed she was there. That would be typical of Heather in that she had great compassion for others, and more than once commented that she felt she had sometimes been 'mother' to her younger sisters. It also means that she was capable of taking on someone else's pain and suffering; a trait that would have extraordinary manifestation in her later life.*

Apart from that episode life fell into a pattern. We used to get the shopping 'on tick'(on credit) – Mum owed a lot. Dad was giving Mum money for food but Mum was getting everything on tick and spending the money on ciggies and tots of rum.

The pub was just across the road. I can remember my mother – many times – giving me this little bottle and a shilling piece and telling me to go over to the off-licence part of the pub and get a tot of rum. They would fill up your own bottle with a tot or two in those days. And I used to get her loose cigarettes when she couldn't afford a whole packet.

There is a long, straight stretch of road leading into New Bolingbroke. The 'fun' game a lot of Sundays was for Dad to drive us to the end of the stretch and then we had to walk back to the house. It took about four hours to get back. Dad would set us games to play like collecting every type of leaf we could. And there were prizes; for every different leaf found we would get a halfpenny. He never came to check up on us halfway, or anything like that.

And we just thought that they loved us and that this was a game for us to play. I suppose we had a lot of fun. We didn't realize until later that they just wanted us out of the way so that they could continue their rowing and arguing.

*In this home Heather found her sanctum sanctorum just as she had on the farm. Not a Secret Garden this time, but an unused attic room. It served the same purpose.*

Upstairs there was a bathroom on the left, then the bedroom and then a few wooden steps to this little door. One day I decided to go up there, opened the door, and went in. There was quite a lot of space and – even more importantly – absolute silence. I couldn't hear anything. I couldn't hear my sisters. I couldn't hear my parents arguing. I thought, 'Oh, this is great. I can come in here and escape.' But I also wanted to share it with my sisters, and later I did. We all went in and I suggested that the room could be our secret hiding place where we could go and just talk together. We found a candle and a tin plate; we heated up some water and had a drink. It was lovely and cosy and quiet. We went there a lot; just sat and talked. Often Dad would say, 'Go up in your room and play,' but if we did we could hear them arguing, so we'd go into the attic room. We couldn't hear them up there.

We all had lists of chores to do, so we did most of the cleaning and preparing the meals: Heather wash, Angela dry, Dawn put away, and so on. One job I hated was to peel the potatoes. I remember peeling them one day and Dad coming in and criticizing. He said, 'What's this? There's half the potato in with this, come here!' And he showed me how to take just the peel off. 'Look at that,' he proudly showed me. I hadn't really peeled potatoes before but that was my job. Every day I dreaded that he would come in and criticize me. I tried so hard to take just the peel off and not to take a lot of potato with it.

*Heather's sister, Hazel, confirmed that home life with the family was probably about as strict in parts as home life in the Homes. Their father was apparently a real disciplinarian. He would beat Hazel – never Heather, in fact – always keeping his leather belt to hand. Hazel can't remember the belt ever being used to punish them, but felt it was clearly there as a disciplinary threat. They were not allowed to talk at the dinner table, or read newspapers. Hazel told us that she was quite grown up before she read her first newspaper. Her father cooked Sunday lunch, he was a good cook, but God help anyone who didn't eat up every scrap from their plate.*

At the time Mum was taking a lot of drugs. At first I was unaware that she was on all this medication, though we knew that Dad gave her her tablets. He would say, 'It's tablet time,' and hand over the pills, but we learned to take that in our stride. Often she kept me off school; she would just say, 'I'm going to keep you off school today, Heather, so you can help me with the housework'. Once, when she had me off school, Mum said that she needed me to help her to break into the bureau to get the tablets. She wanted the tablets, she needed them.

I tried to talk her out of it, 'Don't do it, Mum, you'll be all right.' But I think Purple Hearts were such an addictive drug she couldn't help herself. So between us we broke into the bureau. She found the tablets, took a few, and then asked me to put the rest in the hem of the two curtains. And she swore me to secrecy. 'Whatever you do, don't tell Dad where you have hidden them.'

My father was unaware I was being kept off school. He wasn't there in the morning when we got up to go to school and he didn't turn up until about eight at night. He just seemed to be there now and again.

*A terrible incident happened as a result of the pills; it destroyed everything of the family unity at that time.*

I was trying to do my homework and Angela had some Rice Krispies. They were making a fierce noise, a loud crackling sound. And I could feel myself really getting annoyed and aggravated by this sound. It just got louder and louder and louder. I stood up and in a wild sweep I knocked this bowl off the table shouting, 'I can't stand it any more!' Then I ran out.

Mum came after me. She got hold of me and comforted me, telling me it would be all right. I shook my head, I was nearly in tears. I cried, 'I just can't stand it any more'. I think I realized that something was going to happen; that we wouldn't be home for long.

A little later I heard Mum go out. I ran out after her; she had gone round the side of the house where it was dark, to where we kept the coal for the fire. The rain and sleet and snow was falling, it was slippery underfoot and I went down. Mum helped me up. She told me to go back into the house, that she was going for a walk.

I think I knew something was wrong. I insisted on going with her. It was really cold and wet. And she kept saying, 'No, you go back. You don't want to be with me.' I begged to be with her and eventually she agreed. So I held her arm and we started this walk. We were walking on the road rather than the footpath; it was less slippery.

We walked for a while in silence, just being together, and then Mum said, 'I'm going into town. I want you to go back home. I don't want you with me.' I pleaded again to stay with her, and she agreed.

Mum decided that we were going to thumb a lift, and we tried that. Eventually a lorry stopped; it was going to town. We got in.

All the lights of the cars were coming towards us as we silently drove to town. I was almost hypnotized by the swish of the wipers. Mum never spoke all the way.

After the driver dropped us off we walked to a chemist. Mum put her hand in her pocket and told me, 'Now, you stay out here. I'm just going to go in here and get these tablets.' She was in there for quite a while.

*Heather stood in the bitter cold, wet through and shaking from the night air. She watched through the window where she could see a man dressed in white having a really hard argument with her mother. At one point he went away, then came back with somebody else. Her mother was visibly agitated; she was getting upset about something. The next minute she came out shouting, 'Come on, we're going home'.*

It was as if it was very urgent. I can't even remember how we got home; whether we hitched a lift or not. All I remember was that she grabbed me quick and hard, saying, 'Let's get away from here.'

When we got back home Mum was in a terrible state. She was distressed and shaking; she told us all to go to bed. Then Dad looked in, slammed the door and shouted at us, telling us to get to bed. All four of us slept in one bed, a king-sized bed. We slept two at the top, two at the bottom. The others asked me where we'd been and I told them; then we all cried.

We could hear Mum and Dad shouting and things being banged about. The front door slammed and we heard the car go – Dad had left.

We went to school the next day. It was in the afternoon that I was called out. The headmaster had sent for me. I left my pen and book on my desk and walked to the office. 'Come on in, Heather,' he called. I thought maybe I had done something wrong. Then he said, 'I think you know who this is and why they are here.' It was the first time I realized that there was someone else in the room. I looked at the other man there and I saw it all in those hardened, institutional eyes.

'Oh, not again,' I muttered. 'Yes, I'm sorry, Heather.' He was from the Social Services. They told me Mum had been taken into hospital; I didn't know where my father was. I never even had time to go back and collect my pen. We walked outside to a waiting car; my sisters were already waiting in it for me.

*Heather and her sisters were taken away to another Home. She was yet to discover the truth about her mother, but their last, brief, tortured life together as a family had just ended.*

# Burgh Hall

*For teenagers of around fourteen – as Heather was – 1963 was a Big Year. Every event seemed to make headlines the world over: Kennedy's assassination; Christine Keeler and the Profumo affair; the Great Train Robbery; the death of Pope John XXIII. Martin Luther King told the world that 'I have a dream' and the Beatles told the world that 'She loves you'. There were few dreams, and little love, where Heather was next to find herself.*

*'You will call me Dad. This is your Mum.' The man indicated the woman standing to his left, his hand extended. But his eyes never left Heather. It was Mr and Mrs Crabbe, the couple she had known in Homeleigh – they had run one of the cottages. They were the parents of her 'blood sister', Andrea. Now they were at Burgh Hall; where Heather and her sisters had now been taken to.*

'I've got a Mum and Dad, why should I call you that?' I was shaking even as I asked, but there wasn't much reaction; perhaps he just shrugged a bit. 'That's what you have to call us,' he said.

I never liked having to call them Mum and Dad, but we had to. In the other Homes we usually called them Aunty or Uncle. For a while I would avoid it by not using names, but in the end I had to; I'd have to ask, 'Mum, where is the so-and-so...'

*Heather's return to the Home had been precipitated by the problems of her mother. Heather had known that something bad had happened that cold night while she was outside the chemist shop in Boston, but she had no idea how bad it had been. She had been told that her mother was ill, and accepted that. She wrote letters to her mother, but never received a reply.*

In fact my mother had been put into prison. She was given a prison sentence for trying to get drugs illegally. Apparently she didn't want to answer the letters because it would have had to be written on prison notepaper and she didn't want other children at the Home to know. So we were all unaware for some time. But Mr and Mrs Crabbe knew.

It would have been easier if we sisters had all been together, but Hazel wasn't with us. It was the first time we had been separated. Hazel had been in the car when we had left the school but she stayed in the car when it dropped us off. I asked, 'Oh, where is Hazel?' but they told us that she was too old for the Home, and that she had to go to a working girls' hostel in Nottingham.

Life was very strict at this Home; there were a lot of beatings and a lot of mental torture.

In the day room there was a big library filled with books. Mrs Crabbe told us to dust the shelves. Mary, another girl there, just started dusting round but Mrs Crabbe told us, 'Take the books out. I want the bookshelves dusted.' Every book on every shelf had to be lifted off.

Mrs Crabbe knew how to hurt us. She would say things to us about our parents. 'You're never going to get anywhere in life,' she would tell us.

We all sat at group tables for our meals, five to a table. And there would always be someone watching over us. I was often on Mum Crabbe's table.

You were not allowed to talk at the table so it was always very quiet. All the Homes were the same that way. You had to say, 'Can I have a piece of bread and butter, please?'. You'd have to ask for each round. You couldn't just reach over and get it. And you were very restricted with what you could have; I was always hungry. There were seconds for the boys if they wanted them; they had to be built up into big strong men, of course. Then if there was any left the girls would be told 'OK You can come up'. So of course we never got any seconds, whereas the boys did.

I was on Mrs Crabbe's table one night when she was called away to answer the phone. After she had left, my friend, Mary, looked around, leant over and whispered very quietly to me, 'Shall I put some salt in Mother's tea?'

I was frightened and at first asked her not to. Eventually mischief overtook me and I agreed we should do it. Mary reached over and got the salt, and she started dropping it in – it was as if she was pouring it in. It looked far too much and I said, 'That's enough'. She sat back quickly and only just in time, too. The door opened and Mrs Crabbe came back and sat down. We were kind of preparing ourselves.

After a while she drank from her tea. Her face just screwed up and she winced and made a choking, drawn out noise. She spat the tea out and shrieked, 'Who on earth did that? Who did that? You, Bradley?'

I denied it. She went round the table. 'Harris, was that you?' From each one she demanded an answer. 'It was one of you on this table, wasn't it?'

Suddenly she just picked on Michael. 'It was you,' she said, and still shaking with rage she picked up the rest of her tea and threw it straight in his face. 'Here, have a taste of your own medicine. Now get out of my sight.'

When they said 'get out of my sight' we usually had to stand outside the office or in the kitchen.

When dinner was over I had the job of stacking all the pots in the kitchen. I went into the kitchen and found Michael and Mrs Crabbe there.

Mrs Crabbe was telling him to get the kettle on and boil some water. Michael obeyed her.

They just quietly faced each other; Michael didn't know what was coming and Mrs Crabbe wasn't letting on. She spooned tea leaves from the caddie into the teapot and poured in the boiled water. She took a spoon and stirred the tea. It was as if she was going to make a cup of tea. Then she just picked up the teapot and poured the lot over Michael's head.

Boiling water, running all over his face and hair, all over his clothes. And she got hold of him then because he was screaming; you could see the tea leaves running through the liquid and that it was burning him and he was screaming and screaming. I couldn't believe what I was seeing. I just stood there and I think she said something like, 'You can have some too. There's plenty to go round,' or something like that. But with Michael screaming one of the Aunties came running through and told her that it had been Mary that had salted her tea.

Mrs Crabbe asked the Aunty to bring Mary through. I stood there, and Mary came through. But she didn't touch her. She just said she had got something better for Mary than a hot cup of tea. It was a mental rather than a physical punishment though; she took away from her her one precious thing. That was very cruel. It's difficult to describe how painful it could be. Everything in the Homes was handed down, second-hand. But you were bought one thing new for yourself – I had a jacket – and if you were deprived of it it hurt so much. I had my jacket taken away once. Awful. So painful. Those things meant so much to us.

*Other sisters recalled these deprivations. Dawn, in particular, told us she*
*was unhappy more due to emotional suppression than physical punishment,*
*and mostly caused by Mrs Crabbe.*

There was another Aunty there who took a real delight in hurting
people. If you were walking through the hall she would chop you in
the back of the knees and make you fall over. Or if you were waiting
in line for something she'd do the same thing. She would also just slap
you a lot, often for nothing.

I told Dad – my real Dad – about it on one of his few visits. 'If it
happens again just put a little flower in the corner of your letter.' He
knew that all letters were read by the staff and if you wrote anything
they didn't want you to say they wouldn't let the letter go out. I
couldn't just write a letter and send it to him myself because I didn't
have his address. I suppose he contacted Mr and Mrs Crabbe every
now and again.

One beating really shocked me. Another girl in the Home, and
Angela, were fighting over a rag doll and it got tugged apart. Angela
was left with the head, it just tore off. Mother just happened to be
walking by and turned on Angela. She was quite frightened and said,
'I'm sorry, I didn't mean it. It was only a game.' Mother Crabbe got
hold of her: 'You Bradleys. Get through here into the day room.'

We went through and automatically took The Stance; arms behind
your back and looking down.

'I'm fed up with you Bradleys, lying, running away, breaking
things, not toeing the line. I'm going to beat some discipline into you.'
She stared at us for a while, very quiet.

'Angela deserves this. If you don't think she does I can give you
some of the same.'

She took Angela and pushed her over the edge of an armchair, and
she held her neck and shoulder down. Her arms were pinned underneath her. With her other hand Mrs Crabbe pulled Angela's knickers
down and lifted her skirt up. I watched Angela trying to move her
hands to cover her bottom, but she couldn't move. Mrs Crabbe told me
to take my plimsoll off. She just kept saying that she deserves it. Then
she used my plimsoll to hit her. I thought maybe it would just be one,
two, three or so hits. But it went on and on; her backside, the back of
her legs, her hands when she got them back there over her bottom, the
small of her back. And it just seemed to go on and on and on. Angela
was crying and I was getting quite angry and incensed. It was building
up in me that I was going to retaliate. I thought, 'I need to protect my

sister.' Then she just let go of Angela, chucked the plimsoll back at me and said, 'There, now don't you think she deserved that? Don't you?'

I didn't know what to say. If I started to resist I could have done anything. I could have hit her I think. I just stopped myself. I kind of just stood there and muttered 'Yes, Mother.'

Then she just said, 'Get out of my sight.' Angela had bruises all over her back. I wrote a letter with the flower on it. Dad turned up about a week later. The staff didn't know he was coming, I don't think he warned them. I was in the day room, just day-dreaming and looking out of the windows. There was a big, pebbled driveway with trees either side and I saw the bonnet of the car coming round the corner. As soon as I looked over, I knew it was Dad. 'It's Dad! Dawn, look, it's Dad!'

We ran to the office to tell them. We knocked on the door; you had to wait until it was opened and you were told to come in. They called us in and I told them that my Dad had arrived.

They spent some time talking without us in the room, then Mother Crabbe stormed out shouting, 'Take no notice of those Bradleys. Your daughters are liars and thieves.'

Dad demanded to be taken to see Angela. He was told Angela was in the isolation wing. We had to go there if we had chickenpox, or something contagious like that. But my father insisted on seeing her and they brought Angela to him. They told him she had something – scarlet fever, I think. They had explained the bruising by saying she had fallen down some steps. She was red on the back, the bottom, the legs and part of the hands. And this was a week after the beating, but all the marks were still there. Dad lifted Angela's dress up, pulled her knickers down a little bit and pointed at her back, looking at Mrs Crabbe. 'You're not telling me, woman, that that's because she fell down a few steps. Heather told me she'd been beaten, didn't you?'

He knew what the flower in the letter had meant. But now I couldn't bring myself to say it, that was the mental hold they had over you. I was standing there, Dad was there, the marks were on Angela, all I had to do was talk up. And I couldn't. I couldn't say a word.

Dad kept pushing me. 'Didn't you? That's what you said, that's what you said in the letter.'

I couldn't say a word. I couldn't make my mouth work. I knew that Dad would be going soon, and then I'd be defenceless in her hands. Mrs Crabbe suddenly knew she'd won. She smiled, and she said, 'Well, there you are. You shouldn't listen to their lies.'

*Cruelty in the Homes wasn't always so obvious; sometimes it might even have been unintended. But to young girls struggling through puberty there were unpleasantnesses that even years later made them shudder: Dad Crabbe apparently had an unfortunate habit of needing to inspect the wash-rooms when the girls were having strip washes.*

*Heather's father had a few surprises of his own for Heather, and they were every bit as painful as the beatings. He was at Skegness now. He had got a job as a redcoat at Butlins, about eight miles away.*

Dad turned up out of the blue one day and introduced us to this woman who was with him. I thought she was one of his girlfriends; I would have been ready for that. But he told us that she was his wife; he had remarried.

*Heather's father told us that he thought he had sent a letter to the children pre-warning them. But Heather's mind was swamped with images of her mother. Ill, very ill. Now no longer married to her father. Heather was well aware that her mother had tried – within her own limitations – to keep the family together and to provide for her children. She hadn't succeeded: they had spent their lives in Homes and in care; they had rarely seen her or their father; and now the family was irretrievably broken up – her parents were no longer married. And worse than that there had been no warning, no way to adjust to this new truth. She had found out by being introduced to the New Wife. But not the New Mother – oh no, not the new mother. She wasn't being asked to accept that, at least.*

*Perhaps a few of the shocks she was suffering contributed to Heather's first health deteriorations.*

I started to have a lot of trouble with my bowels; I was getting up in the middle of the night with terrible diarrhoea. It was usually Dad Crabbe who would hear me, he would come down to see if I was all right. He would ask if I was in a lot of pain. He knew from earlier discussions that there was a lot of pain associated with my diarrhoea. Perhaps it was just the shock, but maybe it was the start of my serious bowel problems in later life.

*In all Heather's troubled life, the one area of happiness and achievement was at school, and it is highly likely that given a better series of opportunities she could have excelled; at least she managed to enjoy her school-life.*

I was happy at school. There was one teacher who took a shine to me; I was her pet in a way. This was the first time I had been given any kind of attention, or love, at school, and it was lovely. I worked hard to please her and in some subjects I did really well. I was surprised how easily I got into the schoolwork, considering this was my fifth secondary school. Sometimes I was ahead of the other children because I'd already done the lesson they were doing when I had been in another school. But sometimes I'd go to a school where I was behind. I've got quite a few of my school reports still; one says 'Heather is becoming a fine young lady with a great sense of humour. She will go a long way.' Another says 'Heather has an excellent brain'.

I kind of led a double life in that I gave everything I could at school, I thoroughly enjoyed that, but when the final bell went and we got on the bus back to the Home, especially Burgh, I would be sitting there quite frightened thinking, 'What will I find I've done wrong? What's going to happen when I get in?'

*Heather's 'double life' was the beginning of the emergence of the adult from the child. The Homes were treating her like a child, while she carved out her development as an adult through her lessons. By the same token she was free to act as a child at school, but she had been deprived of her childhood needs, wants and fun by the Homes. The Homes were providing a poor environment for caterpillars to turn into butterflies – certainly they were not encouraging the self-development that makes confident adults. In fact they were breeding grounds for crippled caterpillars.*

I was still having problems with my bladder. I wasn't wetting myself any more but I was always going to the toilet. One time we got off the bus and walked the mile to the Home and all the way I was bursting for a wee. I only just got there in time and I ran in, took my shoes off and threw them in a locker, took my coat off and went straight to the toilet. When I came out Mother Crabbe was there. I nearly knocked into her running to report in. So I was kind of scurrying round the corner to say I was back and I nearly bumped into her. She was holding my shoes and coat over her arm.

'Oh, good evening Mother. I'm home', I said. Almost at the same time as I said it she slapped me round the face. It just happened so quickly. I didn't know what I'd done, I was so shocked I just stood there with my mouth open. She kind of backed away and shook my clothes at me. 'Here, take those. Get in the hall! You know you have to hang your coat up by the hook and put your shoes away.'

I told her that I was sorry, and that I had been bursting for a pee. She shouted back at me that that was no excuse. You always had to miss a meal or something like that for a punishment; and I missed a meal then. There was always a cost if you did anything wrong in these Homes; usually it was a money fine. If you left your toothbrush in the washroom, or left your hairbrush or your gloves or scarf somewhere you had to pay a fine to get them back. You got pocket money – two shillings for fourteen- to sixteen-year-olds. The Home took threepence for the church and then they would clock up your fines; toothbrush, toothpaste, that's threepence each, and so on. I'd hardly ever get any money after paying to get back my toothbrush, and other things. If you couldn't pay for them you couldn't have them back. I know I missed cleaning my teeth many days.

Mary, Michael and I ran away together once. We caught a bus and went to Skegness, walked around for a while and then it started to rain. Mary suggested that we go and find some shelter at the local cinema, the Odeon.

We looked through the doors and saw that there was nobody around; the film was already going. It was nice and dry, we were just drying off. We mooched around a bit, and went upstairs to the landing just outside the Circle. The ice-cream lady had left her tray that she carried the ice creams and lollies in. I looked at them, and Mary asked if we wanted an ice cream. When we said 'no' she told us that she was going to have one anyway. I pointed out that we had no money, that we couldn't have one. She just dipped in and took one. I protested, 'No, don't, don't take one.'

Mary got a handful and put them under her arm, in her pockets, all over the place. She handed me one and some to Michael. I just laughed, unwrapped this choc-ice and was holding it up to my mouth when suddenly the door opened and an usherette came out onto the landing.

'Have you just taken those out of there?' Pockets bulging, all three of us holding ice-creams, Mary said

'No.'

I just shouted 'Run'. Two staircases went from the landing down to the foyer. We separated and ran down both stairs; the usherette didn't know who to go for. We bumped into each other in the foyer, saw the lady was running down after us, shouting at us, and we ran as fast as we could out of the cinema and into the streets outside.

Ice creams were falling out of Mary's pockets all over the place and by now all three of us were laughing almost hysterically.

Mary's pockets were full of all those ice creams and she had the cheek to say 'No'. It was just so funny. We were running and laughing and giggling. But it was cold and wet and getting dark; we'd been gone for four or five hours. I'd learnt something from my past runaways though; I had plenty of jumpers on, and a bit of money. I knew to prepare for survival.

But we had to give up. We decided to go to the police and give ourselves up. They were very nice and made us a drink. They asked the usual questions about what made kids like us run away.

*It was, for a moment, as if time slowed down or even stood still. Heather listened to the question and tried to frame an answer. How could she explain about the Homes, the beatings, the hunger, the deprivation? She could hardly explain about the loss of dignity, the loss of control, the lack of self-respect or respect of others. At that age she couldn't even frame the concepts properly. Perhaps the policeman saw something of the inner struggle in her eyes; there was a short silence between them.*

*Suddenly Heather saw herself as nothing more than a young teenage runaway, demobbed from the Orphan Army. And she knew they just weren't going to listen to her. It wasn't their fault; there was no way they could understand her credibility.*

I think I did say, 'If you lived there you'd know, the things that they do to us, what goes on there.' But they didn't seem interested.

They gave us a towel and we dried up. By that time Mr Crabbe arrived.

'Thank you Officer. Come on you three – in the car! You know you're in for it.'

We knew what he meant all right; we were going to be handed over to Mrs Crabbe. Dad Crabbe was all right most of the time, but Mrs Crabbe was the hard one. When we got back we were all slapped across the face. We'd been standing waiting for her in the room in the stance position, eyes down. The others kept their heads down when they were slapped, but I didn't. I lifted my head and my eyes up. Despite the look from Mrs Crabbe to grind me down, I didn't waver. I was feeling hard and angry. The slapping stung, there were tears in my eyes, but I stared her out.

'Get out of my sight. I'll sort your punishment out later. I'll make you pay.'

*Heather was beginning to fight. Her rebellious spirit was beginning to externalize. The next time she and Mrs Crabbe were to lock horns Mrs Crabbe would know that Heather would not back away again.*

We all had different tasks to do each week. One week Dawn and I had to put water jugs out on the table for meals. The bell had gone to call everyone in from outside. When the bell went you had to come straight in, wash your hands, then come and stand in the hall to show your hands; they checked them and then we were given a 'pinny' and sent in to eat. I was late, I think I'd been in the toilet, and when I got into the dining room I realized we'd forgotten the water jugs.

So we got the tin jugs, filled them and came back as quickly as we could. Dawn went first, I'd over-filled mine and it was spilling all over. As I was walking in Dawn was coming out. I asked her what was wrong. Dawn told me that we weren't going to be allowed the water because we had been too late.

'We've got to take them back,' she said. 'Why?' I asked. I heard the scraping of a chair; someone was getting up. I could hear Mrs Crabbe thudding towards the door. She came out.

'You Bradleys! I'm sick of you Bradleys. Why? Why? Why? That's all you ask, why, why, why? I'll give you why.' She slapped me across the face, palm of the hand and then a back-hander. 'Take it away, it's too late, nobody is having any water now.' I just looked at her and something cracked. I just poured both my jugs of water all over her legs, all over her feet. All the time I was just staring her in the eyes.

Suddenly I realized what I had done. And she was so enraged, just the look on her face. I ran like a bat in hell, ran out of the hall and into the kitchen. She followed me.

In her office I was standing, waiting, with my eyes down. She stood in front of me. I just felt myself slowly just lifting my head and she warned me, 'Don't you dare.' Looking up was just something you didn't do. But I did. I just felt my head lifting. It all seemed to be in slow motion.

'Don't you dare look me in the face.' But I kept my eyes on her eyes.

I said, 'No more, no more, you're not going to hit me anymore.' I stared her out until she actually looked away and said, 'Go on, get off, get out of my sight.'

She looked away! She looked away! I'd won. I went out, shut the door, leant back on the door and thought 'I've got her. I'm not taking any more. I'm not having any more and she knows it.'

*Heather had to face other problems.*

It was noticed that one of my legs was longer than the other. A doctor suggested that I needed surgery. I was having problems and was in a lot of pain. I was nearly sixteen and they had to operate while I was still growing.

What they did was to cut into my leg, remove an inch and a half of bone, pin the bone together again and stitch me up. I think I was under anaesthetic for about five hours; it was a new operation. I asked about it and they told me there would be a metal pin in it. I thought it would just be a little thing, but they said it was fourteen inches long. They had to hammer it down into the leg, into the hollow middle of the bone where the marrow is.

When the nursing sister came to take the bandage off there were three nurses there to hold my leg down. I asked why they were doing that.

'Because your leg has been straight for that long a period it's going to spring up.' When they took the bandage off and slowly took the pressure off where they were holding my leg it just sprang up and stayed like it. And it was covered in long, black hair; you could have put rollers in it.

After the surgery I was told that I wouldn't be going back to Burgh Hall; I was to go to another Home.

'They can't accommodate you at Burgh Hall with your crutches and your wheelchair,' they told me. I had spent sixteen weeks in hospital. I was taken with my sisters straight from the hospital to Barrow Hall, another Home.

# Barrow Hall

I never went back to Burgh Hall to say cheerio to the friends I had made in the last two years – I just got in the car, Angela and Dawn were already inside; they picked me up from the hospital. We drove to Barrow Hall. Like many of the other Homes, Barrow Hall was a beautiful mansion, with beautiful grounds, lovely old trees, bluebells along the drive, and so on. But they were all prisons; the horror inside the buildings wasn't visible from the outside. Birds would sing and chirp in the air, but if anyone could understand them, perhaps they were crying out for someone to come and rescue the children from the lives they led within those walls.

My leg was still bandaged up, not in plaster, and I was in a wheelchair. I was shown my bedroom, which had four steps I had to negotiate, then we were shown to my sisters' upstairs room. We had been to visit Barrow Hall for a short while some months before, so our only introduction this time was, 'You've been here before, so you know what goes on.'

We settled in; again there was a very strict regime. When meal times came we had to line up; we had to show our hands; we actually had to show we had cleaned our teeth. Then we'd be told, 'Turn, march, go in, sit down, be quiet.' I soon got out of the wheelchair; I didn't like it. I had already got crutches and I had been told to practise using them when I was ready. Within a week, I was on my crutches but still unable to put any weight on my leg. But I still had to line up; I wasn't allowed to go in separately.

We would all sit together for meals. There was always some child in trouble. I remember one meal time when, as we stood in line ready for a meal, we could hear somebody in the office crying, and there was slapping and shouting. One boy came running out of the office to run down the steps into the hall where we were.

There was so much noise we all turned round. The boy tripped over coming out of the door; he was trying to get away from Mrs Waters – Ma Waters as we had to call her. She was there shouting and kicking him. He was crying and trying to cover himself and she kept on kicking him and hitting him while he was down on the floor.

The Aunty who had just checked us shouted, 'Come on. Eyes to the right, don't look. It's nothing to do with you.' So although the Aunties didn't actually do any physical punishments, they were aware of all of this. They were around, hearing and witnessing the same things we did. We could always hear slaps and crying somewhere in these houses. You learnt to expect slaps and thumps; it was just part of life, often for nothing; if someone felt like slapping you or pushing you they would.

I had written to Mum a couple of times to say I was going into hospital and that I was having surgery. It was then that I found out Mum was in prison. I wrote to her from hospital and I sent her a gonk toy that I had made.

She wrote back, saying, 'I'm going to come and see you soon as you come out of hospital. When you go back to Burgh Hall.' Of course, we didn't go back to Burgh so when we got to Barrow I wrote and told her where I now was.

Her reply was a sad one: 'Hello darling. Why have they moved you so far away? There's no way I can come and see you. I can't afford it. It's too far.' And that was to be the last letter I ever got from her.

I had to be able to get up and down a few steps here and there in Barrow Hall, to get to the toilet or the day room where the kids played.

Much of the time I stayed in my room and my sisters would come to me, but any spare few minutes I could find when there was no one around I would practise going up and down these stairs. I would hold my crutches and shuffle up on my bottom.

I wasn't consciously thinking about running away, but somewhere inside me I knew that I needed mobility; somewhere deep inside me I think I was planning to run away.

I must have pushed myself too hard. One day I decided I could get myself all the way to the day room; and I set out up the steps.

They were all watching telly up there; several Aunties with the children. I surprised everybody by walking in on my crutches into the day room and shouting 'Da da!' with a theatrical flourish.

One Aunty turned round and in a surprised voice called out, 'Hey Heather, have you done that? That's amazing.'

She called me into the room and asked me to sit down. She could see I was exhausted. As I moved to sit down on the chair I screamed out with sudden pain. I felt with my hand and I could feel a bulge. The pin in my leg was working its way out.

They called Ma Waters; she got the doctor out and I was rushed into hospital, the same hospital where I had had my operation.

The doctors there told me they were going to have to remove the pin. They were going to have to operate the following morning. They X-rayed it and in the morning told me, 'We can't remove it, we are going to have to put it back.'

They were literally going to push it back and do something else that would hold it more permanently.

I was only in five or six days and then brought back. I had still got the crutches but they had given me a stick and told me, 'Just take it little by little or you'll do yourself permanent injury.'

Only a few weeks later, getting ready to line up for tea, Ma Waters said, 'You Bradleys, stand outside the office. I've got something to tell you'. We all thought, 'Oh heck, what have we done wrong?' Angela thought maybe she had made her bed wrongly, or some such thing. We each thought, 'We've done something wrong.'

Then Ma Waters opened the door and beckoned Dawn and me in. She said, 'You two come through. Angela just stay there a minute.' And so Angela stayed outside.

I went in on my crutches and sat down. Ma Waters looked at us coldly, 'I'm afraid I've got some bad news for you.' I was kind of looking at her but she was not really looking at us. She just said, 'I've got some bad news for you. I'm afraid to say that your mother is dead.'

I said, 'What? What do you mean, she's dead?' And she turned round and repeated, 'Your mother is dead. She died yesterday.'

The shock was just unbelievable; Dawn started crying straight away, and I pulled her to me. 'Ma Waters, what do you mean, my mother is dead?' I demanded. 'She died yesterday and you are telling us today. What did she die of? What happened? What are you saying?'

'She committed suicide. That's all I know. I'll get Angela in now and tell her,' Ma Waters said.

And that's when I blurted out that I wouldn't let her tell Angela the way she had just told us. It had been so cold, so without feeling. I felt I had to spare Angela that at least. She argued a bit, but she agreed in the end. She called Angela in and left us alone for a while.

Angela asked, 'What's the matter with Dawn?' Then I did start to feel the tears.

'Angela, I've got something sad to tell you. It's about Mummy.'

'Oh no, she's not dead, is she?' I nodded gently. 'Yes, she is. Mummy is dead.' I didn't tell Angela that our mother had killed herself. My sisters both sobbed, asking 'Why?' and 'Didn't she love us?' 'Why did she die?' and so on.

I was just consoling them, holding them both, and the office door opened and Ma Waters looked in. 'Is that it then? Right, if you three just want to go in the main kitchen. You don't have to sit in with the others for your tea seeing as you're crying.'

I was just so dazed; it hadn't really sunk in. We went down into the main kitchen and sat there, still crying. One of the nice Aunties came through with some bread and butter, and some cake, and said, 'Oh, Heather, I'm so sorry. I'm so sorry for you. Just sit here quietly. Don't worry about the others.'

She went back and of course we couldn't eat, we were just crying and asking no-one in particular, 'Why?'

A bit later on that evening, when an Aunty came through, I asked if I could go and pay my last respects – would it be possible to see my Mum. I told her, 'I just want to see her again; it's been over a year since I saw her.'

She said she'd see what she could do. The next morning I asked again and Ma Waters told me that there was no way we could go.

Later on she advised us to remember our mother as she was when we last knew her; that if we saw her in the state she was in now it would not be good for us.

I cried, 'I don't care, I just want to hold her hand. I want to see my Mum.'

I was told that I couldn't see her because I was not strong enough. They insisted that was the case, but I kept protesting that I was strong enough and that I wanted to see her.

It was the first time I had ever asked for something; it was so important. I wanted to see my Mum and I know my sisters did as well.

*It was only later that Heather found out the details. Hazel, who was then living in a working girls' hostel nearby, had to go and identify their mother. When she went to the morgue and they pulled the sheet back, Hazel saw that they had not tidied or cleaned their mother's body up in any way. Her hair was uncombed, and matted with vomit. Her lips were blue and swollen, her eyes were open. Heather assumed that was the state that they were protecting her from seeing.*

I went back in the day room and told my sisters, 'We can't see Mum'. And I told them that I was going to run away, but couldn't take them with me. They wanted me to take them too, and asked me not to leave them. It was difficult for me to leave my sisters.

I remembered the protective feelings I'd had a few days before when I heard a slap and crying. I knew it was Dawn; I recognized her crying. I shouted, 'What was that?'

Ma Waters shouted out, 'What do you mean, what was that? I just slapped Dawn for running. You all know you are not supposed to run.'

*In fact Dawn confirmed that it was more than just running, though it was still a minor incident. Ma Waters had been inspecting the children's clothes drawers for tidiness and had made what Dawn regarded as an unnecessary comment. Dawn had muttered 'What a to-do!' and Ma Waters had reacted very heavily. As Dawn put it, 'She just gave me the hardest slap across my face I have ever had, it nearly knocked me off my feet.'*

I asked, 'Are you all right, Dawn?' By then she was at the top of the stairs and coming down really sobbing. She came up to me, I was still leaning on my crutches. Dawn pleaded, 'I didn't mean to run.' And as

Ma Waters came down the stairs I just looked at her – I was still holding Dawn, who was crying – and said, 'You are not going to hit my sisters ever again, not while I am here. You are never going to hurt them again!'

Ma Waters came down and just walked past me. I had reached a pitch over the years where I wasn't bothered about myself and things they did and said. But whenever my sisters were hurt it was an instinct to protect them.

Coming back to telling my sisters that I was going to run away: I wasn't really well enough, or strong enough, but time was running out and I wanted to find Mum.

There was no way I could have managed to take my two sisters with me; I was still using my crutches, or my stick anyway. I promised, 'I'll keep in touch.' I didn't have to say, 'Don't tell anybody'. They would have understood that. They just asked when I was going.

'Tomorrow I'm going to ask if I can go into the village,' I told them.

The next day I said 'Cheerio' to my sisters in the morning as they, and the other children, left for school. I wasn't at school – I was convalescing and would usually rest in my room or sit in the big kitchen with the cook, preparing the meal. We'd just talk or I'd sit and help her with the veg.

Knowing I wouldn't be able to take a bag with me in case it made them suspicious, I had put on lots of extra clothing, including warm clothing. I was wearing my extra supplies. I'd also been to the First Aid Kit and taken some paracetamol. I was wearing these long knickerbockers, red trimmed with black lace, and I lined them with the tablets. I don't think at that time that I consciously thought of killing myself if I couldn't reach Mum – I don't really know why I took the tablets.

*After her mother had used Heather to break into the bureau to get at the tablets Heather's father kept there, Heather had been instructed to hide them in the lining of the curtains. This seems to have been to allow her mother access to the tablets whenever she wanted them – a form of taking control of her own life. It is possible that in hiding her stolen pills in the hem of her knickerbockers Heather was subconsciously emulating her mother's actions in her own bid to control her own future; she was setting up a 'security blanket' for herself.*

To the cooks and Aunties I said, 'Would it be OK for me to walk to the village? Does anybody want any cigarettes or anything?'

Two of the Aunties said, 'Oh yes, you can get me some ciggies.' But they added, 'Are you sure you're up to it?' I assured them I was and that I really wanted to help them out. I was playing up to them, making them feel easy about letting me go.

Telling them I wouldn't be long, I left and, reaching the gates, looked back. I thought that if anyone up there is watching they are going to see me turn right, though the village was to the left. But I thought 'now or never'. If they do see me I've had it. But I hoped I'd given them no reason to be watching me; they should just be getting on with what they were doing.

I turned right out of the gates and round the corner, about fifty yards, and onto a straight road through open fields. This road seemed to go forever; it was quite daunting. But I was determined to do it, though I had in mind that I might be able to get a lift.

It was warm for the time of year, though of course I had all this extra clothing on as well. I remember passing fields of pretty flowers; autumn flowers. Blues and whites and yellows. For a while not one car went by me, but I was still determined. I hobbled along slowly, each step leaning on my stick. Suddenly I heard a car approaching from behind and I moved off the road, to the grass at the side.

The car slowed down and stopped nearly level with me. It was quite a big car, a nice looking car. The driver was smiling really warmly. He seemed a gentle man. He had a full face and a smile full of laughter lines. His eyes smiled as well. He wasn't an old man. He was smartly dressed, with an open shirt and neat trousers.

He wound the window down. I looked in, smiled at him, and said 'Hello'.

He asked me if I was going for a walk. I hadn't thought of what I would say in that situation; I just hadn't planned it in that detail. I just made something up on the spur of the moment; I told him that I was going to Lincoln, and that I had just missed the bus. 'So I thought I'd just take a slow walk and wait for the next bus to come past.'

He asked me where I was going to in Lincoln. I told him that I was going to my Mum's, that I was on my holidays. He made the point that I hadn't got any luggage, but I told him that had already been sent on ahead.

He said 'Well, I'm not going into Lincoln but I'm going near enough. Would you like a lift? I could do with the company.'

I looked at him and the car and somehow I felt okay about taking the lift. It wasn't as dangerous in those days but – all things considered – most of the abuse that a person might do to me in that circumstance was, I felt, happening in the Homes all the time anyway. What real harm could I come to? I got in the car. He offered me a mint from a packet of Polos and we drove off, chatting about nothing and everything. It took about an hour and three-quarters to Lincoln. During the talk he asked about my stick, and I told him it was because I had twisted my ankle, and that walking was a bit difficult. About four miles outside Lincoln he said, 'Oh, what the heck. I could do with a haircut, and my barber is in the city. I'll take you into Lincoln.'

He dropped me in the city, and checked with me that it was okay to leave me there. I told him it was fine and that I would catch a bus from there.

Of course, I really intended going to my Nana's; I hadn't seen her for three years. She had been going to come to see me when I was in hospital but, sadly, she'd written to me saying that she'd received a gas bill for nine shillings and ninepence, and couldn't afford the fare.

I took a bus, got to my Nana's and knocked on the door. Uncle Tom – Nana's son – came to the door.

'Come in, come in,' he said. 'Look who is here,' he called to Nana in the kitchen.

I didn't have my stick with me; I'd got rid of it earlier. I hobbled, limped, over to her and had a hug. I asked if I could stay the night. I told her I was doing the Duke of Edinburgh's award and that I had been told that if I wasn't back by ten o'clock they would know that I was staying over. 'Can I stay?' I asked. She said that that would be lovely. So I knew I had got a bed for the night. We talked about all sorts; she gave me a meal and I slept with Nana that night. We had breakfast together in the morning. By now, unbeknown to me, police all over the country were out looking for me. They thought that maybe I had been kidnapped, or that I had had an accident, or collapsed because of the surgery, and was in a ditch somewhere.

After breakfast I told her, 'I'd better get off and catch the bus.' I stood in front of the mirror; I was combing my hair and Tom was stood behind me. And I knew that he knew that I had run away. At the same time I felt that he didn't mind. I was just kind of combing my hair and looking in the mirror at him, and he just smiled at me as if to say 'I know. But I am not going to say anything.' And I just turned round and hugged him. I left then and went to a phone box. (In fact I was wrong, I discovered later that out of concern for me Tom did in fact ring the police.)

At the phone box, I rang a girl called Denise; I felt close to her because I had spent sixteen weeks in hospital with her. I had to ring the hospital and they called Denise to the telephone.

'Denise, is that you? It's me, Heather.' She told me the police were there. They were looking for me.

I asked her not to tell them it was me on the telephone. She promised that she wouldn't. 'Where are you?' she asked, 'What are you doing? Where did you stay last night?'

I told her that I had been at my Nan's. I wasn't sure where I was going; I told her that I had run away to find out where my Mum was so that I could go and see her, and talk to her, and hold her hand. I realized then that I wasn't going to get very far. I was still quite weak but I didn't want to be taken back. 'I'll tell you what, Denise, if I come to Boston, if I come to see you, can you get out of the hospital grounds for a while? I need to see you just to talk to you.'

She promised to try but said that it might be difficult because of the presence of the police.

'Well, promise you won't tell the police that I'm coming. Because if you tell them and they find me I've got all these tablets and I'll take them all. There's no way I'm going back to Barrow Hall. I promised Dawn and Angela, I've got to do something for them because they've still got years to go. I'll ring you again when I get to Boston.'

So I caught the bus to the train station, got off and there were quite a few police about. You could see that they were kind of looking and I thought that they were looking for me. I thought that they might have a photo of me, and that they might get me.

Then I saw a woman, a young lady with a baby and a toddler, and struggling with a couple of cases as well. She was about a hundred yards or so away from me.

I went over to her and asked, 'Excuse me. Would you like a hand?' She was grateful for the help. We chatted; she was catching the train to London.

I told her that was where I was going. She held the baby and I took hold of the little boy's hand. We took a case each. I walked with her and the policeman didn't even look at us, even though we went close enough to him for me to feel his breath.

So that got me through. We bought our tickets and got on the train. I helped her and sat with her for a while. She was going to London but I got off at Boston. I got to a phone and rang Denise again. 'I'm here. I'm not very far away from the hospital. Do you know those two toilets in the grounds?' I was hoping to meet her there, but Denise told me that the police knew I was on the telephone, and that I was going to the hospital. She promised me that she hadn't given the game away.

I was despairing. 'That's it then. I'm going to take these tablets. I know I'm not going to be able to see Mum and I can't go on without her.' I still had the paracetamol I had taken from the First Aid Box in Barrow Hall.

Denise pleaded with me not to take them but I just couldn't go on and I told her so. I said I was sorry for letting her down.

*There is little doubt that Heather was in a confused state. She was certainly frightened by what she saw as captivity in the Homes; with the death of her mother she probably felt that it was all the more likely to be permanent. Heather never saw her father as a likely homebuilder for the sisters; her hopes had, perhaps subconsciously, been pinned on her mother, who she always believed had tried to keep the family together. Whatever the truth of this, her hopes had now been dashed. Now she had become obsessed with seeing her mother, and was realizing that she was to be deprived of even that. The only future now was back in the Homes, and with no mother to hold out the chance of a home life, back to the Homes for the rest of her teenage life.*

I was in a bit of a state. I was prepared to take an overdose and die and yet that would mean that I would leave Dawn and Angela to their fate. I had been with them all those years, protecting them and being there for them. I was just so upset because although I had had a few letters from Mum I hadn't seen her and I loved her and we had shared some times together. I suppose I was just thinking of myself; because of all this and the surgery as well I was pretty desolate and probably full of self pity too, but I was just so unhappy. I just wanted to end it all. I don't think I particularly believed that if I killed myself I would be with my Mum; I'm not sure whether I believed much in anything after death at that time.

I remember putting the phone down and going into some public toilets, locking the door, just sitting on the loo and taking one tablet at a time. I was eating them like sweets, just chewing them without thinking. I was holding each tablet, putting it in my mouth, and eating it, like a robot. Mechanical. Unthinking. I just ate the whole lot and there was a lot. I would think about eighty pills. And then I just sat there for a while. Then I blanked out.

*Heather had chosen to use her 'security blanket' for real, and in doing so had copied her own mother's suicide. However, one psychiatrist we spoke to, who dealt with Heather's case, was sure there was no real evidence of genuine suicidal tendencies. She was sure Heather made 'cries for help'. In this case*

*the 'suicide' did not 'work'; perhaps it was never really intended to. Heather*
*may have been desperate, but essentially she was a fighter, not a quitter.*

On coming round I opened my eyes and found I was on the floor. The
tablets had taken effect. I had slipped off the loo and had fallen on the
floor. I had banged and cut my head. I woke up shivering on the floor
and I think I must have bitten my tongue, because my tongue was
swollen and I could taste blood. I was cold and shaking. I felt awful. I
felt so ill. But I thought, 'I've got to get to Denise.' So I pulled myself
up; there were bells ringing in my ears and everything was blurred,
images in triplicate, all merging and moving.

I seemed to be walking on air, on sponge, nothing was real any
more. I don't know how I got about. I don't think I was crawling, I
think I just kept putting one foot in front of the other, thinking 'I've
got to ... want to ... see Denise. I've got to get to her.' That's all I
remember.

Denise was at the hospital main gate, so were the police. She saw
me and called, 'There she is, look, that's Heather.' I had already collapsed. I woke up a couple of days later in intensive care.

Paracetamol poisons you once it gets in the liver. When this reaction starts, even in hospital with all the drugs, it sometimes cannot be
stopped. I was lucky. I came out of intensive care into the ward for
three to four days. Those days were quite hazy; it was some time
before I was quite with it. The nurse would come to me and talk every
now and then; she asked once why I had tried to kill myself.

'I didn't want to kill myself,' I replied. 'I did it so that I could bring
to attention what's going on in the children's Home where my sisters
are. You've got to listen to me. I've gone to this extreme. You've got to
believe me. You've got to listen to me.'

Psychiatrists also came to talk to me. They kept asking the same
questions, 'Would I do it again?'

All I kept saying was, 'What are you asking me? Aren't you listening to what I am saying?' And I told them about the things that went
on. But they would just smile and turn away; they hardly even looked
at me.

Once, one had his back to me and said, 'Oh, come on Heather, I
think you are exaggerating. These things just don't happen.' He was
basically saying, I think, that I was exaggerating, and that I just took
the overdose to try to kill myself and that I was now trying to cover it
up. I knew I was beaten. I gave up. 'You don't believe me, do you?'

Somewhat unconvincingly they tried to assure me that they did believe me. I was in there for a couple of weeks. Ma Waters brought Angela and Dawn to see me which was great, and then she told me that she would be seeing me back in the Home in a few days.

I blurted out, 'You won't! There's no way I'm ever coming back there. That's it. Angela and Dawn, could you just go out?' I gave them a hug, and told them I wanted a word with Ma Waters.

When they had gone, I told Ma Waters, 'If they bring me back I shall just run again. There's no way I'm coming back to you. I've told them everything that's going on there. I've told them what you do.' The look in her eye told me that she believed me.

I think for the first time ever I had really won. When a social worker came a bit later on she told me that I was going home.

'No way, I'm not, I'll run away again. You'll not keep me there'.

But she said, 'No, you are going home, to your father.' They had obviously got in touch with him. And that's what happened; he turned up with Dot – his new wife – and took me away.

## With Dad, and with Nana

*1965: Heather was sixteen when her father picked her up and took her to Scunthorpe to the house he shared with his new wife Dot.*

Dad had shocked us by introducing Dot as 'our new Mum'. I was only there, with Dad and Dot, for a few days. One day, Dad and I had gone for a walk in the village. When we came back we found Dot was having one of her 'sessions', throwing jam jars and all sorts of things around the house. I later heard that she was a schizophrenic.

All my clothes were on the lawn; Dot was screaming and shouting and throwing things at my father's car. It was a Jaguar, and she must have known that he was very proud of it. Dad got in the car and drove it out of her reach.

He told me to get in, for safety I suppose. So I got in the car and sat waiting while my father went to Dot. I watched Dot at the window; after about ten minutes I saw her disappear from sight. I think Dad was pulling her away from the window. Then Dad came out, and came towards the car, scooping up a few of my clothes from the lawn. He threw them in the back of the car.

I asked him what was going on. 'I've rung for the doctor and the ambulance. They will be here in a minute. They will have to take care of her. I've locked the doors and windows so that she can't get out till they arrive. You can't stay here now. I am going to take you to Nana's.'

I thought about it later. I think Dot had probably been having one of her 'attacks', that she had just gone a little crazy for a while. Although we didn't like each other much, I didn't feel that it was particularly directed at me.

So we got to Nana's. We were invited in and I hugged Nana. Dad went with Nana to the kitchen to explain the situation and I went with Tom.

'You wouldn't have thought that you'd be seeing me again so soon,' I said to Tom.

Dad came through, saying to Tom and me, 'I've got to get back. I'm going to go now. Heather, you are staying here with Nana till we sort things out.' Then he disappeared.

Staying with Tom and Nana was wonderful. I kind of forgot about all my problems. We talked about Mum and all sorts of things.

It all came pouring out of me, everything that had happened over the years in the Homes: how we had been made to feel that we weren't wanted, that that was why they were looking after us.

I also shared with Nana that I thought I was ugly and not wanted. 'I'm never going to marry or have a boyfriend.' Nana reassured me, 'No, you're not ugly. And of course people care about you.'

*That feeling of not being wanted, of being cared for by people for whom it was a job rather than a pleasure, was the result of the cold, authoritarian attitudes in the Homes – attitudes that Heather had so long battled against. Even the housemothers we interviewed were, at the start of their careers, more depressed by this than by the elements of physical abuse that they encountered. When Heather eventually married, as described later in this book, it was after a long period of nervousness in the company of others, and a warm sexual relationship was something that took literally years to develop. Openness, trust, self-confidence, self-esteem; these are all qualities needed for an open and easy relationship. The Homes had provided for none of these basic human needs.*

I stayed with Nana and uncle Tom for about three weeks. By now I had left school. I had enough exam passes to take up nursing. I was due to start nursing at the beginning of the year. I got in as a cadet at Scunthorpe War Memorial Hospital, where I would be living in their residential accommodation. I only planned to stay with Nana and Tom until I moved there.

I went into the town one day, into Woolworths, and I met Mary there. When I had been in Burgh Hall, she was the girl who had run away with me to the picture house, when we pinched all the ice creams. 'Mary! It's Heather!' I called out. We were quickly discussing our lives since we'd been apart. She told me she was staying in a working girls' hostel. I told her that I was staying with my Nana.

In her dinner hour we sat and talked. The old times flooded out. It wasn't long before the old moods and attitudes flooded out too.

Mary said, 'I'm going to run away again. I can't stand it, I've had enough. Will you come with me?'

Even now I don't know why I said that I would. I was with Nana; I had everything ahead of me. I wanted to start nursing, and I had a nursing career mapped out in front of me. I hadn't seen Mary for two years and here I was making plans to run away with her. I couldn't understand myself even as I said 'Yes'.

She said, 'I'll meet you here this time tomorrow.'

*Even Heather couldn't understand herself. For once she had all the cards stacked up the way she wanted them, and now she was self-destructing. But in fact her actions were no different from their earlier, childhood, versions. A structured home life, a plan of a career, these might just have represented cages of constraint to Heather's rebellious spirit. And she had developed in her an instinctive talent to resist captivity. The Homes had one more thing to answer for; not only had they failed to encourage her to find her best talents, they had driven her to fight against even herself.*

The next day I left a note where I knew Tom would find it, but not find it too quickly: 'I love you both very much. I have run away because I'm not worthy enough to stay here, you deserve better than me. I know you care but I don't want to be a nuisance or a burden to you both.'

I met Mary as arranged and we took a train to London. We hadn't got much money so when we got there we just walked round for miles and miles. The hours went by slowly, we spent most of the few pounds we had on bits of food and drink.

We went into a cafe and had a drink, with almost the last of our money. We had nowhere to stay. We were sharing a cup of coffee at two o'clock in the morning when this man came in and started chatting to us. During our conversation it came out that we were exhausted and looking for somewhere to stay. He was a bit unkempt, not that well dressed, but he was charming, he seemed an intelligent person by the way he spoke. He said, 'I've got a flat. I can give you a bed for the night.'

We didn't sense any danger because he seemed so nice. The flat wasn't very far away. When we got to the flat it was upstairs, up about eighty steps. We climbed these and followed him into a room. 'There you are, there's two beds. You can stay here tonight.'

The room was quite rough. The sheets weren't dirty or anything but it was quite rough. I thanked him, and he left. He told us he would be back in a minute. We were so overwhelmed, thinking that we were in luck.

*Considering the upbringing Heather and Mary had gone through it seems remarkable that they could have been so naive; at least part of their 'innocence' must surely have been an indifference. Was there anything that could happen here that hadn't already happened in the Homes they had been sent to for care?*

When the door opened again a short while later the man came back in with another man. This other man was quite heavy-set with long greasy hair. They shut the door. We heard this bolt slam over.

'What's going on?' We both stood up. 'You don't think you're going to get the bed for nothing, do you?' he said. Then of course we realized what was happening. I thought it would be pointless screaming. We were right at the top of the house, up a mile of steps, but I thought, 'Don't panic.' I kind of looked at Mary; we both knew The Look – we'd used it before in the Home. It was a look that said 'Shut up, just pretend to go along with it.'

I said, 'Okay. Why not? No problem. I'll tell you what though. How about a bottle of wine or something? Let's make it fun. We'll have a drink and really have a party. Let's make the most of it. Enjoy ourselves.'

*If the Homes had taught Heather anything, they had taught her to think on her feet in situations of captivity and threat. After all, she'd found devious ways of running away from more secure places than this before.*

They fell for it. But I told them I hadn't got any money. One of the pair told us that the off-licence was just at the bottom of the stairs and round the corner. He unlocked the door and opened it to go out. For those few seconds they were relaxed, they weren't expecting anything. I shouted 'Mary!' and pushed the door, kind of knocked both the men aside. 'Run!'

*It was the picture-house all over again. The teenage Heather and Mary had created for themselves an older version of the ice-cream incident; a room upstairs, a flight from danger, an escape down a flight of stairs. This time the stakes were, in reality, higher. To the pair they were probably about the same; the usherette chasing them from the Odeon must have seemed a terrifying threat in her own way at their, then, younger age.*

I shot down those stairs – I don't think we touched any of them. Mary was right behind me. We ran and ran and ran. That had really frightened us.

We made a plan to try to find an all-night cafe, and just stay there if we could. We had just about enough money for a drink. But after a while, still in the early hours of the morning, when we were just falling asleep, the cafe owner told us he was shutting and he turfed us out onto the street.

So there we were again standing on a dark street in the middle of London. Again, a man came up to us. You would think we would have learnt our lesson by now, but we were tired and desperate. This man had a suit and a hat, a trench-coat and brown brogue-style shoes. He was very smart and very well spoken. It seemed safe. He came up to us and started to chat: 'Do you want somewhere to stay? You don't want to worry about me. Nothing's going on.' He was so convincing. I forget what it was that made me feel that it was okay. He pointed towards the parked cars. 'The car is just here.'

He opened the door. Mary got in. As I went to get in he pushed me hard, throwing me into the car. He slammed shut the door and we realized that we were in danger again. He got in the driver's seat.

'What are you doing? Where are you taking us? Let us out! We don't want to go.' We were screaming. And we were hitting him on his back and he started up the car. It wouldn't start and he was swearing. The engine caught, and we started moving. We were still hitting him, screaming and banging on the windows.

All of a sudden this car came out of nowhere, screeched past us and parked in front of our car's bonnet. Our driver had to slam the brakes on. We were thrown forward.

It was the police. Unbeknown to us, the police had been keeping an eye on us. I suppose runaways stand out a mile. Perhaps the cafe owner had called them. Wherever they came from, we were glad to see them.

They had seen what had happened. Straight away these three plain clothes men got out, opened our driver's door and said, 'Come on you.' They manhandled the driver out of the car and then got us out.

We were crying. They drove to the police station. 'Come on, let's get you a drink.' They took us into a room, got us a drink and asked us where we had run away from, who we were and a few other questions. 'Do you realize that you could have been the next nude bodies in the Thames?' Of course we hadn't thought of the dangers. 'You come here, to the bright lights I suppose. Will you ever learn?'

*A good question. And he didn't even know about the ice creams and the Odeon!*

The policeman was ever so nice. For a while we talked; I told him a bit of what was going on in the Homes. I told him that was one of the reasons I had run, that I'd been running all my life.

He told us, 'You are going to have to spend the night in the cells. We'll get in touch with your social worker and let your Nan know that you are here. I'm sorry, but you've got to stay the night in the cells till we can get you sorted out.' He took us down a long corridor. As we walked past the cells we could see blackboards on the cell doors, used to describe the cell occupants; drunkard, drugs, or whatever written on the boards.

He showed us to our cell and showed us what he was writing on our board: 'Runaways'.

'In you go. There's a bell there. Ring if you want us. There's a blanket and a toilet.' We had to give our shoe laces, belts and our bras to a police-woman. I suppose that was so that we couldn't harm or hang ourselves.

*The mischief wasn't over yet. Of all places, the cell was literally a cage of constraint, and Heather was planning her escape bid probably before the key had turned in the lock. She was escaping from, of all things, safety. But her safety seems to have meant little to her compared to her freedom, such was the teaching of the Homes.*

We kind of looked at each other. 'We're not going to stay here, are we?' I said.

Mary was worried about what I might be planning. I just wanted to get out of that cell. There I was, planning to get out of the cell, even though for the first time in London we were safe. But I was saying that we had to get out.

'How?' Mary asked. 'Ring the bell and when they come tell them that you feel sick. Ask if you can you have some fresh air; point out to them there are no windows in the cell. Then I'll come out with you and we'll just run for it.'

Mary nodded, obviously excited. She started making a fuss. Very soon, we heard footsteps along the corridor. A policeman appeared and asked us what we wanted, what was the problem.

I called out, 'Mary feels sick. She doesn't feel very well. Can she get some fresh air? She feels really awful.'

I make a good actress, I suppose. Click, click; he opened the door and beckoned us out of the cell. It happened just how we planned it. He offered to open the window and of course the breeze came in straight away, lovely and cool. 'Just take some deep breaths,' he said.

I was looking down to the end of the corridor, and I noticed he was relaxed. We stood there just breathing deeply.

'Now!' And we started running. Mary pushed past him. We ran straight up this corridor. And straight into this huge policewoman. She was as wide as she was tall and she must have weighed twenty stone. She blocked the whole of the doorway but we were running too fast. We bounced off her and ended up back on our bottoms.

'Where are you going, you scoundrels?' By now, of course, the other policeman had got there. He told us that we wouldn't get away with that again and took us back to the cell. The following morning we had our breakfast in there. A social worker came to the cell and talked to us. I asked him what would happen to us.

'Mary, you're going back to Wordsworth Hostel. As for you Heather, we have spoken to your Nana and Tom and they don't want you back. You'll be going to Steep Hill, a working girls' hostel.'

I asked why, if I had to go to a working girls' hostel, I couldn't go to the one Mary was in.

'Now, come on, Heather! Why can't you? Just look at why you can't. This is what... your ninth, tenth time, of running away? You've run away from every place. Both of you together sometimes. And now you want to know why you can't be together again? Come off it, girls.'

So we left on the train. Somebody from the hostel was waiting for Mary, and took her off. 'I'll be seeing you,' she called out. And I was taken to Steep Hill.

# The working girls' hostel, Steep Hill

It's the human touch in this world that counts
The human touch of your hand and mine
That means far more to the fainting heart

Than shelter or bread or wine.
For shelter is done when night is over,
And bread lasts only a day,
But the touch of the hand, the sound of a voice
Live in the soul away.

*(from the 60,000 words or more of channelled and other writings Heather recorded during her years of the stigmata)*

So I was taken to Steep Hill. A beautiful house, but as far as I was concerned then, just another big house with big doors and big bolts. Steep Hill, in Lincoln, leads up to the magnificent cathedral and the castle that dominates the skyline of the city.

It was then a working girls' hostel, but it had once been a remand Home. There had been bars on the windows and a lot of the rooms were just one-bedded rooms. Almost like cells. Some still had the little peephole in the door from the days when they actually were cells.

I was introduced to the staff, including Aunty Anne – she seemed very nice – and also to the nine other girls who were there. I was to spend the next two years, until 1967, at Steep Hill – up to the time I was eighteen.

I was shown upstairs to my room, a little bedroom all of my own, which was lovely. No dormitories, no sharing. A time and a space to be alone for the first time.

The rules were explained. When you arrive at Steep Hill you have five weeks' training. They keep you inside the place and you clean, cook and do a few chores. They assess you. And, of course, they are keeping an eye on you – the front and back doors are locked.

In training, the rule was to be in bed at eight o'clock; it was later when you were working. After two weeks you could have one evening out. You had to be back by ten.

You were called in the morning at seven, breakfast was at half-past. If you weren't sitting down at half-past seven you just didn't get breakfast. You couldn't just come in and say, 'I'm sorry I'm late,' and sit down. If you were late, you stayed hungry. You had to ask for everything. 'Could you pass me the sugar, please?', 'Could I have a round of bread please?'; only then, with permission, could you reach for it. You had to ask permission to have a bath.

If you smoked you had to ask permission to light up. In training you were allowed two cigarettes a day; if you were working you were allowed five.

You weren't allowed to chat. You ate, then you packed your plates away and somebody washed them, somebody dried them, these were chores usually done by somebody on training.

*Rules like these had a terrible effect on Heather. Perhaps they might be appropriate for prisoners, or for those with criminal tendencies. But Heather had committed no crime, and should not have been a prisoner. What Heather needed, and worse, what she knew she needed, was the freedom to find her own limitations and skills. The freedom to own her own life, to own her own plans, to own her own future.*

*There may be people for whom these rules and regulations provided a structure and a security that they needed, but they were inappropriate for Heather's rebellious spirit.*

*For the Homes and the hostel to have developed her in a benign and constructive way they should have concentrated on teaching her assertion. Assertion means knowing how to stand up for your own rights while respecting, and not violating, the rights of others. It means knowing how to value the desires, ideas and needs of others as well as yourself. It means teaching people how to avoid win-lose situations and create situations where everyone gains. But it was the alternatives that Heather was taught: aggression and passivity. She was taught that brutality was right, or at least normal; that punishment was the response for those who took initiative; that threat was the response for those who sought to own their own lives.*

I went to Steep Hill in March, having just been brought back from London. It was the time of an Ideal Home Exhibition, which is an exhibition showing annually in London. All the girls – with Aunty Anne – were going for the day. Aunty Anne asked, 'If we take you with us, Heather, will you promise you won't run away? We don't want to leave you here. We'd like you to come. I know you'd enjoy it. Mrs M. has given up her seat for you so you can come.' So Mrs M. couldn't go. The vendetta I felt she had against me from that day was unbelievable; whether it was connected to this or not I suppose I'll never be sure.

So within a couple of days Aunty Anne was trusting me, and I got to go. And I kept my word. We went on the bus, we sang songs going there, and we had a good time looking round the exhibition. Aunty Anne kept with me even when I went to the toilet so I knew there was no point in running. I didn't want to anyway because Aunty Anne was trusting me. It was a great day.

In another fortnight I was due to start my nursing. I told Aunty Anne, 'I don't want to do my nursing. I just haven't got it in me. I don't want to do it.' She tried to talk me round, telling me that I had potential and I was intelligent, but I was quite adamant.

*As her later life was to prove, caring for others, sharing other people's problems and meeting their needs, was latent in Heather. It was her true self. When she later acquired the security of a home life and a loving husband she involved herself in so many activities that gave of herself to others, that many were amazed at her energy. She would, almost certainly, have made a fine nurse, and a real healer. But at the crucial moment she turned away. And there can be little doubt about the reason: she had never been told she was worth anything of value, she had never been allowed to develop confidence and self-esteem, she had never been told that she could trust herself. And her life in Steep Hill was not going to improve on that.*

A typical day would be: I would have breakfast, then I would wash or dry all the pots. Then whoever was in charge would say, 'Okay Heather, I want you to do the backyard, sweep it and scrub it and then I want you to do all of the west wing, the brass knobs and the brown lino there. Buff and clean that up. Then I'll give you something else to do.' And this was hands and knees work, scrubbing the yard outside, swilling it down and sweeping it. It would take an hour or so.

Then I had to go and find Mrs M. You didn't just say 'Excuse me'; you'd find where she was and you had to walk up and just wait to be spoken to. And I stood there twenty minutes with her sometimes. Eventually Mrs M. would turn round and say 'Yes?' and then I would have to ask her to pass my work. She'd usually say, 'In a minute, in a minute.' She'd sometimes make me wait another ten minutes; eventually she would say 'Come on, and let's go and pass your work.' But she always found fault with it, whereas when I did the same work with Mrs K. she'd say, 'That's lovely, Heather.' Mrs M would just say, 'It's not good enough.' She'd go over and kick a bit of the muck off the garden and then say, 'Sweep that up.'

My periods were very heavy. I had bad periods with a lot of pain. I had been at Steep Hill a couple of months and they got me a job as a private nanny. One day I had started a period and I was in so much pain the mother sent me home. It was in the afternoon and Mrs M. was on duty. I was in agony and bleeding heavily. But she picked on me; I can't remember now what she said. I know I replied, 'Why don't you leave me alone!'

I just wanted to sleep, to be left alone. She gave me two paracetamol and told me to go to bed. I don't know what she told Aunty Anne but the next day she said, 'You won't be going to work, you've got somebody visiting you.'

It was a psychiatrist. Mrs M. had told him that I had lost my temper. I hadn't sworn at all, but she had told them that I had lashed out at her and that I had gone crazy.

The psychiatrist asked me many questions and obviously he had done a bit of research. He knew that I had once taken an overdose and been in hospital only four, five months before. He told me that he thought it would be good for me to spend two or three weeks in hospital.

I protested that there was nothing wrong with me; that I was just having my period, and that I had been in pain. Here I was; I had been sent home from work because I was in a lot of pain and bleeding heavily and because I had said, 'Leave me alone', Mrs M. had blown it up out of all proportion. And now I had a psychiatrist saying, 'I think you ought to come into hospital for two or three weeks.' To help me! And a couple of days later, I told Aunty Anne, 'I was just in a lot of pain, Aunty Anne, nothing happened. I had a bad period, why am I going into a psychiatric hospital? Nothing happened.'

She just said, 'They know what they are doing. You can still come and visit us whenever you want, and you will be coming back.'

I went to St John's. I was in a ward where you go for breakdowns or assessment and though I settled in there I could not believe it. I was absolutely dumbfounded by the suddenness of it all. When the sister came down, she had obviously read my notes; she asked me if my mother's name was Winifred. I told her that it was. She also asked if my father's name was George, and I confirmed that it was. She said, 'I remember your mother very well. How is she?'

So I had to tell her that she had killed herself six months ago. The sister was devastated. Having known my Mum she kind of took me under her wing. 'I know you shouldn't be here,' she told me.

I suppose her hands were tied with bureaucracy and the rules. All I did was stay there three weeks; every day I'd visit the psychiatrist in his room. He asked me all these questions and I answered them, but I thought, 'How dare you! You've got me in here because I had a period. I just had a bad period. Who do you think you are?' So I didn't actually lie but I just played along with him. I went through the motions for three weeks.

*Perhaps Heather suffered from unfair 'labelling' by the psychiatrist. Her mother had committed suicide; she had perhaps tried the same – at least she had made cries for help. If the psychiatrists had looked beyond her history they might have found out what her true needs were, and encouraged those around her to develop her benign potential. But they seem to have stuck an easy label on her and 'treated' her accordingly.*

Twice a week I'd catch a bus back to Steep Hill just to have a cup of tea with Aunty Anne, then catch the bus back. After the three weeks I was told 'Okay, you can go back now, Heather.' I returned to Steep Hill. I felt strange, as if it was all new again even though I had been visiting.

Things went from bad to worse with Mrs M. Take making the bed for example. You had to make your own bed, of course, but there were tight rules: the pillow had to be in just the right place, the covers had to be smoothed over just right, and so on. You then had to stand by your bed and wait for someone to come along and pass it. If Mrs K. came to you she would usually pass it easily; 'That's lovely Heather, you can go down for breakfast.' But Mrs M. wouldn't even look at the bed the first time; she would just get hold of the sheets and covers, yank them away and say, 'Not good enough. Do it again!' I would have to do it maybe eight or nine times before Mrs M would pass it.

It was the same with, say, buttering bread. No matter what I did, Mrs M. would tell me 'You've not buttered that right. Look at the corners. You haven't got the butter in the corners.' So I'd have to butter the bread differently. But it was just done to oppress me, not because it was wrong or badly done.

*Heather admitted that she often worked harder to please Mrs M. Heather was possibly exhibiting 'hostage-mentality', that leads captives to try to please their captors. She was also exhibiting a need for love; hardly surprising given her upbringing. But the Homes had no concept of giving love.*

*To a person living in the comfort of a 'normal' home these oppressions, these restrictions, might not seem too awful, might even seem necessary for efficiency. But to growing, maturing people leaving childhood and finding their adulthood they were horrific terrors. Just when mind, body and spirit were yearning for growth, the Homes provided cages of constraint.*

I had a habit of saying 'Tut'. It was just a mannerism, I wasn't even conscious of it. But Mrs M. took it very personally. She'd say something and before I replied I'd apparently make this 'tut' noise. When she pulled me up for it I'd do it again; I didn't mean to, I couldn't help it.

'There you go again. How dare you!' she would say. 'I'm sorry, I didn't realize.'

*Perhaps her 'tut' was a subconscious rejection of the rules, and perhaps Mrs M. detected that. But now not even her unconscious mannerisms were Heather's own.*

At the hostel we were given ten shillings a week. Even if we worked, our wages had to be handed over and ten shillings were given back. But you were very lucky if you got even that. You would be fined for any items left in the wrong place; for every such item you would be charged one shilling. We were told this was to teach us to be neat and tidy, and keep everything in place. But they took liberties with the rules; Mrs M. would follow me and pick my things up as soon as I left a room or if I just dropped something. I would just drop something and she would dive for it, grab it, and hold it up like a trophy.

At the end of the week Mrs M. would add up all my fines; it might come to nine shillings and sixpence. Then she'd give me sixpence change and all my stuff back. I remember once she even said, 'Two shillings if you want your gloves back.'

I told her that I didn't want them back, that she could keep them. I decided I just wouldn't wear my gloves. I'd realized that there was nothing she could do about that, but she made me pay for it later in other ways. In the hostel there wasn't any actual physical abuse, it was all mental.

Dawn and Angela were still at Barrow. I had written to them and spoken to them on the phone and told them where I was. They told me that things were still the same and wished I was there.

I ran away from Steep Hill many times, maybe ten times. One time I ran away to my father, who was now working in Grimsby. I had searched all day for him knowing the shop that he was working in, but not where it was. I wanted to stay with him, but he said it wasn't possible. He rang up the hostel and told them where I was. I asked him not to put me on the coach; to let me stay with him. But he said it wasn't possible and put me on the coach. I sobbed and sobbed and sobbed; but he said, 'You've got to go back.'

*Heather's father was at this time having a few difficulties with his wife; to have taken Heather in would have possibly created more problems than it would have solved. To Heather though it was just a further rejection, and meant going back to a place she could see as little other than a prison.*

I got back in the afternoon. It was three o'clock; Mrs K. was on duty. 'I'm sorry, Heather, but you've got to go straight to your bedroom.'

I was left on my own. About every hour or so I was aware of somebody moving aside that piece of metal over the peephole in my door, to look into my room. They didn't actually disturb me, but they kept looking in at me. No privacy. I couldn't have got out of the hostel anyway because they locked the outside doors.

I couldn't stop crying. I got on my knees and something opened up inside me. I was talking out loud; saying that I couldn't cope and please, please, somebody help me. Saying I'd lost everything, even my Mum was gone. I was asking what I had done to deserve all this, why me and why all of this? I was asking why I had been born so ugly. I was crying and talking out loud; I was sobbing. My hair was wet from my own tears rolling back across my cheeks.

'Please if you are there, God, please help me.' It was the first prayer I had ever said.

*And it was about to be answered. From this point on, Heather's life would never be the same again. Her future would be one of self-development and giving; and it would come about in an extraordinary way.*

I was praying and sobbing and crying and opening my heart when Mrs K. knocked on the door to tell me to get ready for bed. She came in, gave me a kiss and asked if I was okay. I was still sobbing, so she knew I wasn't okay, but I think she also knew I wanted to be left on my own.

I put on my nightie, got into bed and just lay there. I had calmed down a bit, I was relaxed, I had stopped crying. It was near Easter; the two Easter eggs for my sisters on the top of my wardrobe, just near the bed. It was a small room. Then I saw this mist, not like smoke, just this mist that appeared. I was laying in bed. I could hear movements in the house, and the occasional person walking outside.

Then I was aware of the room going quiet. It was a strange quietness. There was some light from outside coming through the curtains, which were partly open. My room was lit up a bit. But there also seemed to be a light like a broken light. It was like stars in the night, but it wasn't stars. And a different atmosphere; this quiet and the lights, and this strange atmosphere.

The mist seemed to just appear; it went up past the wardrobe. I was following it, just looking at it, and I heard a voice: 'You are not alone any more.'

I spoke in my mind, not with my voice, 'I am not alone any more?'

And I heard the reply, 'You are not alone any more. You will not be alone any more.'

All this happened, I think, in a few seconds, but I really felt then that my life was going to begin at that point, that there was going to be a new beginning for me. The past was erased at that moment, the pain and the worry gone. As I was seeing this mist and this light, and hearing this voice, I also knew that my pain and suffering were being taken away. The mist then seemed slowly to disappear.

I laid back and looked around the room. The silence ended with the mist; I became aware of sounds in the house again, of movements in the rooms around me. Everything came back to normal.

But I felt different; I knew there had been a major change in me. For a second I thought, 'Did that really happen? Did I dream that?' And I knew – with certainty – that I hadn't. It had been real. And I just smiled. I remember just kind of smiling, turning over and going to sleep. I'd never been able to sleep easily at Steep Hill before that; usually I tossed and turned, there was so much on my mind. But this night I just rolled over and went to sleep.

I had a good night. I woke up in the morning and the first thing I did was look around the room. I asked myself again 'Did that really happen?' But I knew that it had. I knew I had experienced something unusual. I was just so excited.

*At last the caterpillar was about to emerge as a butterfly.*

I got dressed, made my bed and waited for someone to come and pass it so that I could go down to breakfast. Aunty Anne came in and passed my bed, and I said, 'Aunty Anne, can I see you after breakfast?'

I couldn't talk at the table, so after breakfast I looked over at Aunty Anne as I put my knife and fork down. She said, 'Yes, okay Heather. Do you want to come into the office?'

I went into the office and told her that something strange had happened to me during the night. I told her that I wanted to share it with her. Then I told her exactly what had happened. 'I want to share this with you because I know you'd understand. It was as if I was being told that you would understand. That you would know what it was.'

She didn't really say a lot, but she smiled. 'I'm really pleased you shared that with me, my dear. I know what you have gone through, how much you have suffered. Things will get easier now. Things are going to change now.'

I was sure then that Aunty Anne was psychic. She told me, 'What you have experienced, I believe that to be a gift, that things will start for you. You'll start to see things.'

She said it was a gift, that she would help me not to be frightened, and to accept it. She'd help me all she could in that way.

I knew I was going to begin to live now, that I would grow up. All this from that first experience. My book of life was open now. This was a beginning, the first page of that new book.

And I knew that the voice was right; I wasn't on my own. I was aware of a presence with, or within, me.

'*You will not be alone any more.*'

# CHAPTER TWO

# *Spirit of Love*

## Opening up the paranormal

AFTER HER VISION, *her revelation, Heather found that her mind appeared to be open to what might loosely be called the paranormal: ESP, clairvoyance, out-of-body travelling, and other phenomena. These perceptions and new-found beliefs were to stay with her from that time onwards.*

*She was, in the working girls' hostel, to find a special relationship that meant much to her development of those feelings and abilities – in Aunty Anne she found a special friend.*

When new girls came to the hostel I would look at them and in some strange way I knew exactly what they had done. A lot of them had been on drugs, had been into prostitution, or they had stolen.

I seemed to have a rapport with each girl. I was there the longest, until I was eighteen. Some would just come for a couple of weeks. No matter what they had done, when they came to Steep Hill House they were just like I was really – frightened. Frightened little girls – still little girls, because if you don't have a childhood or you are not able to live your childhood, surely you are missing out on something – we were all just frightened, lost little girls.

I'd introduce myself to a new girl and say 'What are you here for?' While she was telling me I would be thinking, 'I knew you had done that.' It made me feel good that I knew, and that they were confirming it and sharing it with me. Sometimes I would tell the girls a lot about themselves and their family before they had said a word; they would be astonished. 'How did you know all of that?' I was asked.

*Heather's experiences with psychic phenomena turned almost into experiments when she arranged a 'test' with Aunty Anne, who she believed to be psychic. When Aunty Anne was on holiday Heather would feel uneasy; they arranged something to reduce that unease.*

'At ten o'clock,' Anne said, 'wherever I am, whatever I am doing, I will be thinking about you. And you think about me.'

And I did that. In fact, Aunty Anne actually forgot a couple of times, yet I still homed in on her. One time she was in a car and I felt I was in the car with her and her husband. She had the window open and the breeze was blowing her hair; I was feeling this breeze as well, so I was there and yet watching at the same time. But Aunty Anne had forgotten to be thinking about me. I was mentally trying to say, 'Hey Aunty Anne, I am here.'

I also remember once that she was on a long walk. Anne and her husband were out walking late one night and again she had forgotten to think of me at ten o'clock. At ten o'clock I closed my eyes and was thinking of Aunty Anne. And I picked her up; I was actually above her, in an out-of-body experience if you like (but I wasn't aware what an out-of-body experience was then).

When she came back after her holiday I spoke to her. 'It worked, didn't it? But twice you forgot, didn't you, Aunty Anne?' And she questioned that. I told her, 'Yes, once you were in the car, and I was there behind you. I could feel a breeze. And then on Thursday you had forgotten again and you were walking with your husband.' I explained where they were walking. And she couldn't deny it.

I think Aunty Anne could have taught me more but I still had Mrs M. on my back and was still running away.

*Heather was able to trace her blossoming into the paranormal to the first time she prayed, the first time she received what she felt was a confirmation that she was not alone.*

That first vision in my bedroom in the hostel happened on Thursday; on the Sunday I had a second strange thing happen while I was in church. If we went to church we could have half an hour later up at night, so we always went down to church, though I wasn't very religious at that time.

This Sunday we kneeled down to the prayers, Aunty Anne was behind me. I sat with my friends. I suddenly turned around and blurted out, 'The vicar is going to die after Christmas, Aunty Anne. The vicar's going to die two weeks after Christmas.'

She silenced me at the time. Then after the prayers we sat up, and she touched my shoulder and told me to tell her about it afterwards.

We were walking out of the church in twos and Aunty Anne asked me to stay back. She talked to me about it. I even asked her, 'Why did I say that? I know he is going to die even though I don't know how I know.'

The vicar had a heart attack thirteen days after Christmas. The feelings were strong then; I knew it was going to happen.

It was true, it would happen. I was really convinced and knew it would happen. I was quite excited.

Aunty Anne explained that she believed me; she believed that I was on the spiritual path to becoming psychic.

I asked, 'Why now? Why not before?' 'Because the time is right now,' was her reply. 'Your need is there.'

# Pop

*It was 1967 and Heather, almost eighteen, was soon to be ejected from the hostel. She was hardly prepared to cope with the adult world. Her first and most immediate problem was the sudden necessity of getting a roof over her head. She had a week to sort out her future, then she would be on the streets. A hard social regime that had spent over a decade ordering her every movement was now declaring itself finished with her; she was no longer their problem.*

It was pouring with rain. I had just been telephoning the adverts in the paper, looking for a flat. I was drenched, and seeking cover. Pop just turned up.

At first I saw this man hobbling along the pavement on a stick. He was wearing a woollen tweed suit – thick, with quite a big pattern but beautiful- with a hat to match. He wasn't very big but he had presence; a very proud looking man, walking upright with his stick rather than bent over it.

He came straight up to me, held up his hand, and asked, 'Could you ring for a taxi for me?' He would have trouble dialling a telephone; I could see he had lost some fingers.

I did that and then he asked me what I had been doing. He said that I had looked unhappy. I told him that I was looking for somewhere to live.

He waited for me to say more. 'I've been in care. I've got a week to find somewhere. Every time I ring the number of an advert in the papers I'm told "that flat's just gone."'

He seemed to think for a bit. 'Why don't you come and live with me, gal?'

I was astonished. 'But you don't even know me.' But there was something about him; he just looked at me. I said again, 'You don't even know me.'

And he looked at me closely, smiling. I'll never forget what he said – just 'Oh, but I do.'

*It was the start of the first loving adult relationship in Heather's new life. She was not alone anymore.*

He gave me his card. I told him that I would have a word with my social worker, and checked with him that it would be all right for them to visit at some time, to check the house.

'Yes, any time. I'm not going out for the next couple of days. I don't usually get out much, I can't walk very far.'

So I went back to Steep Hill and told them. My social worker came the next day. I gave her the address that Pop had given me and we went there together to see that it was suitable in their eyes. It was a lovely house; Pop was there, he was on his own. He told the social worker that he had a room for me. The social worker looked around and checked the place out. She pronounced that she was happy; I was thrilled. I asked if I could move in there and she admitted that 'In three days we won't have any say, anyway.'

Pop's house was a little terraced one in Ashfield Street, in Lincoln. We shared a passage; the door to our house was off the passage, to the left. He lived in the room at the front, had his telly and his bed in there. To the right was a sitting-room and a small kitchen. The stairs were in the room in the corner. You'd open the door and go upstairs to two bedrooms and a small box-room. No bathroom, no toilet upstairs; The house had an outside loo. There was a coal shed next to it – we had coal fires. No hot water, no immersion heater, boiler or anything like that. Strip washes were the order of the day, water boiled up in a kettle or saucepan on the fire. I'd have to boil up water when I washed. For clothes washing I'd go to the launderette.

Once a week I used to go to the public bath in town and pay my few shillings and get a little bar of soap and a towel. You only got so long, and only so much water. I really used to look forward to that. I'd pay my money, throw the towel over my shoulder and I would be singing all the time.

For Pop, I'd bring a bowl through every morning for him to shave. There was something moving, almost mysterious, about Pop. He was well into his eighties, but still active, still pretty fit.

I was still working at the factory when I moved in. I settled in very quickly. Pop was pretty fit in that he was able to make himself sandwiches and care for himself. When I came home I would cook us a meal, then we would sit through the evening watching the telly, just talking. He would do a lot of reminiscing.

For three years I was with him. In that time I was really just working; I neither had, nor wanted, a social life. I wasn't interested in boyfriends, or anything like that.

Pop would reminisce about being a drummer in the Boer war. He told me he had the DCM; in fact he promised me that he would leave me his medals. I think he said he was one of the 'Old Contemptibles'; I remember going to a parade with him once in Lincoln.

He was a man who understood people. For example, I wasn't someone who – at least at that age – could discuss my body, even with him. But when I had my periods he would understand. He would see that I was in pain; I never had to say, 'It's that time again.' He would know, and just boil the kettle and get me a hot water bottle and two paracetamol.

There was no central heating in the house. We'd sit in front of a crackling, real fire each morning and each night. In the first few months, Pop would often be up before me in the morning and he'd have the fire lit. It would have been laid the night before; I'd often sit up with him the previous evening, twisting the papers to make the sticks and the firelighters. He showed me how to do all of that. It was always lit, or just beginning to get warm, the flames would just be licking up the chimney and I could feel the warmth as I came downstairs.

'Kettle's on, gal. It's cold out there this morning. You get wrapped up,' he'd say.

During those three years Hazel, my sister, came on the scene. She was pregnant – not married – the result of a brief relationship with an airman at RAF Mildenhall, the local American airbase. She wanted to know if we could put her up. There were a few men in the house where she had a flat and they were bothering her.

'Do you think Pop would let me come and live here for a while with you?' she asked.

I told her that I was sure Pop wouldn't mind. I promised that I would ask him.

Pop lived and slept in a room downstairs because he couldn't manage the stairs. We knocked on his door. 'It's only me, Pop,' I called.

'Come on in, gal.' I introduced Hazel, who was obviously pregnant. 'Can she come and stay with us for a few weeks; she's got problems where she is.'

All he asked me was if I minded, and of course I didn't. It was to be for a few nights until she sorted herself out; she ended up staying over a year. Pop was wonderful, so kind, so sharing. He took her in with open arms. Soon she had her daughter, Donna.

I was still working at the beginning but we needed a bit more money. The only way I could work, still have some pocket money and be able to provide food was to take on a milk round. I would get up at half-past four, make myself a bit of breakfast, get ready for work and I'd work from half-five in the morning until three in the afternoon. Then I'd cycle home, prepare Pop's dinner and later on give him a little wash.

I arranged with Pop to give Hazel a nice surprise. Hazel and I shared a double bed in the big bedroom; I said to Pop, 'Would it be okay to paper the room for Hazel and the baby? Then I'll move into the little room. She'll want to be with the baby on her own.'

So I'd go on the milk round, leave the dairy at two, get home about a quarter to three, prepare tea for about half-past four. Then I'd go upstairs and paper and paint for about an hour. It was quite a big bedroom. Then I'd walk up to the maternity unit. It was husbands only at night in those days but I asked permission and they let me be with Hazel. All these husbands and wives and me with Hazel. She stayed in ten days and then came home. That had been enough time to decorate the place and Hazel was thrilled with it. But I never went into that little room. Hazel asked if I would sleep with her the first night until she got used to it. She wanted to know one of us would wake up if Donna cried. But she was such a flipping sound sleeper I ended up helping at night. When Donna started to cry I'd say, 'Hazel, come on. Donna's crying. Hazel!'

All I'd get in response would be a grunt. I'd think, 'Oh well, just for tonight.' So I'd feed and change Donna and put her back. Of course, I was working on the milk round so I was feeding Donna and then getting up to work. But I didn't mind. I think I babysat for about three months before Hazel met her future husband, George, and moved out.

Because I had a way to go to work, I went there on an old bike. It was about two-and-a-half miles to cycle. I'd leave the house about 5am, and always gave Pop a hug, 'I'll see you later, Pop.' I'd cycle off, get to the dairy and load up the float. It was near enough to a thousand bottles of milk. I was the 'mate' of the man who drove it and delivered the milk; I was the helper. It was a lovely, pretty, quiet, country round. So often I remember doing the round as the dawn was rising. It was lovely. I remember the dawn chorus; so many birds singing. And when it was pouring with rain we used to say, 'Rain before seven, fine before eleven.' And I'm sure that was always right; if it rained before seven we knew that around eleven o'clock it would stop raining and we could take off our flipping oilskin clothes and gloves.

I thoroughly enjoyed that job until one day a dog attacked me. We had quite a few calls where the dogs were chained up. There was this one place where a guard dog was outside. It was on a long chain. I hated doing this one delivery. I'd kind of go round the corner and I'd hear him bark and he'd run for me. Of course I knew that that chain would stop him quite abruptly a foot or so away from me so that I could go past and just put the milk down and come back. But even though he was on a chain, just his barking and snarling was frightening. But this one morning I walked very slowly with the crate of milk, I couldn't see the dog yet, but he had already started to snarl. For some reason I knew he was going to get me this time. And as he went to pounce on me the chain snapped. He was coming towards me, flying through the air. I screamed out and lifted the bottle carrier up – a metal carrier, it held eight bottles – and it knocked him out. I fell over and he fell on me. I gave my notice in at the end of the week after that. It was a shame because I loved it, but I was so scared. And I think I realized that Pop was needing a lot more attention, so perhaps I knew I had to give it up anyway.

Over time Pop's health had deteriorated. He'd been mustard gassed during the War. He couldn't walk very far, and he had trouble breathing. On one occasion I had the doctor out to see him, and after he had finished with him he took me aside.

'What's a young girl like you doing looking after an old man like this? It's too much for you. Tell us when you have had enough; and we can put him in a Home.'

I was so angry. I suppose they meant well, but did they realize what 'a Home' meant to me? A Home to me was an institution, a regime. Pop had given me a real home; the first real home I'd had for years. He was the father I had never had. Pop never went to their sort of Home, needless to say.

Pop really wasn't safe and I didn't like leaving him. He'd stumbled a few times. He wasn't exactly bedridden but I had to do a lot for him: feed him, bathe him, change the bed, help him shave, just keep him clean. And we spent a lot of time just sitting together, reading, and so on. I spent a lot of time with him.

Pop told me he was leaving me the house. 'This is your home, gal, when I go. I'm going to leave you this house, gal. Anything happens to me I want you to have this house so that you've got a home. You've got a roof over your head, somewhere to live. You've been more of a daughter to me than my family ever have.'

I never got the house. Pop had family, though I never got the impression they bothered with him. But when he was ill I contacted some of them and they were round him like bees round a honeypot; they saw he had property and I think they decided they wanted it. When they saw me they said, 'We know why you've moved in with him; you want his money.' For a time his daughter and her fellow moved in with us.

Pop told me, 'They're coming in, gal, there's not a lot I can do.'

I was moved into the little room, they took the big room. They had only been in two or three days when I was woken up in the night by this screaming and crying from their bedroom. I knocked on the door and called 'Are you all right?' Pop's daughter didn't say anything and the bloke just swore at me, told me to mind my own business. The next morning the daughter was downstairs in some pain. She had cigarette burns on her back.

They didn't actually stay very long. One night, because of all the crying and screaming, I told Pop. He hadn't heard it all because he was quite deaf. Pop had a go at them, and the fellow came for me, really vicious. He just kept banging my head against the window until the glass actually cracked. Pop came through again with that heavy stick of his, and laid into him. He was old and weak, but he'd been a big and strong man and he still had some power in him. They moved out soon after that and we never saw them again.

During the time I was with Pop I had been writing to Angela quite regularly, she was still in a home of course. I wrote to see if she could come for a holiday, which we arranged. She came for two weeks the first time; neither of us wanted her to go back. We did a lot together. I'd write every week and then she would come visiting on her school holidays, so during the three years I was with Pop, Angela actually spent quite a bit of time with us.

Once my father turned up with Dot and the son she had had with him. They popped in for what we thought was the day. By the end of the day my father, Dot and David, the son, were sleeping overnight. Then my father talked Pop into letting them move in for a month, which they did.

I was quite happy for Dad to come but I had to remind them that Angela was coming to stay for a couple of weeks. He and Dot and David only stayed for a short time.

Another of my 'visits' was from 'Steven', the person that had raped me when I was a child. He turned up one day – I don't know how he'd found me – and he forced his way into the house. I thought I was going to be raped again; certainly he came on tough. Pop heard the commotion, came out with that heavy stick and beat him off. I never saw him again after that.

I continued to share so much with Pop. Everything really. Pop took my past and made me re-think it. There was no hatred or bitterness in him, and he took so much hardness away from me. I had been hurt by my childhood, by the way I had been treated. At that time I didn't realize I had missed out on love because I had never really known what love was. It was only by talking to Pop that I came to find myself. Over those three years I was able to share with Pop all my experiences; he would listen for hours and then talk me through my feelings and show me that it wasn't me; it hadn't been my fault. I needed to know that. It wasn't that I had been a problem or a nuisance; it wasn't my fault I hadn't been wanted by my father. That had been his choice based on his own needs, not a rejection of me.

One night when I was around twenty, coming on twenty-one, Hazel worked hard on me to get me out dancing. She thought I needed some social life, and I suppose I was getting ready for it.

'Come on, it'll do you good. It's ballroom dancing, it's great,' she said.

She met George at the dancing, and a few months later left us and married him. She took Donna with her, of course. The start of another chapter of her life, and a change for Pop and me. In fact it was to be the start of a new life for me too, because while at the dancing I met Ray, who was to become my husband.

*'Would you like to dance?'*

*Pop had helped Heather come to terms with her emotions; these were the first words she heard from Ray, the man who would help her come to terms with physical contact.*

*It was 1969, almost 1970. Heather was now nearly twenty-one and had left her teenage years behind. The adolescence that had started in Homeleigh had been so mutilated by the pressures of Home Life that it is perhaps significant that in her last teenage years Heather did not go out dancing and disco-ing by her own choice – if she really had any choice. Many of her patterns of life had been formed by repression. She had spent her last teenage years caring for Pop; the first of many giving, caring, sharing episodes in her life. But she had forgotten to care for herself.*

*Thanks to Hazel, Heather went out dancing one evening, and it led to the meeting with her future husband, Ray Woods.*

He came over to me and I realized straight away that I was quite frightened. I hadn't really mixed with boys at all. I think I had cut myself off from them after 'Steven' had raped me, and after what had happened to me in the Homes. The men and women had been violent; in fact, physical contact for me meant violence.

But somebody asked Hazel for a dance. That left me alone, and Ray came up and asked me.

I wanted to say, 'Oh no, I'll sit this one out,' but I didn't. Throughout the dancing we boxed around with the usual chat-up lines; 'Do you come here often?' 'No, it's my first time.' That kind of meaningless talk. He was shaking, so was I. But I actually held him – lightly – and I danced. I had had no lessons but I danced with Ray as if we had been partners for a long time. I also had one or two dances with other people that night but it was kind of clumsy, stepping on toes and so on. It wasn't much fun. All I could think of was Ray, and how we'd danced so 'together'.

The hall was loud and noisy and smoky, I didn't really like it, yet I hoped we'd meet again here and dance more. He said he came every Thursday.

'Are you going out next Thursday, or can you come here? I want to see you again,' he asked.

I found myself promising that I would be there; I was so excited. We were going out together for a few weeks when he told me that he loved me.

'I don't love you,' I replied. I hadn't exactly meant that; I had to try to explain the curious feelings inside me. 'I think I will love you. I don't love you now because – honestly – I don't really know what love is. What it's supposed to feel like. I'm fond of you.'

He was so understanding, so wise. He knew that my being fond of him was me giving everything of myself that I had to give. He said he had enough love for both of us and that he knew I would grow to love him.

We were engaged just six weeks after we met; within eleven weeks we were married. I was twenty-one. When I met Ray, Pop was very happy but I know he was also quite distressed. When I told him that we were getting married he wanted us to stay with him; for us to be married but live with him. It was an emotional time for us all. I didn't really want to leave Pop even for my Ray, but I knew that it was right that I had to. Ray and Pop got on so well but I knew that to marry Ray I had to leave Pop. I didn't know how to deal with that at first; it was a new set of feelings for me to deal with. Ray had his own house. We knew that if we stayed with Pop it just wouldn't work. We needed to be on our own together if we were to grow together.

I wanted Pop to give me away when I married, because he'd been more of a father to me than my own father had ever been. So Pop gave me away, which was lovely. My father was living in a village nearby. I found out his address and sent him an invitation. He didn't turn up.

When I went to collect the cake the day before the wedding the man there had sold all the cakes, taken the money and run away. So it looked like there would be no cake. I ended up running round on the wedding morning to find a cake; I managed to get the top tier off a five tier cake. The photographer didn't turn up either; Ray's Mum had an Instamatic camera. We got one wedding photograph out of it.

Even after I left and married I visited Pop every Wednesday. I'd go down and chat with him for hours. And Ray and I often picked him up for tea. Pop lived another two years after I moved out.

One Wednesday just before Christmas I couldn't get down to see him. Some other thing took me away for that evening, but I expected to see him the following week. But I never did. A few days later a friend came round to our house.

'You used to live with Pop, didn't you?' she asked. Just thinking of him warmed me, comforted me. It made me look forward to going to see him in a few days. I smiled as I nodded.

'Yes, for three years. Why?' 'Sorry to tell you if you hadn't heard. He died last week. Last Wednesday.'

I was blank inside. Cold and crushed. If I had gone to see him that day, would he have died? Could I have at least been with him at the end? Could I have held his hand and said 'goodbye' gently? I was devastated.

I didn't go to the funeral, to the burial. I didn't want to see him put into the ground, I didn't want to remember that. I paid my last respects in the Chapel of Rest, where he was laid out. It sounds silly now, but I bought him a Christmas card and a present and when I got there I put them in his hand. I was so pained inside, I can't remember if I was actually crying. 'I was going to give you these,' I said, 'Why did you leave me?'

*But sad though his death was, and the fact that Heather had not been with him as they might both have liked, Pop had left her reborn, feeling better about her life, and her own value. And he had created a world for her where she had met Ray. He had left her, but he had not left her alone.*

# Living with Ray

We settled down to our life together, finding out about each other. Ray was keen for a hobby; he had been talking about pigeons. He wanted to keep racing birds.

'Ray, I can just see it now,' I said, apprehensively. 'The neighbours putting their washing out and then coming to us saying, "Your pigeons have just messed over the clothes," and so on.' I didn't really like the idea. But if he really wanted to keep the birds I wasn't going to stand in his way. We had to get a loft to keep them in. The loft we chose was sixteen feet long in three sections. It took a week to get it from the house we bought it from, and build it. He sold his bike and his camera to buy it, later I found he'd sold my camera as well.

We bought four birds, two pairs for breeding. And it was brilliant – we started to read books about them and Ray soon got me interested. Eventually we had eighty or ninety birds. It wasn't just the racing. We'd use the eggs. Tiny eggs – we'd have them scrambled.

But it's not really a hobby; it's a full-time job. In the end I knew the birds better than Ray; I spent more time in the pigeon-loft than he did, given he had to work.

In the first few weeks of our marriage I explained that I was absolutely petrified of making love because of the things that had happened to me. He said he understood, and that he'd be gentle.

Ray's own background made it easy for him to understand my problems. He had been a war baby; his father was an American-Italian who had been married but had got Ray's mother pregnant while stationed over here. They shipped Ray's father back to America. Ray's mother raised him for a couple of years but then she got married, and her new husband literally hated Ray. He was often beaten with a poker and forced to sleep in the shed at the bottom of the garden, very ill-treated. Ray also saw his stepfather hit his mother; he grew up being beaten and seeing his mother hurt. He told me that he had promised himself, 'If I ever get married my wife will never be hurt like that.'

There was a time when he had taken an overdose, as I once had. He'd gone out with a girl and they'd got engaged but she jilted him; he took that very hard. He was living in a caravan at that time and his mother found him just in time and brought him round. He was so heart-broken by this rejection. That had been when he was eighteen, three years before we met. It had made him afraid to get close to anyone, though I only found out about this years later.

I do remember his nervousness though; he once said to me, 'You won't jilt me will you? You won't break the engagement off will you?'

I told him that was something I would never do. I had had too much pain in the same way. I knew all about broken promises; the times my father had promised to visit in the Homes, the times I had spent waiting and watching. And he never turned up. I know the value of promises; I would never break them.

So love was also something that we promised each other. We were so in love, but it went further than that. We'd both been hurt, we'd seen in each other something of ourselves. We both agreed that we would never promise our children anything we couldn't deliver. We would rather say, 'No, you can't have it,' than say 'We'll see' or 'yes' and not give them it.

We'd been married four months or so and we hadn't made love. We were kind of working up to it. We were just really lying together and sharing warmth and comfort and security. We were sharing everything else, but I hadn't been able to bring myself to make love.

I told him one day that I would love a baby, and I asked if we could afford to have one. Ray had been offered a new job, so he thought we could afford it. But, of course, we hadn't even made love yet.

He was very gentle but I was so frightened that I stopped him whenever we got close.

The very first time we made love was very painful, I was so tense. But in fact I actually conceived then. After about ten days I knew that I was pregnant. I went to my doctor, Dr Bhanja, and had the tests to confirm it. I was so happy. I kind of skipped all the way home, so light headed and happy. 'I'm having a baby!'

But I nearly lost the baby. At three months pregnant I started to haemorrhage and Dr Bhanja said to rest and not to make love.

'Well we've only done it the once anyway,' I pointed out. We didn't do it again during the pregnancy.

When I was pregnant I wanted something to do. It came out in some strange ways; almost every night Ray came home to find the furniture had been changed around.

'Oh, not again,' was a frequent cry in the house. So I asked Ray if he minded me going out to work. The money would come in handy; there wasn't any real need, but he knew that I needed something to occupy my mind. I got a job working at a transport cafe just around the corner. I started as a washer-up and ended up organizing and preparing the meals and serving them. I changed the menus completely and the numbers of lorries stopping there doubled.

I worked right up to nearly having the baby.

Lindsay was born on the 7th April 1971. He was brain damaged – he was a blue baby.

Ray was at Lindsay's birth (in fact he was there for both births). It was unusual at that time for the man to be in the delivery room, and he had to get permission. I was thirty-two hours in labour, pushing all that time. Today it would be a forceps or Caesarian birth, I suppose. Lindsay was blue and they weren't ready; he didn't cry when he was born. They told me, 'It's a little boy'. But he was the most horrible colour and his head was so misshapen it was unbelievable. Another reason for it being a difficult birth was that his arm was twisted up to his head during birth. You can see the scar on his head in his baby photographs; they told me that if it had been any closer to his eye he could have lost sight in one eye.

I asked if there were any other problems. I pointed out that he didn't seem to be breathing and asked what was the matter with him. They took him from me, I didn't see him for three days, so I knew something was wrong.

When Lindsay was born we were living at Nelson Street; a lovely house with a ninety-foot garden. Lindsay thrived there with all that space. Ray had a good job; he was working at a forge nearby.

Lindsay seemed normal to me. I breast-fed him; he laughed, he cried, he was a quiet baby, a good baby. But his head was a bit big. He had a whooping cough injection and I think that's where the brain damage came from because he had a fit an hour or so after that. His eyes started to roll and he was shaking in the pram. He was rushed into hospital.

From then on he didn't cry. He didn't walk until he was nearly two. He didn't speak till he was three or three-and-a-half. He'd sit and rock to music.

I had to use a pushchair until very late on; and I had to lift him onto and off buses at a late age. And of course he was a big baby – he's over six-and-a-half feet tall now – so I used to hear people saying things like 'Look at her spoiling that kid, why doesn't she make him walk.'

Ray's mum and stepfather had a grocer's shop on Monks Road, in Lincoln. Ray used to drop me off there on the way to work, and I would help out in the shop. Lindsay would stay in his pram, he seemed happy to sit there and play with toys, and rock to music. I spent quite a bit of time there. After work I would either walk home, about a mile, or Ray would pick me up.

I got postnatal blues. I found I was crying and I felt that I just couldn't cope. If Lindsay cried even for a short time I'd be shouting, 'Stop crying. Why don't you stop crying?' I never hurt him; I looked after him, but I just couldn't understand why I was feeling so bad. Ray went through it a bit as well, caught up in my moods perhaps. Dr Bhanja was very good. He suggested, 'I think you ought to go into the mother and baby unit for a while,' but the whole point of that was to take the baby with you. I couldn't, so I rested in hospital for a couple of weeks and friends looked after Lindsay.

After I came out of hospital we settled down to our life together. We didn't seem to need a social life, going out a lot. We were happy using our time to get to know each other. I suppose most people get to know each other and then get married, but we married very soon after we met, and had to get to know each other afterwards. We'd have our tea and then sit down and watch telly – *Dr Kildare* was my favourite – and we'd play with Lindsay. We'd go to bed quite early; half-past nine, ten o'clock. I used to go to bed first, and Ray about an hour later.

We talked a lot, and later we tried to teach our children to talk a lot. It's so important to talk and share your feelings with each other. We never went to bed on an argument.

The second time we made love, about sixteen months after we'd married, was so wonderful. So together. So warm. So healing. So uniting. It was me that said to Ray, 'I would like to make love to you.' It was such a thing just to be able to ask – to ask for contact. Human contact to me had meant violence and pain for so long. But I just knew that it could be wonderful with Ray, and so it was.

It was like you now see on the telly sometimes. The passionate embraces, the moaning and the groaning and the closeness. I'd seen those films but I thought there was no way it could really be like that. But this was. We were together for over an hour just holding and caressing. I don't think of it as intercourse – we made love. We both reached a climax together. And from then on it was wonderful. We made love maybe only once every five weeks but each time was wonderful. It would build slowly, would last so long, be so full of feeling.

There were sleeping problems because Ray was so big and I was so small. He was eighteen stone and six foot eight. When he got into the double bed it would drop about a foot. The mattress would tip slightly,

I'd roll over towards Ray and be squashed right up with my nose pressed into him. And his feet and half of his legs were out of the bed.

We were very playful; he used to be Tarzan and we'd do silly things and muck about. One night he came into the room beating his chest and making the Tarzan-call and he leapt into the air and onto the bed. It collapsed of course; it was completely destroyed. The side folded up and I rolled over the sloping bed and off onto the floor. But it was so funny.

Ray got these four inch nails and was hammering them into the bed at about one o'clock in the morning, trying to repair it. The next day, Fran from next door asked, 'What were you doing at one o'clock this morning?'

'Let's just say we broke the bed,' I told her. I imagine she had a quite different image of what we were doing that night to what really happened.

We agreed the bed was so old it needed replacing and we decided to get single beds so we could sleep more comfortably, given our different shapes and sizes. So after the first year we had single beds all the time. Because of his shift work he could get into bed as I was getting up. We didn't disturb each other either. But it certainly didn't hamper our love-making; that was wonderful, something very special.

We bought a house right on the top of the hill. But we were only there a year or so because in the winter it was hell. When it was snowing there was no way you could get down with a pram. You couldn't get out, so that didn't work. We moved off the hill, to round the corner.

We had both kind of clicked together and said to each other that we wanted another baby, and we planned for another.

In the meantime, I was thinking about the promises I had made to myself to get my sisters out of the Homes.

Angela had been a bridesmaid at the wedding, and at the time she had told me she was unhappy about life at Barrow Hall. She was much younger than me, and still there of course. I talked to Ray about it.

'What do you think about us having Angela, about getting Angela from Barrow Hall? Could she stay with us for a while?'

I thought we could perhaps get her away from Barrow, and prevent her having to go to a working girls' hostel.

'I don't want her to have the two years I had.' But I promised him, 'You know, it's up to you Ray, whatever you say. I'll abide by that.'

We talked it over for quite a few nights. There were benefits after all: Angela could babysit, and we'd get out a bit which we were beginning to enjoy. So we agreed and Angela came to live with us.

We only had one bedroom, but we had a huge bathroom. In the bathroom was a toilet and a bath and a sink. Lindsay's cot was moved in with us for a while and Angela slept in the bathroom. Eventually we had the toilet removed, Social Services hadn't been keen on that being where Angela would sleep.

Angela lived with us, very much part of the family. She was good with Lindsay, and she was working as well. Ray got on with her.

One day I realized that I was again pregnant. I told Angela that we soon wouldn't have room for her to stay; that she'd need to find a place of her own.

'Angela, I'm having another baby.' She said it was great, and that she was pleased for me. She was less pleased when I pointed out, 'The thing is, you know, we are going to need the extra room. You have to make some plans.'

It made her angry. 'You've got pregnant just to get me out of the house, so that I have to move.'

*Angela confirmed that for a time she had believed Heather had manipulated her pregnancy against her, but it was a teenage thing, not a problem that lasted into her adulthood.*

We helped find her a place. It was above a jeweller's in the middle of town. There was one really big room with a fold-down bed, a toilet, a bath and a kitchen. She was happy there. She was in work, we'd visit her, and her boyfriend, Des, would go there and stay the weekend with her.

Three years after Lindsay was born we had Barbara, in October 1974.

I had the blues worse than ever after her birth. But I didn't dare tell the authorities. I thought they might put me in a ward where they could watch over me, even take my child away. It petrified me. So I acted in the maternity ward; I was crying over her one day when the nurse came in and said, 'Heather, are you okay? Come here.' I told her that I was just crying with joy because I had got a little girl and a boy. But I wasn't crying from joy, I was sobbing because I was depressed.

I had counselling, though Barbara has never been aware of this. The counsellor believed that I kind of rejected Barbara in a way. I didn't reject Lindsay because even with the blues something somewhere inside me had told me I could cope with him in the end. But with Barbara there was a form of rejection. I didn't want her.

The counsellor said it was because I'd had a girl; that something deeply subconscious was happening.

'No, that's got nothing to do with it,' I told him. 'That's not what it's all about. It's not that at all.'

But he thought that it was the childhood I had had that caused the feelings I had towards Barbara.

We still played as a family, we did everything together and basically we were happy. It was just now and again I had these feelings towards her. I shared them with Ray. If he thought that we needed to share it with the doctor or the counsellor we would. We were determined to go on until we could understand it. Lindsay was good with Barbara, he never felt jealous as some first-born children do when another comes along. He helped with feeding her and changing her.

When Lindsay started to walk he kept falling over. They said he was flat-footed so we had inners fitted to his shoes.

Later on he started day-dreaming at school and he didn't really mix with other children. He was a loner – he still is – quite happy with his own company. The schoolteachers asked to see us. 'Is there a problem at home?' they asked. We told them there wasn't and asked why they wanted to know. They told us about Lindsay being a bit withdrawn. They were concerned and that made us think, and we decided that this was the time to find out more. Lindsay had an ECG test and it confirmed a permanent brain damage. The side of the brain that is damaged relates to initiative. He can respond intelligently and easily, but he doesn't take the initiative.

*We discovered this is still apparent in Lindsay. He is very pleasant to talk with, but rarely initiates any conversation. In fact when Lindsay walks into a room he rarely acknowledges people already there, but if they greet him, he warmly responds. Heather told us sometimes she would struggle with a heavy box of shopping and Lindsay would just watch her without offering to help, but when asked would immediately throw all his efforts into helping.*

We got him into a convent school that dealt with special cases. They taught phonetic reading, not straight ABC. He picked that up straight away. It was hard for us to understand it when he brought his homework to us to read but we soon got used to it. They told us, 'Lindsay is very intelligent. He is a very bright child. He is willing, he wants to please.' He stayed there two years.

Even today, he is sometimes drawn to a light. As soon as you switched a light on you would find Lindsay slowly start to look at it, then he would stare at it. I told him, 'I'm sure you were a moth in your last life.'

He will stare at clocks, or at the telly for hours, without seeming to watch it. He can stand in front of you without realizing he's done it, until you ask him to move out of the way.

Nowadays he doesn't have fits as he sometimes had when he was very young; he just sleeps a lot. He just switches off. He is registered disabled and where he is working now he is supervised. His work is good; he's got a City and Guilds qualification in Construction – six passes and a credit. Once Lindsay has been shown something he picks it up well. He can cook, sew, create lovely things in wood, and he's a wizard with computer games.

Lindsay and I have been able to share a lot about feelings as well, something I missed in my childhood. We've talked about love and sex. I have told Lindsay that it is making love that is so special. 'You will know when it's the right person. It's not just sex.' There are too many films today where women are used. It should be beautiful, something shared, something special.

I have been Lindsay's friend as well as his mother. His friends would come round to talk to me about those personal things they couldn't talk to their own parents about.

*Heather was beginning to find her ability as a counsellor and healer to others; something that would develop as part of her ministry and her life.*

# A spirit of giving

*When she had the support of a loving husband, secure perhaps for the first time in her life, Heather immediately turned to helping others. It was a fore-runner of the helping, healing Ministry that she would one day believe to be her 'mission'.*

*Along with many other activities she was a member of the Royal Observer Corps, wrote to prisoners in jails around the country, and sought out a variety of ways of giving to others.*

*In 1973 she applied to the City of Lincoln to become a registered child-minder. This application was approved on 8th January 1974. There is no evidence that she did childminding as such, though the application may have been to help Heather and Ray have Angela with them at home, thus achiev-ing Heather's ambition of getting her sisters out of care.*

*Heather was also a Samaritan (Motto: 'To help the suicidal and despairing') at the Lincoln branch. Anonymity is strictly enforced by this group; Heather was 'Heather 463', her 'supervisor' was 'Marilyn 322'.*

*Unfortunately she had to give up this work due to personal circumstances of her own; a deteriorating family situation and her own stresses, withdrawing from membership on 28th November 1978.*

*Heather's most extreme involvement at that time was with an operation she devised and ran called SCOPE: The Senior Citizens Own Prescription Enterprise.*

*It followed Heather's successful attainment of a First Aid Certificate and was set up with the blessing of the Practitioners' Committee, and the support of the County Social Services Department. It was started in 1977, when Heather was twenty-eight years old, and lasted more or less until Ray's death created a radical turning point in Heather's life.*

*It received considerable local press coverage and acclaim, as in one article: 'An ingenious scheme called SCOPE ... is in full swing in the Monks Road area [of Lincoln]. The idea is the brainchild of Mrs Heather Woods, of 62 Monks Road, who saw the need for this service of collecting and delivering prescriptions to the elderly, housebound and infirm. Not only does it provide an excellent service but it also brings about personal contact – a much needed commodity.*

*'To help in this work – which is entirely voluntary – Mrs Woods has just completed – and passed – an extensive ten-week course in home nursing and first aid.*

*'It keeps the elderly and housebound in contact with the outside world. Heather's husband, Ray, took a housebound lady into town for shopping; it was something she had not done for many years and her delight had to be seen to be appreciated.'*

*Heather's own interviews at the time confirmed that these outcomes were part of the reason for SCOPE: 'We hope to give the elderly a much wider service than just collecting prescriptions. It is vital that people who cannot get out of their houses have some company sometimes.'*

*SCOPE ended up with a large body of voluntary helpers – it had acquired fifteen in its first year. Heather was not reticent about finding support for the scheme either. In March 1980 she wrote to the then Prime Minister seeking her support, and received a reply from Downing Street, which said, 'Mrs Thatcher was interested to hear about SCOPE and hopes that you will convey her very good wishes to your group and to the Senior Citizens'.*

*In October 1980 she wrote to Buckingham Palace asking if they could change the Queen's schedules for her visit to Lincoln to include a visit to SCOPE members. The Palace assisted by – in their words – organizing for the Lord Lieutenant, who was looking after arrangements, 'to see if there is any way in which members of your group could be provided with a place on or near the route so that they may have a glimpse of the Queen and Prince Philip.'*

*Apparently it was a great success, as Heather, in the local newspaper at the time, described it: 'I was able to take eight housebound senior citizens on the route, to see the Queen ... the Queen stopped to have a word with two of our group.'*

*It seems that Heather was looking to use her new-found personal security as a base for helping and giving to others. But her own personal difficulties often prevented, or hindered, her attempts. What was to follow suggests that some other aspect of her was developing within.*

## A spirit in transformation

*Changes were happening to Heather. Battered and bruised, mentally and physically, from her time in Homes and hostels, she was now going through healing processes. Pop had helped heal her self-respect, Ray was helping to heal her mind, body and spirit. In those changes Heather also became aware of other developments – psychic developments. At the end of her time in the hostel there had been a few moments of psychic ability; 'seeing' the vicar's impending death in the church, 'feeling' the past experiences of new girls joining the hostel, and so on. With Ray, and with her new-found awareness, these abilities blossomed.*

The first time that I saw something when I was with Ray, I woke up in the night and there was a smell of apples, very strong. It had woken me. I sat up in bed and saw the silhouette of a man near the window. I could see the outline of his hat and nose, and a bit of a pot-belly. Although it was only a silhouette he was really there. I woke Ray up.

'Ray. Ray. What's that man doing in the bedroom?' He couldn't see him; after a while he asked if he was still there.

'Yes, I've been looking at him for twenty minutes.' Then I had the strangest awareness, and I told Ray, 'He's going to be assassinated.' He didn't tell me that, in fact he never did anything. But I was so certain. He was just there and I knew – for certain – that he was going to be assassinated. After half an hour or so his form disappeared. I went back to sleep.

In the morning I asked Ray if he remembered me waking him up and asking him if he could see the shape of the man. He clearly remembered me waking him up, and he remembered me saying that the man was going to be assassinated. I thought on it at the time, and I felt that he was foreign, but I had no other real identification about him.

Ray told me, a few days later, that someone fitting that description had been killed.

There was no special time for these premonitions. It didn't just happen at night. I could be on the toilet, in the middle of baking, washing, whatever. Once I had a vision of a plane crash, and I said to Ray, 'There's going to be a plane crash. The plane is going to take off, flop over, crash and burst into flames.' I had this vivid picture; I was seeing it as though someone was telling me. Ray and I would make notes, we would jot down the time of the premonition.

In a lot of these cases I not only saw these events, I experienced them as if I was in them as well. It was more than just watching them happen. In the plane crash I was also in the wreck, pulling a chair off a person who was trapped. And I was watching myself do that ... I found I cried a lot when I felt like that.

The next morning Ray shouted at me from downstairs. 'Look, look, that's that plane. They're saying that it took off and it seemed to run out of runway and kind of only got so far and then the weight of it flicked it over and it slid onto the grass.'

*This relates to the early days of their marriage, from 1970 onwards. Heather may be referring to the crash of a Trident 1-C at Staines reservoirs, on 18th June 1972. Having failed to take off successfully from nearby Heathrow Airport the plane crashed and 118 people died.*

I had two other experiences. I was sitting up in bed one night – Ray was snoring away beside me – and this park bench appeared in the bedroom. A tramp was laid across it and he was looking at me as if I was invading his space. I just looked at him and asked, 'What are you doing here?' He replied, 'This is my bench.' And I said, 'This is my bedroom,' and with that he just smiled, he didn't apologize or anything. Then the tramp and his bench just slowly disappeared.

On another occasion I saw a boy climbing into my bedroom through my mirror. Wherever he was I think he was climbing backwards out of a window. He saw me, we smiled at each other, and he climbed back again.

There was so much coming to me, and happening to me, at that time that I went to Dr Bhanja. He just told me that it was my subconscious working overtime, but I knew from my earlier experiences with Aunty Anne that something was happening again and that I should follow it through. It was then that I began yoga. By now I was around twenty-five or twenty-six years old.

Ray was an atheist. He didn't believe in God and my faith wasn't that strong. I believed in God but only went to church at Christmas for

Midnight Mass, and Ray was happy to take me. We were just busy bringing up the family. But in this time a lot was happening to me spiritually; a maturity I was learning and growing into, without knowing it at the time. I needed other support and guidance during this period; guidance to learn how to understand what was happening to me.

I was introduced to a lady who taught yoga. I went to a lot of seminars and was able to share with her what was happening to me. She took me under her wing and helped a lot in putting things in perspective for me.

With premonitions, she said, there wasn't a lot we could do. I asked, 'How can we warn these people; how can we say, don't get on that plane, or that train, or this ship because it's going to sink?' But she told me that we couldn't; all we could do was pray for their souls. I was upset about that because I was seeing these things before they happened but there was no use to which I could put the knowledge.

I had an out-of-body experience when I was with my yoga teacher. It was as if I just slipped sideways; and suddenly I was looking at myself, from next to myself. It didn't last long.

The first lasting out-of-body experience I had happened when we were sitting doing mantras, meditating, doing visualizations, relaxation exercises and so on. The teacher had said we should keep aware of something: her voice, the ticking of a clock, something like that. You have to be aware of something, she told us, or you can drift off, but she didn't explain exactly what she meant. I found out. My visualization was very beautiful: a brook rippling by, the sun on my neck, my feet splashing in the water. Time seemed to slow down, and I lost touch with her voice. I couldn't hear anything. Then there was a pressure in my head and I seemed to be sucked, head first, down a dark void. I felt very heavy; then all of a sudden there was warmth, a different feeling, a lightness. I liked it. It was better than swimming – it was weightlessness. Then suddenly I felt this pain in my foot, on my ankle. I became aware again. I opened my eyes and found I was about three feet above my yoga mat, looking down on myself. The teacher was sitting in the full lotus position; gently holding my ankle. That pain in my ankle pulled me back to awareness. I was fuming; I wanted to stay where I was, it was so beautiful. The teacher had realized what had happened and had pulled me back. When I came fully round, inside my body, I could hear her saying 'Nice deep breaths, Heather. Come on.'

Another trip I did was with a leading guru from overseas who visited the group. When he and I first shook hands, when he was intro-

ABOVE: *The Bradleys. From left: Hazel, Heather, George (their father), Dawn and Angela.*

RIGHT: *Heather's children: Barbara and Lindsay.*

BELOW: *Happily married couples. From left: Warwick and Hazel, Heather and Ray.*

*Examples of Heather's channelled writing and drawings. Over the years of the stigmata, Heather produced over 60,000 words of religious writing. She channelled these drawings of Christ baptised, and Christ crucified within days of the onset of the stigmata.*

The 3rd page...
gave you.

The vision if numbered would be page 111 = 3

The 3rd vision of the lady and two men
if numbered would be no 63 = 9.

Add 111 + 63 = 174 which total 12 = 3.

There is three years between my last
book and the prophet published 1923.

The only book published in your birth y...
is not the lady, not the man, but you
in 1949.                    KAHLIL

1MAY 1992 STARTED  30.4.92

A friend visiting Heather's house-church took this photograph
showing a strange light effect. Heather said she could always
see it around her, and she believed it to be the Holy Spirit. It
was not visible to the photographer at the time the photograph
was taken and to date analysis has not explained the image.

*Heather with Father Eric Eades, the most influential figure in her spiritual mission.*

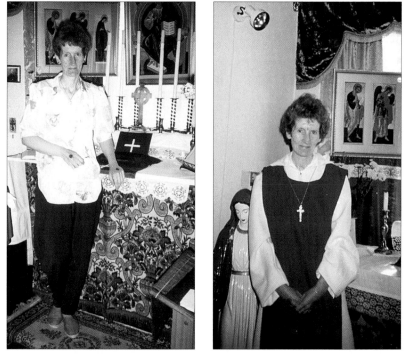

*Heather in her house-church. The signs of the stigmata are clearly visible: (left) the wounds of Christ's crucifixion on her hands, and (right) the cross on her forehead.*

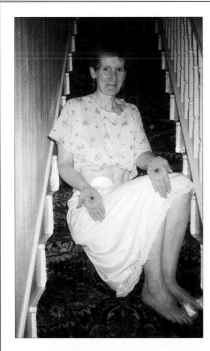

*Heather displaying the stigmata marks for the camera. The marks on her hands and feet are evident.*

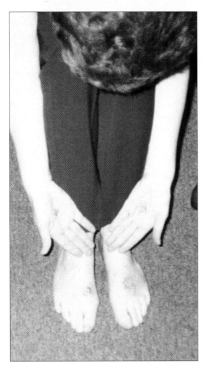

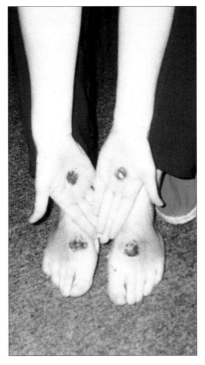

RIGHT: *Heather, clip-miked during interview with the authors. At her own insistence we interviewed for long hours each day: 'Telling this story to the world is part of what it's all about,' Heather insisted.*

BELOW: *A frame from a television documentary featuring Heather. Heather is showing the 'spear-mark' stigmata on her side.*

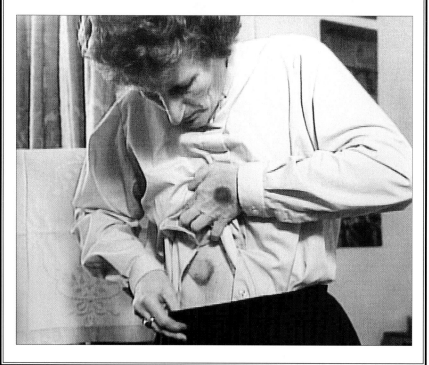

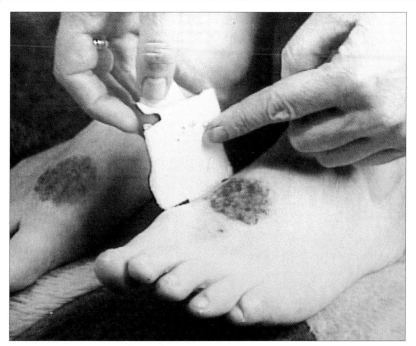

*The blood oozed through the skin like a fountain, according to one witness. And the heat coming off the stigmata was tremendous: six inches above it, it was like putting your hand in a candle flame.*

*Heather with the authors during a break in interviewing. At the most intensive period of interview, Heather stayed with us for three days and dictated 130,000 words of notes and recorded twelve hours of video-taped interview.*

*Heather.*

duced to the group, he put a hand on my shoulder. I said I felt quite honoured, but he just looked into my eyes; something very important and special passed between us.

He took us from that room, to the ceiling, to the roof, to the sky, beyond the planets, beyond this solar system and to another galaxy. He kept gently asking who was still with him from the group of eighty who started in the room, there were only about six or seven of us that kept with him. I had a wonderful feeling of oneness, warmth, completeness. Then we came back, although I remember feeling so strongly that I wanted to stay where I was. I knew I had the family to come back to, that they needed me. Slowly I just opened my eyes and I was back.

*A life together with Ray, which might have been Heather's fondest dream, was not to be. And Heather's sense of the paranormal alerted her to what was to come.*

One day we were planning what pigeons we were going to send to a race and I looked over at Ray and he seemed to just slowly disappear. He was still there, but I could see through him. I said to him, 'We're not going to grow old together sweetheart.'

He laughed. 'Don't be daft, I'm going to live to be a hundred. I'll outlive everybody.' But he realized I was serious.

I said 'I want you to promise me that if you die before me you'll let me know you're okay.' He pooh-poohed it, saying 'You know I believe when you're dead, you're dead, and that's it.' But he could see in my eyes that it meant a lot to me so I got him to promise.

Ray was dead a year later; I didn't think it would be that soon. It was early 1982; I was just thirty-two years old.

By the time Ray died I had forgotten about that promise. I nursed him for four months at home. The night that he died we had a Marie Curie nurse with us, and my sister Hazel had been helping me so that I could sleep a bit.

An hour before he died Hazel screamed out; I thought a mouse had run across the floor because she went, 'Aaagh, did you see that?' I asked what she had seen. She described that she had seen this grey, dark wisp of smoke – quite vivid – which seemed to come from Ray's chest, slowly move to the top of his chest and upwards. The bed was in an alcove downstairs and this wisp of 'smoke' followed the curvature of the arch and then just drifted through the ceiling. I was fuming because I hadn't seen it.

I told her that I believed it to have been Ray's soul. He was in a coma, the physical body was relaxed, there was no tension and it was a natural death so the soul was moving on into the transitional stage.

Ray died an hour later, at ten-to-three in the morning. I didn't ring anybody to tell them he was dead until nine o'clock, but at a quarter-past five that same morning, a couple of hours after my husband had died, his cousin was 'visited' by him. This cousin and he had grown up together and shared a lot. She had become very restless; she got up, lit a cigarette and had a cup of tea. She went downstairs and became aware that Ray was in the kitchen with her. Like Ray, she did-n't believe in anything paranormal. But now she was aware that he was in the kitchen with her. She knew that he was very ill, but she was not aware he had died. And she said she saw – in the corner of the kitchen – a little wisp, three or four inches high, like white-grey smoke, in the corner. And a voice was saying 'It's me, don't be fright-ened. It's me, don't be frightened. Can you give Heather a message for me?'

She replied, 'I can't do that, it would frighten her surely?' But he told her that I would understand; that it was something he had promised me.

'Will you tell her not to worry, I'm all right and it's lovely here. Just promise me you'll tell her not to worry.' And she told me that with that he just seemed to disappear, just go away. She had sensed him in the kitchen with her and that feeling went away as well. She wasn't frightened; she said it was a lovely feeling.

Ray had been a big man, a strong man; you'd have thought he would have gone on for ever. And yet suddenly he was gone.

## Growing without Ray

Ray died in February of 1982. I was okay for a couple of months after Ray's death and then it took me; it was delayed shock. Ray was gone and not going to walk through the door. I didn't want to live any more.

I went to my doctor and told him that I felt I might take my own life to be with Ray. I suppose that was a cry for help. I don't think Dr Bhanja took me seriously although he knew me and knew I had taken an overdose in the past.

I was concerned for the children, not for myself, so Dr Bhanja got the psychiatrist in. The psychiatrist talked to me, he said he wanted me to go into hospital for a complete rest. He feared I was on the verge of a physical and mental breakdown brought on by the strain of nursing Ray through his illness.

I agreed, but I had to arrange for the children to be looked after. My father agreed to have Lindsay, who was then aged eleven; but knew he couldn't cope with Barbara, a girl of just eight years old. My friends, Ron and Jan, said they would have Barbara for the couple of weeks I would be in hospital.

That was arranged, I was waiting to go, and then for some reason I did take an overdose a day or two after these arrangements were made.

A friend just happened to come in and find me; I was taken into hospital and put into the psychiatric wing. The two weeks became three months.

When I came out I was fine; Lindsay was already home and I said I wanted Barbara back. But Barbara refused to come home. I felt that they had spoilt her, having a television and a bike, and she did not want to lose these. I don't know what they said but, anyway, Barbara stayed with them.

It was hell; for two years I couldn't cope with the rejection by my daughter. She didn't want to come home to me. Social Services were informed. A social worker came to me; Barbara had told them that if I made her come home she would run away and just keep running back to Ron and Jan. This reminded me of my childhood, though I had been running to my own parents. Barbara was, at eight, saying, 'If you make me go back to my mum I will just keep running away and come back to Ron and Jan.' I didn't want Barbara to have the pain I had had; I wanted for her to be happy. If she was happy there, as long as I could see her I was happy for her to be there. She has been with them ever since.

I asked to see her, and Social Services told Ron and Jan, 'You must bring Barbara and leave her with her mother for a couple of hours.' But she wouldn't stay without Ron and Jan being there. She would just sit for the two hours; I felt there was no love or affection shown for three years. Social Services thought Ron and Jan were leaving Barbara and I alone together, but the only time we were alone together Barbara cried the whole time.

I couldn't cope with the distress of her not wanting to stay with me so I rang Social Services and told them, 'I can't go through this; I've been through all this myself. She doesn't want to come, she doesn't want to stay. This is not on, I want for Barbara to be happy.'

I would sneak along and watch her at playtime but Barbara caught me looking at her. I kind of just waved, I needed to be close to my daughter, but she told Ron and Jan that I had been there, watching her. I believe that Ron and Jan asked if they could move her from the school after that.

They were saying, 'She has a new home, a new life with us. You are intruding, you are a nuisance. She has to get on with her life. We want to move her from the school.'

Although they brought her to see me I think they made sure that she chose to stay with them. She had a new life and new aunts, uncles, grandmas, and they did not want me. The odd time that I was invited for tea, I would actually sit at the table with my daughter, eat with her, but Ron and Jan's parents would be there and I could see Barbara's love for them. She wouldn't sit anywhere near me even when I asked her to. That was so awful for me.

I asked Ron and Jan things like, 'Will you tell me when she has her first period.' I just wanted to know what was happening with my daughter. It was happening to her as it had with me, although I had been in care. I was an observer on the outside looking at my daughter, and missing what was happening to her. That was very painful.

She never called me Mum until three years ago; I've been waiting all these years. I'd have birthday cards addressed to Mrs Woods; it wasn't 'To Mum' until three years ago. We got very close when my illness got so bad and I was in the hospice. I asked for Barbara to come and see me. The ward sister rang her; Ron and Jan brought her and left me with her and I think we had five hours together. And we sobbed and everything came out and we had both really been fretting and worrying over something that hadn't happened. We had both assumed the other had done the rejecting. It was very sad that it took all those years before we understood one another. And the bond was there, all the lost years. I never saw her grow up. I suppose that for the first time Barbara realized that she was going to lose me and there were so many questions she wanted to ask me, like 'Did you really want me?' All the things I wanted to share with her and to say, 'I did love you and at no time did I not want you.' Because at eight I think this is what she felt, that I had pushed her away.

No-one was able to counsel Barbara over the years as they did with me. There was no counselling, so she grew up, I suppose, doubting my love.

Out of everything that happened to me in the Homes, losing Ray, all the physical pain and surgery, that has been the most painful event. Those years of not knowing what she felt; that hurt the most. It doesn't anymore. And we are so close. She is nineteen next month and she brings flowers and cards. She is not trying to make up for the lost time – this is genuine. It did take a while but she has her own key now so she lets herself in. She has settled down in herself and she knows where she is going and where she belongs now; college and work and everything is going well. She is hoping to join the police force.

*We spoke to Betty Eades, the wife of Father Eric. In the years she had known Heather she had watched her try to repair the wounds with Barbara. 'Heather tried very hard to treat her as a daughter, very much wanting to show her the love she felt, I do know that.'*

Lindsay and Barbara were, of course, split up and do not have a normal brother and sister relationship. They are not close at all; there is nothing at all between them. There is no love, no hate; there are not even friends. He doesn't seem to be comfortable with her. He will tolerate her.

*Heather's view of Barbara and Lindsay's relationship is a very negative one. This is partly brought about, no doubt, by Heather's belief that Barbara 'rejected' her, a belief supported by Heather's friends and relatives. Lindsay confirmed he believed that had been the case also, however he was much easier about their relationship; 'We get on,' he told us. 'Basically I'm all right about her coming round.'*

*Searching for something to keep her from vegetating, Heather turned to seeking ways to help others just as she had done years before, during her time with Ray.*

I was living with Lindsay, just the two of us together, and I decided I needed to do something so that I didn't vegetate. I bought a Honda Melody, a moped, so that I could get around a bit. I went to the Social Services and asked, 'Is there any course I can do where I can help people with their reading and writing?' They said there wasn't but they gave me leaflets and some reading material: 'Read through that; if a course comes up we'll let you know.' I then went to the library and spent a period of about nine months reading up on literacy and dyslexia. I felt I then knew enough to be able to help somewhere along the line.

I went to St John's Hospital where I had been twice as a patient. I was still in touch with the Sister. I asked, 'Do you think there is any chance that I could help here?' She replied, 'I'll tell you what, we've got two lads in Colby ward that you might be able to help.' I knew that Colby was a lock-up ward. 'These two have been sniffing glue and played hookey – didn't go to school for two years – and they are kind of withdrawn. They have been saying they wish they had gone to school because they missed out and are now regretting everything.'

I told her that was a good case for me to start with and that I wanted to help. So it started there twice a week. They were very enthusiastic; we worked on a one-to-one basis.

One of the lads, when I met him, was covered in cuts and things all over his hands and legs. He opened up to me later, saying, 'Wasn't I daft to do all this, slash me wrists and everything...' They were in there six months. I went every week, I didn't ever miss a week, and we got on really well. I didn't feel threatened although they were apparently supposed to be quite violent, these two lads. There was a male nurse sitting not very far away while we were talking. I then went to the YMCA to see if I could help the young men that lived there, and I did for a while. I used to go once or twice a week.

I was very upset by this one lad; he was twenty-one, and struggling with two-letter words. I thought, 'I've got to do something earlier, help the kids earlier so that they do not get to this stage.' I saw it was so painful for this lad that he just could not pick it up, and yet he was so bright in everything else.

I think that's when I decided, 'I'll go and see what Mr Williams – at the local school – thinks.' I told him I was an Adult Literacy tutor, and explained what I had done at the hospital. 'I'm just wondering whether you'd like me to come in and listen to the children read, just let them read to me?' He was very agreeable to the suggestion. He knew Lindsay from school and he knew me as Lindsay's mum. I asked him when I could start. I started on the following Monday, one hour a day, two mornings a week. I started in Miss Taylor's class of five-year-olds, and later took the six-year-olds. Eventually I was helping on four mornings.

I found that I got on better with the six-year-olds. They were more receptive. I found my niche with the six-year-olds. The last two years I stayed with these two teachers; a hundred children a week read to me. I wanted to concentrate on the children that were struggling, then the other kids who could read wanted to come to me as well, so in the end I had to include the good readers.

I helped with the Christmas plays as well; getting the children changed, and walking them into the hall and so on. I was asked to help with the coach trips, but I was afraid of the children hurting me when they hugged me with the excitement of the outings so I told the staff I wasn't a good traveller. I had to be careful; I had had operations and they had left me a bit delicate.

I asked Lindsay, 'Would you like to come to school with me one day and listen to a few of them reading?' He agreed he would like to do that. I asked Mr Williams and he also agreed. So one Friday I told the class, 'On Monday when I come and see you all I'm bringing my son with me. He is a giant. He is as big as the doorway. He is really big.' They asked me if he was a real giant. I told them they would have to wait until Monday, and then they would see.

When Monday came round Lindsay came with me. I went into the class where the children were all engrossed in their work; I just walked in quietly. I never knocked on the door. Lorraine, the teacher, just smiled. I just stood there until one child said, 'Here is Mrs Woods, Mrs Woods is here.' One or two would always just come and talk and chatter about things. Then one of them asked, 'Where is the giant then? You said you were going to bring a giant.' And I called out, 'Lindsay, would you come in?' He came in. And of course, being over six feet tall he did look a giant to the children. As each child came up I asked 'Do you want to read to Lindsay or to me, it is up to you?' Some chose Lindsay, some chose me. So once a month when he wasn't working Lindsay came with me.

I gained so much from the children. Parents would let me know how their children had improved. That was my reward and what I wanted.

I applied to Children In Need, asking for five or six hundred pounds to buy a computer for the school, knowing it would help hundreds of children. The charity asked for Mr Williams, rather than me, to be the proposer. Sometime later, the secretary rang up and told me, 'Oh, Mrs Woods, I am just ringing to say that over the holidays Mr Williams went to Yorkshire TV and to Lincolnshire radio to have his photo taken as they handed him the cheque for £600 that you applied for.' I wasn't invited; I didn't know of the event. I was upset, thinking Mr Williams or someone could have told me and didn't. But I was pleased anyway that the children got their computer. I feel I did that for them.

*The end of Heather's work at the school was, for her, a traumatic and unexpected one. As we shall see in this book, the manifestations in her later years were to produce some varied reactions.*

I remember leaving home one Monday morning at about ten o'clock on my moped to visit Barbara, thinking I could get there, see her and come back for my dinner. I remember going along this country road with not a car nor a person in sight. And I don't remember anything more until I woke up in hospital. What the police think happened was that I hit one of these lumps of mud left by a tractor and it threw me up into a ditch. My moped went on for another hundred yards or so and went along the verge and laid down, so that it wasn't seen. And they think I must have been there twenty minutes or so before this man had come by. He was driving along and just happened to notice this big pile of rags or clothes. He got out of the van and found me. He had to get to a phone and ring for the ambulance; they picked me up and took me to the hospital.

It was Monday tea-time when I came round. There I was in hospital with a drip and a collar on my neck wondering what on earth had happened. I was in hospital about five days. I wasn't too badly injured but I was quite badly bruised. I had hit the handlebar and caught my side here where my pancreas and spleen are, and that was particularly badly bruised. Every half an hour they had to keep measuring me because I was swelling up a bit. And now I am having problems with the pancreas and spleen.

## The onset of physical change

In 1988 I was diagnosed as having ulcerative colitis. I had the large bowel removed and an ileostomy; that should have been all I needed. But complications set in and everything that could go wrong did. Adhesions, Crohn's disease, and then because the rectal stump and anus weren't taken I had yet more surgery to remove them. Before that operation I went to a reflexologist, which led to my meeting Father Eric Eades, a bishop in the Celtic Church.

*Father Eric was probably the single greatest influence on the religious and spiritual years of Heather's development. His involvement with Heather extends right through the spiritual chapter of her life. At first, however, he offered a needed hand during her illnesses, as Heather shortly describes.*

I have had eight major operations, three smaller ones and I have been in hospital many, many times. The last surgery was a hysterectomy; the womb, the ovaries, everything was taken away including the pelvic floor and the cervix, part of the small bowel and some of the bladder. There were two masses there as well, as big as melons, that had adhered to the abdominal wall, so they had to be cut away and removed. I looked as though I were pregnant. They were growing by the hour. The surgeons found that the masses had damaged a kidney so that's not working very well. But for all of that my heart is strong.

So I have my heart, a kidney and my liver and pancreas, a bit of small bowel and half a bladder. I am constantly in pain, but kept comfortable with painkillers like morphine. I need more surgery but I am not strong enough to have it and I won't. I don't want any more. Enough is enough. I can't take any more. They have touched every organ in my body except my soul and I've told them they're not having that! So I've accepted that I will just have the pain relief. I know I must later die with dignity but I am not ready to give in, or to give up, yet.

*Heather had left her working girl's hostel, and a life of institutionalized care, and had found very special people who had come to mean so much to her: Anne, with whom she found what she believed to be special abilities within herself; Pop, who gave her her first real home; and Ray, who provided a normal loving home and relationship within which she could heal her earlier wounds. But all had left her now, for one reason or another. But she was still not alone; her vision was still being fulfilled. She had met, and would meet, people who would nurture her through extraordinary changes to come.*

*Now she was suffering illness, but her need for healing was to lead her to a new phase in her life. She was later to feel that even her illness was a part of preparation for a life of focus, serving the Lord.*

*From then on, every aspect of her life – including some incredible paranormal experiences – were directed to that end.*

# CHAPTER THREE

# Spirit Within Her

## A healing ministry

I HAD NOT REALLY BELONGED to a church up until 1985. I would say my prayers at night and went to the Methodist Church at Christmas – just the Midnight Mass, really. Then when I moved to Spa Street the church was just around the corner in the next street so I went to see the minister. I wanted to start to go to church. I liked the minister, and I liked the church, so I started to go. Everybody was nice, I ended up becoming a member. Lindsay became a member as well. They were a great bunch of people and I enjoyed church every Sunday. I sang with the choir; I loved singing. Then I got involved in a lot of the church activities.

*In the same spirit that Heather had adopted towards SCOPE and other voluntary, giving, sharing, activities years before, she became a fundraiser for the Methodist church. Her energies were once again being directed towards giving to others.*

I was still going to the Methodist church when I fell ill in 1988, and when I went to Father Eric Eades for healing. I met him through a friend who I had gone to for reflexology. She knew that I was in a lot of pain and asked if I had ever had healing. When I told her that I had not she offered, 'I know a priest who does healing. Would you like me to introduce you?' I said that I would. So I was introduced to Father Eric.

Through my illnesses I had healing from Father Eric. Sometimes he would invite me for tea. Once, when Lindsay and I were having tea with him, he told me, 'We've got a service here tonight.' It was a house church – a church set up inside Father Eric's house – and I thought at first that maybe it wasn't a real church and that Father Eric was playing at it. But I asked if I could stay and join in and he agreed. I soon realized my doubts were quite wrong; it was very much a real church. I so much enjoyed the service and we had communion. The fellowship and the atmosphere there was lovely.

My interest in that church grew from there. There was a oneness with the people and the service, and with Eric. It wasn't formal and rigid. The Celtic group is a home group, a house church serving the local community basically, but we also travel around sharing testimony in services with different churches in Lincoln and nearby.

The Holy Celtic Church is a recognized church in the World Council of Churches. Our saint is St Gregory Palamas. The Holy Celtic Church is your own; you follow your own personal calling, but it is not a church where you just do your own thing, it has rules and structure.

*The Holy Celtic Church is a small, independent Christian church, which, its members claim, goes back to ancient times. Although house based, much of a service would be familiar to Roman Catholics.*

I came away from the Methodist Church because I felt less fellowship there and because everything felt right with Eric and the Celtic Church. But I felt I was vegetating, sitting around too much during my convalescence.

'Think about theology,' Father Eric suggested. I thought about it and realized that it would be good to tax my brain. Father Eric told me, 'It's not what you might think, it's not boring. You will enjoy it, I know you will. It is two years' study.'

So in a way that became a goal to reach, because it was as if Father Eric was at least confirming that he thought I would still be here in two years.

The course is like Open University study. You give as much or as little time as you can. Father Eric paid for me. I promised that I would take the first ten lessons and if I reached the pass mark, I would go on. The pass mark was seventy. I decided that if I found it a struggle or I didn't get that grade then I would stand down, as it would be obvious then that I wouldn't be able to do it.

But I sailed through it over the two years. I studied at the library when I got strong enough; the staff all got to know me there. I almost lived in the reference library; I had a real passion for the study. I later got my graduate degree in theology in 1990.

At the time I was still in and out of hospital. As my illnesses progressed the pain got worse; I was eventually admitted into the hospice. I was given a pump to deliver morphine. And that was the first – and only – time in the last five years, that I have been free of pain.

Because the pump gives you morphine continuously for twenty-four hours a day, it slowly puts you to sleep. You gradually become semi-conscious, then unconscious. I suppose it's a bit like when a vet puts an old dog down; that's just a lot of anaesthetic, isn't it?

Everybody came to say goodbye, but although I was in there and free of pain, I was pretty out of it, drifting in and out of consciousness. Days were coming and going and I was not aware of my family and other people being there and crying and saying cheerio. And yet there was a part of me saying, 'But hey, you know, don't say goodbye. I am not going anywhere.' And I don't know what happened next.

Something happened and I was lifted above the effects of the morphine and of the unconsciousness into a different state. I was observing myself; I didn't seem to be in this time at all. And then I seemed to be back in myself. There was still no pain and I knew that there was something for me to do. It was as if there were two of me: and one of me was telling the other, 'You've got something else to do, Heather.'

It could have been my subconscious. I believe it was another self, a subconscious part of my brain, talking to Heather who was unconscious and drifting in and out, trying to rally her. And then this other self lifted me up to see myself, to show me that I was there. My other self was saying, 'Look, we need you. There's work for you to do and we can help you but you have to surrender fully so that we can work with you, for you.'

As much as I thought it might be me talking to myself I also believed that it was God talking to me as well. I said, 'I will serve you, God, but I can't serve you while I'm in pain like this. You know how weak I am.'

There was also another presence. Help was being offered. All I had to do was say, 'Yes, I want to do it. I want to serve you.' And I did that. And I said that I needed to be well, I want to give one hundred per cent.

*The response to her prayer seemed, to Heather, to be a familiar friend.*

This presence was the one that I had experienced in the working girls' hostel when I was eighteen. Then I had heard it as a voice, the voice that had told me, 'You will not be alone any more.' This time I didn't hear it – nothing was said – but as before I got this feeling that I was somebody. Somebody did love me and I was being cared for, watched over. All this happened in only minutes. I came out of my body and the self met myself.

Dr Bob had walked by. It drew the parts of me together into a whole again. It was as if I re-entered my shell. I muttered his name.

Apparently he had been in to see me earlier and I had been semiconscious, drifting into a coma. Now I told him that I had had this vision, and that it was lovely and I was going to be all right, going to get well, that I was going to be helped because I had accepted Jesus. I had said, 'Yes, I want to serve you.' I remember Dr Bob patting my hand and patronizing me, 'Yes, Heather. It's the morphine, you are hallucinating.'

I told him, 'I am not hallucinating, Dr Bob. I am going to get well and I am not going to need this morphine. I am going to walk out of here.' And I think that he then realized something real was happening. I think he knew then that I wasn't hallucinating.

He left and for the first time I relaxed, and slept. I woke up the next day and I found I had been given a prayer. I shared the prayer with Dr Bob, who was amazed. Later I got out of bed with the pump attached to my belt and walked effortlessly to where Dr Bob and the nurses were. The nurses asked, 'How have you got here? You shouldn't be out of bed. You shouldn't be able to walk this far.'

I was brightening up, with colour coming back to me, and I was beginning to eat.

The main thing is that I had told them that I was going to get well within two days. I told them I wouldn't need the morphine but they didn't want to remove it. But I was very insistent. They said, 'We can't, we've got to wean you off.'

I can remember saying, 'But I don't need it. I am not in pain.' Anyway, within a couple of days they were quite sure of a change in me, I was eating well and walking for exercise. I was still out of breath but not in any pain, so they took me off the pump but kept a syringe to hand. When they saw how strong I had got, the same afternoon I think, they admitted I didn't need the morphine. They were amazed that I needed no weaning off.

So from the day I went in to the hospice, it was just three weeks to the day I walked out.

Father Eric had visited every day. I had shared with him what had happened about me being given another chance for life and my belief that I had been called to serve the Lord. I told him that I had asked to be made whole, to be able to serve one hundred per cent, and he could see how well I was after that short time, which for me confirmed the Lord's help. I knew that I had given myself fully.

I also felt there was something out there, something in addition to our Lord. He had sent me my companions, the unseen holy ones who I think had been with me from that time in the hostel. They had been the ones that had told me I would never be alone again.

I think Father Eric had been prepared for something like this for weeks, perhaps in his own prayers. As I told him about all this there was a look in his eye as he looked at me; we just knew each other's thoughts. We didn't have to speak.

I got more and more interested in Eric's church. I asked what I could do if I wanted to get more involved. I had enjoyed the work I had done with the Methodists, and wanted to continue that in this church.

'You could serve in the congregation,' Eric suggested, 'Or serve as a deaconess.' I became a deaconess.

So much happened at once with the healing, my illness, the studying, and becoming a deaconess. It all merged together as one and then when I really gave myself over one hundred per cent, gave my life into the church, I felt it was right. Rather than just be a member of the congregation I had given myself completely. I would serve God in that way. I was sharing services around the country, and visiting the sick in hospital.

Father Eric was a good teacher, a mentor. There were more hours of studying, learning all the time. There was a lot of work involved. I was ordained first as a deaconess, and last November (1992) I was ordained as a deacon, taking the title Reverend.

As a deacon I could share the hosts with the congregation. If Father Eric gave out the bread I could hold the chalice and give the wine after the blessing.

As a deacon I can marry, baptize and I have done five funerals already. I can do everything the same as a vicar or minister apart from consecrate. If I were to be priested, the only difference would be that I would be able to consecrate.

I've registered my house as a place of worship, as did Father Eric. It is also registered for solemnization of marriages; it's actually registered in its name of St Gregory Palamas.

## Becoming a healer

As far back as when I first met Eric, he recognized something special in me. When I shook hands with him, as soon as we touched, he asked, 'Did you realize you had healing hands?' The thought fascinated me but I told him I had not thought of it, and didn't know.

But I had gone there for healing on myself at that time. Father Eric shared healing with me for about an hour. We went into his church and he started 'the laying on of hands'. He had his hands a few inches away from my head and slowly moved them – keeping them a short distance away – all over my body. He stopped every now and again. At those points he would say 'Have you had problems with this part of your body, or that part...?' When he got to down to my hip and leg he asked, 'Have you broken your leg at any time?' So he was picking up on old injuries and problems I had had but about which I hadn't spoken to him.

This quite intrigued me. I had thought I was just going for some healing, and to be topped up to give me enough energy to cope with the major operation I was going to have, but this extra analysis was fascinating.

I asked him how he knew all of this. 'I seem to get a hot spot. It feels hot. And that's The Holy Spirit moving in me, saying that that is where there is a problem.'

He was a very good healer, a very good channel. He could pick up other things, not only what was making you ill but things that had happened to you years before, because there were weaknesses he could see. People who can see your aura say they see breaks in the colours, or they are not so bright in some areas, and that lets them know where or if there is an illness.

When I was in hospital, Father Eric and his wife Betty visited me. It was lovely to see them. We built up a rapport from there on; when I came out they came to visit me at home. They invited Lindsay and me to tea one Sunday. We'd talk about one thing and another. And then Father Eric would share healing with me, saying that he could keep me topped up in case I needed any more surgery, or even if I felt okay I could still have healing to keep myself well. People tend to think that if they are not ill they don't need to go. But even if they are pretty healthy they can still go and have the laying on of hands to stay healthy.

So I was having healing and building up our friendship. We became close friends near enough straight away. Father Eric asked again if I was interested in healing, pointing out once more that I had healing hands. I told him that I was interested; I had benefited from it and if I was able to channel that for other people it would be great.

He explained about the Order of St Luke, the Christian healing ministry. It is recognized worldwide, internationally known. Because of my experiences I wanted to follow this up. Father Eric would ring up and tell me that he had somebody coming for healing.

'Would you like to share this session with me?' he'd ask; often I could just watch. You don't need lessons as such if you have the gift; it's a natural ability. All I did was stand with Father Eric and he would say, 'Just put your hands there ... or there...' It was like a lesson but more like sharing and talking and feeling.

So I shared quite a few healings with Father Eric. After the first three or four it seemed to come naturally to me. I began to feel those hot spots.

Father Eric warned me, 'You have to be careful. When you pick up something you don't always tell the person. You have to find out in each person who comes to you how much you can say and what not to say, because you sometimes pick up on serious things that are going on in their body that they are not aware of and it can frighten them.'

My surgery was on-going so I was in and out of hospital in between all of this, and taking periods of convalescence; hours and hours in bed, resting.

I asked to go to one of Father Eric's church services and I quite liked the service and the atmosphere. I liked how relaxed it was. I had been doing healing with Eric for maybe a year when he asked, 'Would you like to become a member of the Order of St Luke? All I have to do is write to the warden and then there will be a little service of induction. It's a nice service. You are then registered as a healer; you get a badge and a membership card.'

He stressed that we don't charge any money; we don't do it for that. It is to meet the needs of the people who come for healing, but we also gain from it. And we are never drained. Sometimes you read of people who have done healing and they collapse or they are tired; it is not like that with us. We are never depleted ourselves. We don't lose any of our strength helping somebody else. The energy doesn't come from us, it is The Holy Spirit. You are just the hands; the Holy Spirit flows through you.

It's Christian healing. We do it in the name of Jesus Christ. So when you put your name forward to become a member of the Order of St Luke you have to have a letter from your minister, from the church you are going to, because you have to believe. But you can be of any denomination. You write a little bit about yourself. Then your minister or vicar has to write a reference for you. Not everyone can be accepted; it isn't personal, they are looking for quality of healing. I should also stress that while many of us at some time have been interested in the paranormal – and perhaps spiritualist healing – this is not spiritualist healing. It is a Christian healing.

Faith helps of course. If the person who comes to you has faith and believes you can help them, or believes in the healing, then it makes it easier for them. But we have also had many people who don't really believe – they can also be healed. Relatives will sometimes ask on behalf of a friend or family, so although they don't believe, the faith and trust of the person who has asked is there; those people are usually present at the healing.

Father Eric was the chaplain; we are a chapter of seven healers and need a chaplain, a leader to organize everything. People don't always understand what's involved. One lady had been trying to pluck up courage to come. She was frightened and shy but she eventually came. She admitted that she was a bit unsure because she had seen some healings where people were stood up, the healers then put hands on their head, and they'd fall. I told her 'No, there is none of that. You are always sitting down. If you have to stand up to let us get to your back or legs, you are well supported and helped.'

People react to healing differently of course. Some people are sound asleep and stay right out for twenty minutes or so. Others might close their eyes slightly because it's such a peaceful time. Or some talk; you can talk right through it because we are just the channels for The Holy Spirit to move in. Talking doesn't matter, The Holy Spirit is doing the work. We are just the hands.

We always make it clear that it's not our gift to others, it's not our gift to give. Although they ring up or come round and say, 'I feel so much better, the pain has gone, it's absolutely lovely. Thank you very much,' we will always say, 'We are really pleased that you are feeling better and that you have thanked us but we are still only the channel, the utensil. We ask you to thank the Lord.' Even if they don't pray or don't believe, we just say, 'If you can just say "thank you Lord" that is enough.' There is spiritual strength in numbers which is obvious. Usually once a month we have a healing service where all the healers are together. We can share the healing with one person, all seven of us, but that can be too much for them. So although all the healers are there it's often a one-to-one when the people come up. But we can double up, or whatever is necessary.

I would think I have shared about forty healings over the last three years. Some people just come the once and we never hear any more.

Just lately, through my illness, I've been receiving healing from my chapter, from my friends in the healing group, and I benefit from this. I've received healing, so I'm an example, if you like, of receiving healing.

Just recently we have had a lady who has bone cancer. She had been very ill and had chemotherapy and other treatments. Her friend came to me ever so distressed and asked if we could help at all. She said, 'I just love her so much and it's hurting her.' I told her that I couldn't say whether I could help her or not because it would be God's will. Sometimes the illness is something that person will have to cope with so that they will grow in some way. I feel that I have to say that; if I said 'Of course we can,' that might be giving them false hope, so we just say that we invite the Holy Spirit.

So the lady brought her friend. She could hardly walk but she was quite insistent she wanted to go upstairs, she'd heard about the church in the house, I think from one of the stories in the papers, so she struggled up the stairs. She wanted to see the church and sit in the church. Steve – he's another healer with me – and I were with her for about an hour and forty minutes.

They came every week for three weeks, and the second week when she came again with two friends we sat round and just said a little prayer to relax everybody and to invite the Holy Spirit to be in our midst. She seemed to be moving a bit easier. I asked 'How are you? You're not looking too bad, in fact I think you're moving a little bit better.'

This lady replied that the night after her first healing session she had slept quite well, there was no pain and she was reasonably comfortable. Both her friends were quite excited that they had begun to see a change in her. Two nights later the phone rang; it was the friend to say that the lady had gone to the doctor because she had felt so much better. She wasn't even limping and the doctor was quite amazed. That was great and that lady is still coming. She's now bowling and she's back at work.

A lady named Anne came. 'I'm a devout Roman Catholic. Does that matter?' she asked. I told her that it didn't matter, as we went up to the church. She said she was a bit nervous, she was shaking. She told me it had taken her a long, long time for her to pluck up the courage to come. Could she have healing please? I suggested that she come the following day, and we agreed a time. That night the phone rang, it was her husband.

'Is that you, Mrs Woods? This is Anne's husband. She is not coming to your healing sessions.'

I felt quite sad about that. Of course we hadn't exchanged numbers or addresses so I put Anne onto absent healing wherever she was and tried to visualize her face. We have a prayer book with over fifty names now. I mention each by name – that's important to me because then I am identifying each person to God rather than just saying, 'You know all the names in this book, Lord.'

About ten days later the doorbell rang and there was a man there. He said, 'I am Anne's husband. I rang you up just over a week ago and told you my wife wouldn't be coming. I've come to apologize. I am ever so sorry. I shouldn't have done that. Anne has never left me alone since I phoned. I just don't really believe in all that stuff but I've come to say I'm sorry and can my wife come to healing?' I told him that of course she could come. I thanked him very much for coming and apologizing. I told him not to worry; that I understood. It is hard for some people to accept.

For absent – prayer – healing I can't really set a time, because I don't know from hour to hour what I am going to be doing. I do try to find a couple of hours for prayer and quietness, my own space. Sometimes in the church, sometimes downstairs after Lindsay has gone to bed. I always find it's after midnight when the world itself is quiet. The telly is not on, there are no cars going up the street, no children playing outside. So the whole atmosphere is quiet which is nice. I feel that there are no distractions for me, I can be at peace with God. Everybody is sleeping. Of course, God never sleeps, he is watching over us, caring for us. That's when I pray for each person and his or her family, just to get through another day, to cope with their problems.

With absent healing, if we know where the pain is or what the problem is, we will visualize the person if we know them or ask for a photo if somebody has rung up. All I do is look at that person and then I will just close my eyes and see this person in my mind's eye and I just imagine that I am sending through my hands blue rays of healing to that person. I am seeing the rays come from me into them.

We don't want to take people away from their doctors. In fact we encourage people to keep going to their doctors. We want to complement health treatment rather than it being an alternative. And I think slowly the doctors and hospitals are moving towards seeing it that way.

## The channelling, the stigmata, and transfiguration
*Heather's range of paranormal experiences were only just starting. Her earlier ESP, and her involvement in healing, were only the beginning.*

On Monday, 4th May 1992 I found I had a blister in the palm of my right hand. The weekend before that I had been with a friend, Helen Whatton, painting her skirting boards. I assumed the blister was caused by that. The following day I noticed a similar blister on the back of the same hand. On the 6th May, I had a vision, it was of a man who I believed to be our Lord being baptized. Just standing there; our Lord being baptized. It was as if I was there. I could see the water dripping from him, sparkling in the sunlight. It was a very brief vision.

During that night I dreamt of the vision. But that following morning I found I had actually drawn it. I found the paper on the floor with the picture. I had seen His baptism; I had been there. I had been given a vision of the Lord's baptism. And I had drawn it. *(see plate section)*

*Heather believed that these drawings, and many writings which helped guide her on her path, were 'given' to her; her expression for channelling. It was her belief that the presences that had comforted her in the working girls' hostel, and which developed her paranormal abilities, were now guiding her on her mission for Christ. Indeed, she believed God Himself was giving that guidance.*

It was that day that I noticed what I thought was a blister on my left hand.

*This was the beginning of the stigmata, though Heather did not know it at the time. Another, perhaps even more extraordinary, vision came to her.*

That evening I was there on the cross with our Lord. In that time I felt the pain and desolation of Christ, his suffering for the whole world, and all mankind. I understood every line of agony in the face on the cross. The blood, the sweat; I felt all of it. And a drawing was given to me then: a depiction of the crucifixion. It is a very passionate, moving picture of Christ being crucified. And He's not actually on a cross; contrary to popular belief about His death, He's nailed to an upright post. *(see plate section)*

I rang Father Eric and told him about the channelled messages and drawings I had received. Of course, I had told him about the blisters which he believed were the stigmata. He came over to see me.

I showed the picture of Christ's crucifixion to Father Eric.

'Just look at the pain and the agony in his face. I can feel the compassion,' I told him.

Father Eric was moved by the picture. 'Can you remember drawing him?'

I told him that it had just been an urge to draw. I could only remember reaching over for the pencil. I asked Eric what it all meant.

Eric was really excited. 'These drawings are magnificent. They mean something. I believe they are part of what's happening, part of the stigmata.' He went on to add, 'We have now got the drawing of Christ baptized, and Christ on the cross.'

I wasn't even aware I was drawing. But it got to where the urge to draw and write was so strong that it was distracting me. I would be coming downstairs and I would miss some of the steps in my urgency to reach pencil and paper, to get it down in black and white. It wasn't as though there was an urgency or that I was going to run out of time; it wasn't that if I didn't get it down I wouldn't get it at all. It was just that these feelings were so compelling. So I started to keep paper and pen upstairs, or anywhere I might be.

Father Eric had said from the beginning of receiving these drawings and writings, 'Try and make a note of the time as well before you "switch off" or when you "come back" because that is important, that is relevant.' It was hard because there would be times when I'd get up, come downstairs, write or draw, go back to bed, and not realize I had done any of it.

So I tried to keep a digital clock on the floor in my room. Sometimes I would wake up and if I saw the clock I knew I was still here in this present time but if I looked and I couldn't see it then I knew that I was elsewhere.

I am aware of reaching for the pen but I don't know what will come. During the time the writing or the drawing comes through I am oblivious. Those who have seen me writing, or drawing, say that I do it with my left hand. I don't know, I'm not aware; but normally I'm right-handed. And when I have to write it's like a need – like when you have to go to the loo. I've grabbed anything that comes to hand; I've written on a Christian Aid poster, on a piece of cardboard box, on old envelopes and cards and all sorts of papers that were lying around.

*Father Eric's wife, Betty, said of Heather's channelled drawings: 'From what I've seen I've no doubts whatsoever. She didn't do those (consciously); she could do little faces and so on, but what she did with her left hand was amazing.'*

On 10th May the prophecy of transfiguration was given to me. I was given that in sixty-three days' time I would witness a transfiguration that would take me from my old life to a new beginning.

That night I had gone to bed, but I was awakened. I found myself coming down the stairs once again and just sitting down. The urge to write was strong. I knew that I was going to write and I reached for the pen. I was trying to remember to look at the clock to note the time, remembering that Father Eric had told me to try to note times down in case it was important. But I couldn't. I was fighting inside myself, trying to look at the clock and yet I knew then that it wasn't me any more. I wasn't taken over but I had lost my own will. I was under another will. So although I was aware of picking up a pencil or pen and finding some paper, and I was aware I was writing, I couldn't move. I was aware I was writing but not what I was writing. And I wasn't able to look at the clock.

And then it just seemed as though I picked up the paper, as if there was no break. But there was writing on both sides of the foolscap paper. The pen was still in my hand. Then I looked at the clock and made a note. It was too early in the morning to ring Eric up; I put the pen down and went back to bed. I drifted off.

Eric rang me in the morning. I was quite excited, and I told him what had happened that night.

I told him that I was being told, in this writing, that I would witness a transfiguration that was going to take me from my old life to a new beginning. This would happen upon Elul. We did not know then but later found out that Elul is a Hebrew festival around September.

I said, 'I don't know what this is or what it means.' So in the first real mass of channelled writings I was given that a transformation was going to happen. In the writings I am described as the gentile woman; there is also the chosen servant and the woman with insight.

*These phrases were to have significance later; Heather believed she identified the other two who were to join her 'mission'.*

There are two or three times when I've had some extraordinary evidence of the visions. On one occasion, 4th July 1992, the evidence came when I was with others.

I collapsed in a church very early on, while I had the stigmata. I remember going out in the car with Father Eric and Helen Whatton. We'd gone to Stow Minster; it was very big with four chapels in it. I had asked them to take me there. When you go into a church, the Bible is on the lectern, open to a scripture, or some reading for that day. The book was on the lectern, Father Eric went up to it and looked at the pages it was open to.

*Helen described to us what happened next: 'Heather was standing away from the lectern. She told Eric which page the Bible was open to, and as Eric was looking at the Bible, she called out to him what he was seeing, what was actually in front of Eric. Eric said to me, "I think you'd better come and see this," Everything that had come out of her mouth was what was written in that Bible.*

*'And Heather didn't open the Bible, or ask Eric to open it to a particular page; it was opened when he got to it.*

*'Heather had no way of getting to that church; she had no car, no trans-port, and certainly couldn't have walked. There was no way that she could have known that that particular Bible would have been opened to that partic-ular page on that particular afternoon.'*

I don't have a memory of what happened at that time, except what I was later told.

Later, I told them I was thirsty. We walked to an alcove and there I found a glass bottle with some water in it. 'Look, here is a drink; this is here for me,' I said.

Yet I can't remember any of this. We were on our way out of the church, signing ourselves out.

Then we heard this thud. Even I heard the thud. But it was me; I had collapsed. Eric and Helen brought me round, they both helped me to the door, half carrying me, and asked me if I had got the strength to sign my name. I think I did that. Then they brought me home.

They put me to bed. I told them that I didn't need a doctor, although they were quite concerned.

That night I was 'given' – told, through channelling – to ask Eric the following day whether this had frightened him. I was also told to ask what had been shared in the writing on this stone. I was told that if Eric was to reply, 'It didn't worry me, even you blacking out,' then I was to share with him something else. I was to tell him that he was the 'chosen servant' and that his mission, his task ahead, was to be there with me, to help me by reading my writings, to help me by explaining it all. His job was to be collating it all, to just be by my side through the whole of my experiences.

I was never told what to say if he replied that he had been worried. I've often wondered what I was supposed to say then. However, he told me he wasn't worried at all, and I told him he was the chosen servant.

As well as the chosen servant, I had been told there was a woman with insight; I believe that to have been Helen.

We couldn't share the writing or the stigmata with anyone. We were given that it was to be contained within the Ministry. And we never did let it leak out until I was later given that I should do so.

More writings followed; every day there were prophecies – things and events that were going to happen.

It seems that sometimes time is not normal when I'm writing. We went to Hazel's for Christmas and I took Mass. There were eleven of us and that was my first Midnight Mass. I had taken the host with me so we had communion as well.

On Boxing Day I was watching *Orphan Annie,* and about ten minutes before the end I got this really strong urge to write. It was strange because I got a bit angry that I was going to miss the end of the film. As I left the room I asked them to video the end for me so that I could watch it later. I went upstairs. Hazel gave me some paper and I went into my bedroom and just let the writing come. Then I went through to Lucy (Hazel's mother-in-law) and asked her to witness that I had just done the writing. I came downstairs and Hazel said, 'You weren't very long. Weren't you given anything?'

'What do you mean, I wasn't very long?' I felt as though I had been up there about half an hour. She told me that I had only been up there for a few minutes.

I showed them the writings. I think there were three sheets covered on both sides and another sheet that looked as if it was just plain. I told them that I mustn't have used that page.

But then we saw faint marks on the paper; there was a faint pencil drawing on the paper. You could only see it when you held it up to the light, or caught it at the right angle.

*Hazel remembers being astonished at the short time that Heather had been gone, given her prolific output. Lucy was similarly astonished; it is burned in her memory because of the strangeness. As she put it: 'I wasn't very well on Boxing Day; I was in bed, and Heather came upstairs. In a matter of ten minutes she came into the bedroom and said she had just had this ... prophecy, or whatever. I was absolutely staggered by the short time it had taken and how beautiful the writing was. It really was remarkable.'*

I have channelled from many people. For example, Wilhelmina Stich, a German lady. She is in spirit and she told me I could have these writings published. She said they have never been shown; she died before she could show them in print. They are beautiful.

And I have received communication from two priests: Charles Twyning Boyd and Henry George Jephson Meara. They were alive at the same time but didn't work together on Earth. Apparently they are working together now in spirit, so they have communicated to me.

Father Eric wanted to confirm that these priests were who they claimed to be. He wrote to the Archivist at Christ Church, Oxford and to the Diocesan Library in Colombo, as they had suggested he should, and we got back confirmations that they were the people they said they were.

The niece of one of them also confirmed that details given to me from the spirit world were personal, unknown facts about her uncle.

I should mention Helen again. I was flooded out for three days at the same time that I was admitted to hospital. I didn't want to leave Lindsay with all the mess, all the water, but I had to go in. Helen shared quite a bit with me, and came to visit me after I came out of hospital. She had been 'told' to come up and see me and to say to me, 'You are coming to stay with me until the house is dried out and they have got everything done.' A lot happened with Helen. She was the third person in the triangle with me and Eric; as I have said I think she is the one referred to as 'the woman with insight'.

Helen told me then, 'I wanted our friendship to last and for us to be friends forever.' But she added, 'We will never lose what we are sharing now, but there will come a time when we have to part.'

In November, after I had moved in with Helen, I drew the face of a man; also the image of a hand and an eye. A few days later I was given that the drawing was of Spinoza and that he had joined with Helen's soul. Spinoza, in spirit, was linked with Kahlil Gibran, who had used the image of the hand and the eye in his book *The Prophet*.

*Benedict Spinoza lived in the mid-1600s. He was a Dutch philosopher whose writings influenced many prominent poets and writers. He was described by the poet and philosopher, Novalis, as 'a God-intoxicated man'.*

Somewhere along the line, just after Christmas, I was given that Helen's spirit guide was Kahlil Gibran and that he had also merged with Helen's soul.

There came a point, much later, where I believe Helen couldn't cope with it. And like Eric I was told if she couldn't then I wouldn't be given more for her. And so it turned out.

Kahlil Gibran came to me. He was an amazing man, his soul was not unlike mine. He was born before his time. Kahlil Gibran wrote many books. He came to me: 'You can have three witnesses or three hundred but I'll show you, and them, that I have merged with your soul. People are now ready for our books, our sayings.'

I was told to get the book *The Prophet* by Kahlil Gibran. Father Eric rang me up one night. 'I've got it. I've got a copy of *The Prophet*.'

I explained, 'I'm being told you've got to wrap it in some white linen – not cotton – linen. And when you eventually bring it to me don't let me touch it.'

*It had been planned that Eric would bring the book to Heather in a few days' time. In fact he decided to surprise her the following day and took the book to*

*Helen's, where Heather was visiting. Heather had not expected that, and was completely unprepared. Despite this, what followed was thought-provoking and suggested to Heather than Gibran was in control of this 'test'; her own pre-preparation was neither wanted or needed.*

When Eric arrived he showed us that he had the book. 'Have you got some paper and a pen please?' I asked. I was not aware of what was going to happen; I put my left hand a few inches above the wrapped up book. I didn't know what colour, shape, whatever, it was. I counted to nine I think, and with that I wasn't aware of anything else. Helen and Eric watched me pick the pen up with my left hand and scribble away filling the page with writing. Helen told me that she was fascinated, not by my hands or my writing, but by my face. She told me that she didn't feel that I was with them at all, in the real sense. 'You were writing but your eyes were quite ... I don't know ... you just weren't there.' It only took a couple of minutes and yet there was a lot of writing.

*Helen is one of few people to have witnessed Heather's writing, and to be able to offer some supportive evidence of the nature of the channelling. She described these events: 'I gave her a large piece of white cardboard. She wrote with her left hand, and using a red pen, which she'd never used before.' (Helen is confirming that Heather could not have pre-prepared this writing.) 'She was writing quite furiously on this piece of white card – at an abnormal speed, I can definitely confirm that. Eric and I sat with her in the lounge, ate sandwiches and drank tea, and watched her doing this writing. Then all of sudden she dropped the pen, looked up and said, "Oh, tea."'*

Then I came round, and said 'I suppose we had better get started.' I hadn't realized of course; here I was thinking 'we had better get started' and it had already happened – the writing that I had channelled from, I assume, Kahlil, was the proof.

Eric picked up the sheet of paper and read what was on it: 'The image I gave you if numbered would be on page 111.' So Eric undid the wrapping on this book, it was the hardback version and not in print at that time. He read from my writing: 'Next to page 110 is that drawing you did months ago,' but there was no number on that page because it was a plate illustration.

The next thing written was, 'The vision you had, if numbered, would be on page sixty-three.' Father Eric flicked through and sure enough after page sixty-two there was no number; it was the image of a woman with not one hair on her body. It was like a statue; she was naked and her hands were impaled on a man either side of her, impaled on their chests. They stood on a rock under clouds. Now I had had that vision and shared it with Eric and others. When he saw it he said, 'That's that dream you told us all about last week'.

There were about ten things on this paper which Eric checked, and all were spot on.

The writing went on: 'Not the man, not the woman, but the lady whose birth year is 1949.' That was obviously me. I can't remember the exact words but it was saying something like 'You must purchase another book if you can because you are mentioned three or four times in it.' The book was *Spirits Rebellious*.

All my time in children's Homes, all my life I have continually rebelled, run away all the time, because when we were brought up we weren't wanted. Nobody cared about us. So I rebelled as a child and always ran away. And here was this book that Kahlil Gibran had written entitled *Spirits Rebellious*, and which was printed the year I was born, though he had died years before then.

*The book was written in 1920 but one edition – the one obtained by Father Eric – was printed in 1949.*

Father Eric got this book and sure enough it could have been me the author had been writing about.

The most extraordinary thing about the whole business is, two days later Eric came in with another bundle in linen. He opened the linen and there was another copy of The Prophet. But this was the paperback. He opened it up and commented, 'That picture is not on page sixty-three. None of the pages relate to the writing you did'. This fascinated Eric, and Helen, because if Eric had brought the paperback and that had been wrapped up Kahlil would have had to give me different numbers. I said I thought he would have done.

*Helen commented to us on the significance of this: 'I have one of those kinds of minds; I'm not easily convinced. If Heather had had the book at home, memorized it all, and then written it, there would have been no guarantee that the edition she might have used would be the one Eric came up with. This book Eric had borrowed from a long-standing friend of his; it wasn't something Eric had, or Heather had. The chances of Heather having that edition were so remote, I didn't think it was possible she could have faked it.'*

Eric and Betty were going away for four weeks to Malta. They promised to send a postcard after ten days. About six days after they had gone to Malta, I had a feeling – a sense – that Eric was in a lot of pain. I didn't say anything to anyone but I felt the pain for about four days. Then on the Saturday morning, ten days into the holiday, I just knew they were coming home. I could see them coming out of the hotel. I didn't know what hotel they were in, but I could see Eric being helped out of this hotel down the steps by these two men, and Betty was coming out next to him. He had insurance and that provided him with a limousine to take him from the hotel to the plane. I saw all of this when I was on my own and I knew that they were coming home. But only minutes later I was on the plane with them. I could feel that I was with them, right there, on the plane.

So what I had seen – coming out of the hotel and into the car – must have been something that happened a couple of hours earlier. Now I sensed that they were on the plane; I could see Eric sitting there. And I could feel his pain.

Betty was looking out of the window. Eric was thinking about blackbirds and spring and couldn't wait to get back home to England; that was the clear impression I got. I was writing this down as I felt it.

*Heather wrote a note for Eric and Betty: 'Dear Eric and Betty, I have been with you both every hour through your pain. Read the enclosed, given to me on the third. I looked at the clock today at 2.15, Saturday 6th and knew that you were on the way home, yes home. I love you dearly and know everything will be all right. The Lord has kept us in His care while you have been away. Fondest love, Heather. Will ring Sunday.' In the envelope was a channelled piece of writing that Heather had been 'given', for delivery to Father Eric.*

I then rang Steve, who is a member of our healing group. 'Steve, could you come and pick this letter up and put it in Eric's letter box, please?'

'There's no hurry, is there?' he asked, because he thought Eric was going to be away for at least a couple of weeks more.

I told him that there was a hurry; that Father Eric would be coming home very soon. He asked me how I knew.

So I told him that I could feel Father Eric hurting a lot, in pain, and on a plane back to England. 'It's important that when they open the door this letter is on the mat. If you'd do it now I would be ever so grateful. I think they are going to be home in the next half hour or so.'

*When we spoke to Betty she confirmed the story in extraordinary detail, and confirmed her and Eric's surprise when they received the note. 'She couldn't possibly have known we were on our way back by any other means other than telepathy or something.'*

When we told Betty that Heather had described the two men helping Eric down the steps, and the limousine waiting for him, she was shocked even as we interviewed her. The details were indeed correct, but neither she, nor Eric as far as she knew, had ever discussed with Heather the fact that Heather had 'seen' those particular details.

Betty rang the day after Steve had dropped the letter into the letter-box. 'Eric is in bed, the doctor has been and he is going into hospital.' She was crying on the phone. But she asked, 'How did you know all of this?' I told her I had been with them on the return.

Eric had been ill for many years. Like me, he was in and out of hospital a lot. Because of my own illnesses my health was deteriorating. Although I needed more surgery the doctors said they couldn't do any more for me. I told them, 'I don't want the surgery anyway. Enough is enough.' I wasn't strong enough for surgery so it was a case of keeping me comfortable on the morphine and just waiting for whatever was going to happen. In the twenty-one weeks I had the first stigmata I met many people, had a lot of visions, and I was given a lot of drawings. I met a lot of people. A lot happened in those twenty-one weeks. Of course, I was still going to the school four mornings a week, my hands wrapped in bandages covering the stigmata.

## The stigmata: a detailed account

The first appearance of the stigmata, as I have already described, was in May 1992.

We had had a good weekend. I had done some painting with Helen; just some work on the skirting boards. This was the Sunday before the Bank Holiday Monday. On the Monday we were having a drink and talking and I was itching.

'I've got a blister here, Helen, look. It's in the middle of my palm.'

She suggested that perhaps it had been caused by the painting. I thought that made sense, that probably it was. Maybe I had been pushing the brushes too hard against my skin.

About an hour or so later I seemed to be itching again and the mark was a lot bigger. I showed it to Helen. 'You know that blister, look how big it's getting. It's itching a bit too. It's weird, isn't it?'

Helen looked at it. 'I reckon we ought to show this to Father Eric. I think he'd be interested. Would you want to go and see him?'

I thought that was a lovely idea, and that we should go straight away. It was a quite spontaneous decision. So we got in the car, and drove to Eric's, less than ten minutes away. Nobody was in but we left a note to say we had popped round, and asked him to give us a ring when he got in.

We didn't see Eric that day. But he rang in the evening and I told him all about the blisters. He said that he would come round the next day and have a look.

It looked as if the top of a blister had come off. It was red raw. The white skin wasn't there. It looked just like it was raw, but it wasn't sore. It was later on that evening I was given the drawing of our Lord being baptized. I think that when I had finished the drawing it was then that I noticed that both my hands were the same. Both hands, both sides, the same marks.

The following day, when Father Eric came round, I showed him my hands. He just kept looking. Eventually he said, 'I think I know what it is. I think that's stigmata.'

I didn't know what stigmata was. I asked him to explain it to me.

'Well, it looks like the nail holes of Christ when he was crucified on the cross. That drawing looks like Jesus being baptized, although John is not in the picture baptizing him. But I think that's Christ. This is exciting. I think the marks on your hands are the stigmata. I have a feeling that something amazing is going to happen.'

He asked if I was frightened. 'No, I'm fascinated. It's amazing.' Then that night the holes on my hands grew bigger, and they started to bleed. When Father Eric rang me up I explained how I felt. 'The marks have started to bleed, both sides. I feel as if there is a change taking place. Something is going to happen but I'm not sure what.'

He asked again if I was worried, or frightened, but I told him I was not. He asked me to ring him if I needed him.

It was that night that I was 'given' the picture of Christ crucified, nailed to the stake. My hands were bleeding all the time. Thick, deep, red blood. They were not sore, just bleeding.

Eric and Betty were going to France for two weeks. Because of their interest in the stigmata they did not want to go but I told them that I thought they should. Eric left after giving me a number where he could be contacted. 'I want you to keep looking at your feet. I think something is going to happen to your feet, the same as your hands. Just keep looking and if it does happen, ring me.'

That Friday night I was sitting in my living room, watching the telly with Lindsay, when I felt this itching, like ants running over my foot.

I looked down. 'That's itchy. Look at this Lindsay. Eric said to keep looking at my feet.'

Lindsay made the comment, 'But it's not in the middle of your foot, Mum.'

I told him that I wasn't doing it; I couldn't help where it appeared.

Then the other foot started itching as I was talking to Lindsay. I rang Father Eric. 'Guess what,' was all I got the chance to say. Immediately, he guessed: 'It's come on your feet, hasn't it?'

I started to ask him how he knew, but of course I realized that I needn't be asking. He had, after all, told me to watch out for that. I described the marks to him. 'They're like halos. As I am talking to you now it's appearing on my other foot.'

He asked me to look underneath my foot. I told him there was nothing there. He asked how my hands were.

'They are about the same,' I told him, 'but they are bleeding very thick blood.'

We were talking for just a few minutes and again he asked me to look at my feet. I saw that they had started to bleed, just spots of blood.

'They've started to bleed, Father Eric. The blood is just seeping through the skin.'

'We're coming home soon. We'll see you then.' On Saturday afternoon I was at Helen's. I was in the garden on a hammock, laying down. Helen was sunbathing. I felt as if I had been bitten; I was scratching the skin on my right side. By now I was sitting upright.

Helen noticed and asked what was the matter. 'I reckon I've been bitten by them flipping ants.' We had noticed ants running around. 'It's itching.'

Helen asked to have a look, and I lifted my blouse to show her where the itch was coming from.

'Look at that,' she said, 'it looks like a smile.' There was a red mark on my side, like a U-shape, just under my ribs.

Helen told me she was going to ring Eric, she thought that he ought to see this. She went inside to telephone.

When she came back out she told me that Eric and Betty wanted to see me straight away. She asked if I wanted to go, and of course I did.

Helen drove me to Eric's. At this time, of course, Eric hadn't seen the marks on my feet either. We went in, hugged, and Eric asked to have a look at my hands. 'That's quite different to when I last saw it.

Now it's bleeding, whereas it was just the raw blister before.'

I took my socks off and showed him my feet. It was still like a halo mark, and it had come through underneath. I think it had bled a little so that it was stuck to my sock. When I took my sock off it had stuck and I had to pull it off the mark. It didn't hurt, it had just stuck.

Then Eric asked to look at my side. He was fascinated by that; of course I was as well. In fact I was more interested in my side than my feet, because of the shape of it.

Helen told me to breathe in so that she could see it more clearly. The mark sat on the rib cage, and if I breathed in it went under the rib. Eric was smiling this lovely smile. He asked me to lift my arms up.

When I did that I didn't have to breathe in, the mark was clear then. Eric asked me to raise my arms in the way that Christ was depicted on my picture.

I asked, 'Why do you think it is a curve rather than just a cut or a straight line?'

Eric explained it in terms of Christ's wounds. 'Remember that the Bible says a soldier pierced his side and that blood and water came out. Because they then thought he was dead they didn't need to break his legs, as they usually did in crucifixions. We don't know what the Roman spears were like – we're assuming it's a spear, it could have been a sword – we don't know how long the swords were, or what shape they were.' Eric believed that this U-shaped mark on my side was the stigmata of the spear-mark.

Eric took a photo and then said to Helen, 'I think we ought to photograph this if it changes, or when it bleeds.'

I noticed that the wounds came in order; the hands, then the feet, then the mark in the side. That may have been the order of the wounds on Christ during the crucifixion; certainly the wound in the side was the last one.

The hands, and then the feet, and lastly the side started to take on a pattern of weeping. There was a lot of bleeding during the day because of my walking, I just had to be walking. But because the wounds were under my feet as well as above I needed padding there to stop it hurting. I also needed something to stop it spoiling my shoes and socks. Eventually the bleeding got so bad that at night I would take my socks and shoes off and put my feet on a tea towel. I think that was the first time I noticed that the marks were weeping. Something like water was just bubbling up, running between the toes. Whatever it was, it was setting as it was running, it was just like melted sugar.

A lot of people saw that weeping: Eric and Betty when we were there for tea; my Dad; other friends and relatives; Lindsay, of course, because he was usually around me.

It was literally just dripping off both sides, often for up to about three hours. I would feel when the bandage was wet through, then I would have to change it.

And of course the marks were getting bigger every day. A lot bigger, and a lot deeper. They never at any time went right through but it was quite deep and raw. When they had finished bleeding I would bathe my feet and hands again, just to get the blood off and tidy it up. You could see the rawness, and the blood just sitting there. But there was never a scab, and never any pain. Once or twice Eric asked if I would wash the blood away; then you could see it raw for a few seconds.

They were full, raw, crater-like things. Over the twenty-one weeks that I had them, all the marks on my hands, feet and the side got bigger. They were all like open wounds; weeping and bleeding. I didn't put bandages on at night, I wanted to let the air get to them. But I would put a square bit of non-stick plaster over them.

Through the early stages and when my feet started to bleed, I couldn't walk very far. I rang Dr Bhanja, because I couldn't walk to the surgery. I asked him to come to see me, which he did. I showed him my feet and how they were bleeding, and the marks on my side and hands. I had needed his support, and practical help. But I had been given that the stigmata was to be kept in the Ministry, not given publicity. I prayed, and I was given that if Dr Bhanja recognized the marks as the stigmata then I was able to share with him what was going to happen over the month. But if he didn't acknowledge it I wasn't to say anything.

I showed Dr Bhanja one hand. 'What do you think that is, Dr Bhanja?' I asked. He suggested that it looked like a nasty insect bite that had gone septic. Then I showed him all the other marks. And he held my hands and looked at them; then he looked at me.

He recognized it, but apparently daren't say anything to me because he felt it would frighten me. I was waiting. I couldn't share any more with him because he hadn't recognized the marks. He gave me a few bandages and left.

A few days later, when the wounds on my feet opened up, he came out to me again. This time he acknowledged what it was and I was able to share it with him.

'I was waiting for you to say if you recognized it as the stigmata. You knew, but you didn't say so. You didn't want to frighten me.

Now you have said so, I'm able to share it with you.'

Both doctors from the practice at came out at different times and their eyes filled up. They didn't actually cry but they were very moved by it.

I told Dr Bhanja that it had been given that I would witness a transfiguration that would take me from my old life to a new beginning; and I shared with him my writings and drawings.

*Dr Bhanja wrote to Heather, offering a letter for public use saying 'I believe that these were spontaneous lesions of hands, feet and side and can offer no medical explanation for their appearance.'*

Because I was in the church, in the Order of St Luke, Father Eric and I could contain it within the Ministry as I had been instructed through the channelling. Father Eric wrote and telephoned a lot of different people in different churches; Anglican priests and priests from the Church of England. A lot of these people came to see me. One even came from Devon. I seemed always to be at Father Eric's church at that time. A lot of ministers, priests, vicars, doctors and other friends would come and have tea with us, talk to us and look at or feel the wounds. Many had their photos taken with me.

I found it best to leave my socks off because my feet bled so much. I could have just left the bandages on but the blood always seeped through them; it meant dressing them every hour or so.

A lot of people within the church witnessed my stigmata, as well as the doctors. In the writings there were also lots of messages given, and things mentioned from the Bible that we could refer to. It was all really just confirming part of what was happening to me; so many different things were happening to me. And along with all this, of course, I was going in and out of hospital; I was still quite ill.

I think what has helped carry me through this is that it's not all been done behind a locked door. There have been witnesses. People have been with me when it happened, when it stopped or started again. Several people have taken photographs. When I went to one of the services at a Methodist Church, the stigmata was still in evidence though it was drying up; but it broke open. We had sung the hymns, Father Eric had introduced me and I was sharing part of my testimony. Then the sores just broke open and I was in the middle of talking when my hand started bleeding. I wanted to say 'Excuse me', but instead I tried to hide my hands in my sleeves like this. We went to four different churches and a lot of people came to touch me after the services.

*Heather's father, George, and his current wife, Martha, saw the stigmata. According to George, Martha is very religious and was instantly impressed by the marks. George took a sceptical view of the stigmata when he first heard about it, but when he saw the marks he thought, 'There is no way that Heather could have done this to herself.' As George described it: 'You could virtually see through Heather's hands.'*

*Martha challenged George: 'Do you want any more proof?' George was impressed enough: 'I said seeing is believing, and now I'm seeing. I believe it.'*

*Heather's aunt, May Bull, also saw the marks. Perhaps even more importantly she was one of few people Heather had pre-warned about the second appearance of the stigmata; Heather had told her before it happened that it was to occur. As Aunt May described it: 'I saw the holes in both her hands, not just on the top – but right through. What was coming out wasn't blood, it was like a white fluid. She said there was no pain with it, none whatever, and she didn't feel any pain when it happened. I looked at her feet and both feet were the same. But the puncture went right through to the sole; they were actual holes. She couldn't walk for a little while because the hole was underneath and it was getting a bit angry, a bit raw, so she had to keep off her feet for a while. When a fountain has been switched off and then it suddenly starts up again, you get that little bubble starts coming up and it gets bigger and bigger; that's what was happening with her feet.*

*'Then she showed me the mark on her tummy. I asked her "What's caused all this then?" She said she didn't know. She just felt that it was a sign that she had been chosen. I said, "Well, there must be a reason, Heather, for all this." She said, "I can't tell you any more, Aunty May, I'm just telling you how it happened and you can see for yourself." The marks were there for quite a while.'*

When I went to the hospital they often took skin scrapings. I am happy to do whatever anyone wants because I think proof is important. They gave me creams; I think they were a bit annoyed, not being able to accept the fact that they couldn't find a medical reason for it. It wouldn't heal. I'd put the cream on one hand and leave the other, but it wouldn't make any difference.

I explained to them that it had been given by divine Grace and that it would be taken away the same way.

## Transfiguration

In the earliest writings I had been given the name 'gentile woman'; in the writings I was receiving now it changed to 'holy woman'.

Somewhere along the line I said to a member of the church, 'What do you think the transfiguration is going to be?' 'I don't think you are going to witness the transfiguration,' he replied, 'I think you will *be* the transfiguration. You will be transformed.'

The 8th September was when we knew that within the next twenty-four hours I was going to witness this transfiguration. I had been at the service of the Nativity of the Virgin Mary that day and I was so ill there that they carried me out and sat me in a chair. The pain was so bad, I just sat there and my tears poured out. This upset everybody. I think I looked as if I was going to die. It was hurting to breathe; I was struggling to breathe. I think I had got to the point where I just wanted to breathe my last, just die and be with our Lord. I felt I had had enough. Everybody was praying, and wishing me well.

They took me home and Eric and Betty put me to bed; Lindsay sat with me a while.

*Betty confirmed this story to us expressing her great concern for the state Heather was in. 'She was in such pain, she looked so tiny, she was so ill-looking. We didn't think she was going to survive the night, in fact I thought she was going to die in the chair.'*

*But Heather, at home, was having an extraordinary experience.*

I found myself moving, floating. I was moving towards hundreds of people on this river bank. I knew they were expecting me; they were all looking up at me. As I moved towards them there was a warmth, a wondrous feeling of compassion. I had now come down to the ground and turned away from all of these people to see this stream – it was bigger than a river. It wasn't that deep; two men were standing with water reaching above their ankles. One man had his arm out-stretched, I knew he was beckoning me. So I waded in, I can remember feeling how warm it was. It felt like warm oil, it was so soft. There was no splashing, it was smooth like oil. I walked towards this man; the two men were both looking at me. Their eyes were the same. I still felt this warmth, this gentleness from the people in the crowd. I reached out to take his hand and I found myself in a room.

It was an upper room; somehow I knew that it was upstairs. I noticed that the roof was quite low. I saw mud and straw on the walls. And there was quite a warm atmosphere. I was in the house with ten men and one other; each man came forward and embraced me in turn, then just moved away. One man remained sitting. He put his hand out and I reached out to take hold of it. Then I was on the cross.

As I took his hand I found myself on the cross with the Lord. I wasn't with him as if it were the two of us; I felt myself within him, looking out. There was no pain; I felt very light – weightless. But then I also found myself looking towards Christ on the cross. I felt no pain but looked into his eyes and felt his compassion.

It wasn't pain in Christ's eyes, it was compassion. The same feeling as with all of the people and the two men at the river and the men in the room. It was a kind of a oneness. The atmosphere and feeling was the same; Christ's compassion for the world and mankind I think, but also for me.

I was suddenly aware then that it was three o'clock in the morning. I was cold. I found myself sitting up fully dressed and dripping with water. My head was wet through, and this water was dripping on my shoulders and on my hand. I looked down and my hands were bleeding; I was aware I was bleeding also from my side. I hadn't got socks or anything on my feet, and they were bleeding. The holes and marks were bigger than they had ever been, yet only five hours before they had been virtually healed.

Despite the time, I rang Father Eric. 'You're not going to believe it. I'm sitting here all wet and I've been on the cross. I've been in this water, but I wasn't actually baptized.'

I was so excited. 'I feel great. There's no pain. I'm hungry.'

I apologized for having woken him but he told me that he hadn't been to bed. He had been waiting for me to ring him. He told me that he was coming straight round to collect me. He had known something was happening; he had been aware.

*Eric's wife, Betty, remembers the telephone call. Despite her husband's anticipation of Heather's call, when the phone rang Betty was convinced that it would be a message that Heather had passed away, so ill had she been when she had left the Eades' house.*

Father Eric took me to his house. I jumped out of the car and ran in. I hugged Betty. They had been so good to help me earlier when I was in so much pain; now I'd got colour in my face and the bags had gone from under my eyes.

Betty said, 'You're wet through.' She got a towel to dry my hair. The hunger was still with me; I felt as if I hadn't eaten for ages. I asked for a bit of toast and a drink.

*Betty told us, 'I couldn't believe it. All her hair was soaking wet. She looked absolutely brilliant. She had this stigmata on her hand. it was quite big now, and the colour that it was ... It was brilliant red with glinting, golden glows in it. And she wanted more and more food, which was very unusual; any time she had visited before I would try and give her soup, or something that was gentle for her, because she ate so little. I don't know how she kept alive from the little food she had. But this time she wanted more and more.'*

Later that morning, when they would be up and about, Eric rang several people, including some who had been with me the previous night. Many of them thought he was going to tell them that I had died during the night. They were amazed and surprised when he told them that far from being dead, I was sparkling, happy and excited. He invited a lot of people to come round.

*Betty confirmed that when the visitors saw Heather, 'they just couldn't believe the difference in her. And overnight her hair had grown very thick, very quickly; it had been quite short. It was a transfiguration, there's no doubt about it.'*

So a lot of people visited. I was sitting there smiling and eating. I wasn't in pain and I was laughing. I remember saying, and feeling, 'This is great.'

They laughed and cried with me. I said 'I'm healed.' I wasn't in any pain. Eric suggested that I ought to call Dr Bhanja and tell him the news. Dr Bhanja had seen me two or three days before when I was waiting for a bed so that I could go into the hospice. I was just so ill. He came to the house and I don't think he could believe what he saw. I told him that I had not taken my morphine because I didn't feel I needed it. He was really worried at that. He told me not to stop; that I would have to be weaned off it, otherwise I would get withdrawals.

I told him, 'I just don't need it. I am well; I am healed. I feel great. There is no pain.'

We all believed that the visions – in the water, in the room, and on the cross with our Lord – had absolutely transformed me. I was healed. I looked well, I even looked as if I had put on quite a bit of weight, even my hair was longer. This was the transfiguration that was going to take me from my old life to a new beginning. A miracle, and it was a transformation of me. That seemed to be the prophecy fulfilled.

On Thursday I spent most of the day at home. If everything else hadn't already been enough I knew that something further was going to happen, something even more remarkable. But I wasn't aware of what it was, and I didn't know when it would be. In fact it was the next day, but I didn't find out about it until after it happened.

I discovered the next day that Eric had been trying to ring me that morning, and my daughter had come to the door that morning too – in fact several people had been trying to get in touch with me most of that Friday. Nobody had been able to find me, or knew where I was.

And I wasn't aware I was anywhere. I can't even remember getting up that morning.

When I found myself, I was sitting at the top of the stairs with the telephone in my hand. Eric was on the line. I'd just finished saying 'Father Eric, can you come and anoint me?'

'Heather, where have you been?' His voice was concerned. He told me about all the people that had been trying to find me.

'I haven't been anywhere, I've been here. Can you come and anoint me?' I repeated.

Eric asked me again where I had been. 'I've been on the cross with the Lord,' I explained, 'Can you come and anoint me? Then the prophecy will be fulfilled.'

I went downstairs and opened the door so that Eric would be able to come in.

When he arrived I was just standing there in the house. As he came through the door he told me that there was a lustre, a translucent look, about me. He described it as a glow all around me. I was naked, apart from this blue material that was covering me; I think he could see through it, though it seemed to cover my body decently. I just stood there smiling. My hair looked as if it had been permed and set; there were all these curls and it shone. My eyes twinkled.

Eric said, 'You look absolutely beautiful. I wish I had my camera with me.'

I asked again if he would anoint me. And I sat down. 'What is this you are wearing? It is beautiful.'

It was a blue cloth, but there was gold and silver threaded through it. There were tassels hanging from it, full length, all around. It just seemed to be draped over and wrapped around me, like a sari.

I was insistent about being anointed. I sat down and he held my hand. 'You look beautiful,' he commented as he got the oils ready.

Before he anointed me I showed him a little blue glass jar with herbs in it. I handed it to Eric, 'I'll give you this, Father Eric, because I didn't need it.'

He asked me if I knew what I had just said. I couldn't think; I asked him what it was.

'You're saying that you're giving me this back because you didn't need it.'

Eric very strongly believed me to be Mary Magdalene in reincarnation. Christ appeared to Mary first, in the garden. She got to his tomb and found it empty. She saw a man, and thinking he was the gardener asked, 'Where you have taken my master? Please tell me.' The man said her name, 'Mary', and she recognized him saying, 'Rabboni', which means teacher. So it was Mary who saw Christ first after his resurrection. Then he told her to go and tell the disciples.

Eric believed me to be Mary Magdalene; blessed with the stigmata, and now further confirmed because of these herbs.

I believe that the herbs were those used to bathe and purify the body in the tradition of the times. I hadn't needed them because the body wasn't there.

He took the jar off me, put it down, got the oils and anointed me.

Eric asked me to come back to his house with him. 'I want Betty to see you like this.'

I was happy to, and went upstairs to get some clothes on. I didn't bring that cloth back down with me, I can't even remember taking it off. When we got to Betty's, she opened the car door and hugged me; she couldn't believe the change. I hugged her.

'The prophecy has been fulfilled,' I cried. 'I feel wonderful. Just look at me.'

Eric couldn't get in quick enough. I stood there jumping about and even doing a twirl. Betty started to cry, 'I can't believe it, look at you.'

*Betty confirmed to us that both she and Father Eric believed Heather had in some way been transported back to the time of Christ, and had been with him. Betty told us of another experience when Heather recalled to Eric and herself that Christ had come to her and lifted her into a boat, to be with Him.*

Eric told Betty about the cloth, and Betty wanted to see it. I told her that I would show it to her later, when I could bring it from my house. Eric suggested, 'When I take you back, you can get it and give it to me.'

I stayed an hour or so, and had a meal with them. Betty had told me that they were going to have sausages and chips but assumed that I couldn't eat that as I had been on a basically liquid diet. But I told her that I felt I could. And I sat at the table and had sausage, chips, peas and a pudding, and I drank tea. And I never stopped talking.

Eric took me back about six o'clock. He asked me if I would go upstairs and find the cloth that I had been wrapped in. I went upstairs but I couldn't find it. I've never found it to this day. Eric believed it had somehow manifested, and having served it's purpose, disappeared.

There were no photographs of me in that cloth. Eric photographed me shortly afterwards, when I had changed into other clothes. You can look at the various photographs from that time; the difference between then and the pictures from just a short while before are dramatic.

After the twenty-one weeks and the transfiguration things got back to normal. I was still being given writings and drawings. On the Sunday I was given in the writings that there would be a manifestation on St Luke's Day. I was in the Order of St Luke of course. St Luke's Day was the day of prayer. We didn't know what was going to manifest; only that something would.

There was a service that evening and during it a cross manifested on my forehead.

Somebody said it looked like the Cross of Lorraine. It was quite deep, it looked like a burn, the sort of burn you get when you burn yourself on the iron or the cooker. It was an indentation; it didn't blister over and go red, it looked like an early scab. It was quite rough and scabby and deep. After an hour or so it started to bleed. Blood was visibly running down my nose. But it was only visible for three days. One morning I woke up and it had gone.

Even the doctors saw it. I was a bit embarrassed about walking out with it; of course it was something I couldn't hide. I couldn't pull my fringe over it, and a bandage would draw attention to it even more. So I didn't go out, people came to me. Dr Bhanja came and he was fascinated. He suggested, 'It's going to be days before that heals.' But I just got up one morning and it had gone completely, it didn't leave any scar or sign of having been there. The other marks had gone by then as well.

This was in October 1992. People were still coming to visit me. And yet it was still contained; the media hadn't got hold of it. Somebody asked if I had thought about going to the papers or a magazine. But all of us were quite adamant it was not yet the time for it to be shared. The messages I had been given made it clear that it had to be contained within the Ministry for thirty days. Then it could be released. It was fascinating that it didn't actually leak out. Over those twenty-one weeks I wasn't in hiding; a lot of people saw me, such as the children in the school whose reading I listened to, and saw the bandages. But it stayed contained.

## The second stigmata

In 1993 I was given a message, through the writings, that I would get the stigmata again, and that this time it could be revealed publicly. What I was given told me that it could be shared; I telephoned Eric and told him that. The message said that eighteen days before Easter the stigmata would appear, and indicated that something was going to happen on Good Friday.

Eric had been waiting for this for a long time, to be able to share it. He telephoned or wrote to several people, including media and researchers into the stigmata.

Using a calendar to work back eighteen days from Good Friday I realized that if it was going to happen it would be tomorrow or the next day. It actually happened in the early hours of the morning, exactly the eighteenth day before Easter. I woke up feeling a wetness in the bed. The stigmata had appeared and I had been bleeding quite a bit. The blood was all over my sheets; they had to be washed immediately,it was so bad. I telephoned Eric to tell him it was back, and bleeding heavily.

*One of the researchers telephoned was Ted Harrison, who has done a lot of work in this subject. He is a former BBC religious affairs correspondent and the author of a book on stigmata, entitled* Stigmata *(published by HarperCollins) and another, entitled* Marks of the Cross – *the story of another stigmatic, Ethel Chapman.*

He was making a film documentary of the phenomenon and he came to see me that first day. He was thrilled; I believe he had never seen stigmata actually bleeding on anyone at that time, except in photographs. Ted telephoned to arrange to bring a film crew to the house on Good Friday.

Ted asked a few questions in front of the cameras. He asked me if I would wash my hands, feet and side in front of the camera; he was talking to me as I was doing it. On the film they made, you see not me washing my hands but just the blood dripping down into this bowl. They slowed it down, and set it to music. It was beautiful. And the marks continued to bleed and the film crew kept zooming in on them. During the time the crew was there I had to get changed to give a service. I asked them if they minded, and they did not. In fact they wanted to film the service. I had to wear bandages to stop the bleeding ruining my shoes, apart from that I was in my usual clothes for the service.

I can't remember a lot about the service. I remember giving the address, and then we were singing the last hymn. I can't remember any more or even bowing and coming out of the church.

I can remember just this sharp pain for a few seconds, in my side. It hurt so much. I wasn't aware I was crying or anything, just that I felt this pain only for a few seconds. But they must have seen my reaction, or a change in my face, because the cameras zoomed in. You can see on the documentary how the tears were streaming down my face. I looked to be in agony.

As I say, I can remember starting to sing the hymn and then I was in the other room taking my gowns off. I got a cup of tea and then Ted asked if I would mind if we went back into the church where he could ask a few more questions and complete his filming.

'Were you aware, Heather, that you were sobbing towards the end of the service?' he asked.

I told him I wasn't. 'All I remember is this terrific pain in my side for just a few seconds.' In fact I wasn't even aware that I had bowed with Father Eric, or that I had left the church.

My hands had been bleeding throughout, and I had put a bandage on my feet and side. I lifted up my blouse and took the bandage off. The wound was big and deep and the bandage was wet through with blood. It had trickled down onto my vest and the top of my pants. Ted pointed out that the wounds must have opened up, because he and his crew had earlier asked me to wash so that they could see what they were like. There couldn't have been any blood from before then, so it had to have appeared recently.

'I think that's it,' they announced and they began to pack up to go. Then Ted asked his cameraman if he could zoom in on my forehead. I asked what all the fuss was about.

'It's like a red mark,' Ted said. 'I just saw it as you moved past the light.'

If I remember correctly, Ted was saying 'David, zoom in on it. As I'm talking to you Heather, I can see it moving. I can't believe this. It's manifesting now, and we're getting it on the camera.' He described it as quite raised, and asked if I had any idea what it might be. I hadn't been expecting the cross to manifest, but I said 'I think I know what it might be.' I told him of the cross that appeared last time. I told him I was not embarrassed, that I didn't mind witnesses. After all, when you've got a big cross on your forehead, it's not something you can hide. Nor did I want to.

Then I was taken home by one of the members of the church, Steve. Father Eric had come from his bed to be there, and he went back to get some rest. He was exhausted.

It was a hectic weekend. We were having a wedding the next day. The people had asked if I would share the service with Eric, but Eric was so ill that I did the service alone, though Eric sat in. That was my first wedding. I asked Eric if I should cover my hands up. I didn't want them to spoil the day, or to shock the bride or groom's relatives.

'No, just leave them,' Eric suggested. 'Don't do anything because it will mean so much to them.'

I wasn't sure. I checked again with Eric. I didn't want to frighten anyone. But Eric told me not to cover it up.

So the wedding went ahead, and my hands did bleed a little bit. But I didn't need to do anything, no-one was troubled by them. The family videoed the whole of the wedding, about twenty minutes in all. After the ceremony we all got together. Eric had shared it with some of them, and many were absolutely intrigued. We went back in the church and chatted. Some of them had heard about the stigmata but none of them had ever seen it. They took some photos of me with the wounds visible.

Then I went home. I knew I'd be doing a service in the morning, which was Easter Sunday, a very special day. I woke up at half-past four that morning. As I was washing my hands I looked in the mirror and there it was. This huge cross, twice the size of the first one. It was about an inch into the hairline, looking again like a red burn.

I noticed that my hands were not bleeding. In fact the wounds had almost disappeared. The marks that had been so red and bleeding the day before had almost completely vanished. All that was left were slightly pink marks, patches of pinker skin.

Steve had picked me up at about ten o'clock, and Father Eric was in bed. I walked into his room and he smiled. He looked at the cross on my forehead and all he said was 'Beautiful'. I think I cried a little, because Eric had deteriorated over the two days. He was in bed, and I knew he wouldn't be sharing the service that day, or even sitting in.

'Here is some more writing that I was given,' I said to him, and I handed him some sheets of paper. 'This is the last of the writing, Father Eric. There won't be any more.'

I had never hidden my stigmata or my writings once it had been given to me that I could reveal them. Not that I wanted to. I felt privileged to be able to witness it and able to show others.

During the service in his house, Eric stayed upstairs. We left the door open so that he could hear the service. At half-past ten the room was packed; people were in the hall, they were even sitting on the stairs.

I walked in, of course, with this extraordinary cross on my forehead. One of the ladies of the church, Sylvia, was absolutely moved, her eyes filled up with tears and they were streaming down her face. She believed so much. There were a few other gasps and noises of surprise.

When I showed the people at the church, they couldn't believe it. Some of them had seen the marks the previous day, and would have expected the wounds still to be raw, if not bleeding. But they were gone.

I did the service and we shared Communion. Afterwards I asked, 'Do you mind if I go upstairs and sit with Father Eric for a little while?'

We talked about the experiences. 'It's not going to come back any more, Father Eric,' I told him. 'There will be no more writings, and I won't have the stigmata any more.'

'I think you will,' he replied. But I was sure I would not.

*It was later that Father Eric explained how – and when – it would manifest again.*

We both knew that Father Eric was dying. He asked me to take his funeral service when he died. I did cry then, but I said. 'I know we promised that to each other but I thought I was going to die first, and you were going to do the service for me. I can't believe it's going to be this way.'

I agreed to do the service, we chatted a while longer, and then I left. We had both decided together that although we knew he was dying, we weren't going to let on because Betty didn't know. He lived for just four and a half weeks after that.

The cross was already disappearing later that night. You could only just make it out; it had completely gone by Monday evening, at about eight o'clock. There was absolutely nothing there at all. Then the writing stopped as well.

The following Sunday there was no service. We were all watching the documentary. About an hour later Eric rang up and asked, 'Can you come over because the phone has not stopped ringing? There are a lot of journalists and reporters coming.'

Somebody came to pick me up, and took me to Eric's. Father Eric was still in bed. We gave interviews all afternoon and into the early evening. Many times I was asked if the stigmata would re-appear. I was always sure it would not, and Father Eric always said that it would. It was the one and only time that we ever disagreed on anything important.

After everybody had gone we had a soft drink together. Betty was downstairs, and Eric and I sat together holding hands and hugging. We said that we loved each other.

*As Heather made clear, this was a spiritual sharing, the love between two people whose work is love.*

*In a later conversation Heather harked back to Eric's belief that her stigmata would re-appear after her death.*

'I didn't want to sound as if I was arguing with you, Eric, but I'm so sure it's not going to happen again, I had to say so. As you know I've never contradicted you before. And yet you were just as sure when you said that you know it will. Why, or when, do you think it will come again?'

He smiled – he had a lovely smile – and he said, 'It won't be when you're alive. I know that it will manifest when you're laid in your coffin and people are coming to pay their last respects. It will manifest again then. And that is important. It means more than you think.'

*Even after Father Eric's death Heather remained certain that no marks would appear on her after death. In fact the outcome was to be surprisingly ambiguous.*

But I realized then that there would be no more writings, and no more stigmata that I would have to deal with. It was a big relief to think that the mission was over. There had been a whole year of this mission, this task, and at no time did I ever wish it hadn't happened or anything. But it was a relief to be at the end.

Father Eric and I had got to the end together without either of us at any stage feeling we couldn't cope, or that we had to give up. Now it was a relief.

## Father Eric died on the 19th May 1993

A few days after everything had settled down, after the stigmata and the writings had ended, Father Eric went into hospital. He was in so much pain. He was in for about ten days and deteriorating fast. I visited every day.

Eric was then transferred to the hospice. He was in for maybe a week to ten days. I still visited every day.

One day, Dr Bob, the doctor that had looked after me, rang me up, 'Father Eric is asking if you could come and anoint him.'

I told him I would. Betty and Michael, one of their sons, were already there. We drew the curtains and I anointed Father Eric. He was drifting in and out of consciousness then but he was aware I was with him.

Very soon, Father Eric slipped into a coma, in which he remained for about a week. On the morning of Wednesday, 19th May 1993 he peacefully passed away.

I didn't cry, I didn't really feel that it was Father Eric. I knew that he was gone from the physical plane. I saw Betty a bit later on and she asked, 'Do you want to see him? He looks lovely.' I wasn't sure whether or not I wanted to go and see him. Then Sylvia and some of the congregation rang me, asking if it would be all right to see Father Eric. I told them it would be no problem. They asked if I would like to go with them. That made my mind up for me. I agreed to go and see him. Steve came and picked us up to take us to the Chapel of Rest, to pay our last respects. We took Sylvia in the car; we could all be there together.

So I went to see him; he looked so proud, so radiant. He was in his bishop's gown with his hands together, and his cross on. It was just beautiful. His hair was all smartly combed. To me it was as if he was lying in state. He looked like a king.

We stayed a few minutes. I stroked Father Eric's head and held his hand. Sylvia was reluctant to touch him, but she did; she stroked his hair and held his hand. Afterwards she told me, 'I am ever so pleased I did hold his hand.'

I actually went six or seven times, because so many other people wanted me to be with them when they went to see him. He died on Wednesday, the funeral was on the Monday. Even on Sunday, the undertaker, Mr Lupton, opened the chapel to let friends visit Father Eric and pay their last respects.The funeral was at eleven o'clock Monday morning. Eric and I had earlier agreed that I would conduct his funeral service, and I had already prepared the service.

As always, we had two candles lit and we burnt incense as we walked in front of the coffin. I led the procession for Father Eric.

It was a special service, just for Father Eric. It was all about what Father Eric and myself believed. It was not the traditional service. Although he had died, we were only cremating the body; I knew that Eric, the moment he died, had entered the higher realms of our Lord and was face to face with Jesus. He was up in heaven getting to know our Lord more. I felt it was very beautiful. This is what we both believed.

I hadn't taken any morphine before the service because I did not want to be tongue-tied or drift off. So I was in pain, but that kept me alert. I was determined to do the service well.

Father Eric had asked if I would be able and strong enough to carry on with the church after he had died, and I was happy to do that, but a bit sad as well. Father Eric had prepared me for this and had said, a year or so earlier, that he had noticed I had a lovely room upstairs. He happened to say that he thought it would make a lovely house church, or a chapel. I only used the room for hanging my clothes in, and it was full of old boxes and bits and pieces. At the time I didn't think much about what Father Eric was saying.

Now I think that Father Eric perhaps knew the future and what was to be. A week or so after Father Eric died, his wife and son said, 'We might as well move everything.' I agreed to take the church into my house. Everything in the church has been handmade and people have donated things to us, even the cross.

Everything of the church was transferred from Father Eric's house to my house. I had to register for the change of use for the church because it's all done bona fide. Sadly there are a lot of people that think that's it's just a made-up church and we are just playing at it. I thought so myself for a short time; I did at one time say that I thought it was unusual to see a house church. But when you see the wider area we work in you realize it is a very serious calling. There is a lot of work involved. And Father Eric did a lot of travelling; when any other ministers or vicars are on sabbatical, on holiday or sick, Father Eric could be called on to stand in. Although we are Catholic and we do a Catholic service, if we went to a Methodist Church we did their service.

Eric was a wonderful, gentle man who has been a priest and a bishop for twelve years and given everything of himself to God and to everyone around him. I looked up to Eric as my friend, my priest, my mentor, my aide through all of this, but one day he held my hand and said, 'I am your pupil, Heather. If I live another twenty lives I will never reach or attain where you are now.'

I listened to what he was saying but it was too much for me to accept. I can never accept it.

*Betty told us that shortly after Eric's death Heather received a channelled message from him. 'It was actually for me and the family. And it was in his writing, which was amazing. Heather told me 'I have this message from Eric.' This was on the 22nd May, at 4.10am. She said, 'There's one thing about it I don't understand – I've never heard him call you Bet before.' But in fact he always called me Bet when we were at home, alone together. She said she'd never heard him call me that.*

*The message was: I give to you all this greeting and this love so that as one in Communion we shall be inheritors of the Kingdom. What are our lives for but to be in harmony with each other and to know the love that God has put in place. Your hearts beat in harmony and are of those who seek to do His will, and always fresh and ready to do as you are bidden. You are in tune with the Creator and as you draw close towards the new day let your love and healing intertwine with each other in our chapter at the Order of St Luke. It is not only paradise here, but a Garden of Eden. It goes on and on. I love you all. We have enjoyed our time together and it will be so in all the time to come. Have patience, courage and faith and find fulfillment, Bet, in our sons, family and friends. I will always be nearby until our hands touch again, until eternity. Thank you Bet for loving and helping to make this life of mine complete. Ask for strength rather than pain. You are a special person in the lives of so many. No looking back. Look to the future. No regrets. No tears, unless they are tears of joy. You will always be my boys and we will be together again in the new day. That is a promise I can keep. Until then spread the Good News. I am only a stone's throw away from the beach. Share the Celtic blessing always, until we are together again. My love, always, Dad, and your Eric, Bet.*

We asked Betty if she had any doubts about the 'origin' or 'authenticity' of the message. 'None at all,' she told us. 'He always used to say to me about when you die, "No looking back, no regrets, no tears." That was so typically him. And also the expression "only a stone's throw away ..." It was one of his phrases. I have no doubts whatsoever about that message. Eric didn't very often write his sermons but when he did, the faster he wrote the bigger his writing and this (channelled from Heather) is exactly the same. The "y"s are the same ... it is all just the same. And I was so thrilled to have that.'

## Reactions and rejections

*The stigmata was not universally accepted by Heather's friends and others around her. She herself pointed out that there were bound to be those who could not accept these visible signs – even those who would insist she was just a charlatan.*

I had for some time been going to the local school to listen to the children reading to me. The children and the teachers all saw me for those twenty-one weeks with bandages on; I don't think I ever took the bandages off. The teachers never commented, though the children did. When I'd been in hospital and come back they would say how sorry they were I had been in hospital, and they hoped I was well. Every summer holiday, and Christmas, there was a bouquet of flowers and a box of chocolates from the school, and cards from the children. In the week leading up to Christmas I would get lots of little presents they had made for me. I have kept so many of the knick-knacks, they were so lovely.

Then the stigmata was made public through the television programme and some articles in the local newspaper. Initially, the stories don't seem to have bothered anyone. They weren't fully accurate but they weren't too badly inaccurate.

The teachers had not then said anything – Mr Williams certainly hadn't. But a reporter from one of the papers, interviewing me, also asked about my hobbies and interests, and about the school. I told them that I went to Monks Road Primary School to listen to the children read three or four mornings a week on a voluntary basis. I told them I really enjoyed that. That was all I told them. But they published it as 'Mrs Woods, a part-time teacher...'

I hadn't seen that because it was in a newspaper that I don't buy.

I had been off school for two weeks because I had been in hospital. I went back and called into the headmaster's room just to ask if he would praise the children during assembly. They had helped a man that had been found unconscious, and they had alerted the police. I just thought the children should get recognition for that. The headmaster agreed and told me that he would do it, but then he said, 'Would you sit down. I've got something to tell you.'

I thought, 'This doesn't sound very good.' 'We've had a meeting of the governors' board, including parent governors. I'm afraid, because of what was in the paper about you saying you were a part-time teacher, we have decided we would rather you did not come back to the school.'

I told him that I hadn't said that; that they had asked me about my hobbies and that I had told them I went to the school and listened to children read on a voluntary basis. But he was very insistent.

'So that's it after five years? You just don't want me to come? What about the children?' I can't remember much more that was said. I remember that he told me, 'Well, there's only one thing that we can do.' He offered to put my case to the governors if I could get the newspaper to print a retraction, and the correct details. But they never did; and I never pushed it.

*Local people told us that there had been talk among parents of the school-children that they were 'concerned' about the claims Heather was making in the newspapers. They left little doubt that the claims they were worried about were of the stigmata, not the claims of being a part-time teacher. They were sure that that would have got back to the board of governors; that that was what would have influenced them.*

So that was it. I was absolutely gobsmacked by it all, it was such a shock. I went home, holding the tears back. I just got in and shut the door, and leant on the back of the door. I cried and sobbed my heart out. I was angry, but mostly I was so upset.

*Heather talked with some passion about other rejections she believed she had suffered. She described a friend who had for years helped her to go shopping. They had first met in Steep Hill House, the working girls' hostel. That was when she was about sixteen to eighteen; over twenty-five years ago. She had then met her years later when they both did yoga together. They became close friends. Apparently she knew about the stigmata and did not seem at all troubled by it; but soon stopped coming to help Heather. Heather felt she was rejecting her. How much of that was in her mind is unclear. Certainly, the experiences she was undergoing caused upsets in Heather's routines that this friend may not have found easy to accommodate, and Heather herself may have changed to someone this friend found less easy to get along with. But Heather certainly felt something was amiss.*

*Heather also believed that she was rejected by people in Lincoln who rec-ognized her. She described people crossing the road to avoid her, ignoring her when she addressed them. Again, how much of that was in her mind and how much was real is unclear. But it troubled her to think that her mission for Christ could not be accepted more widely.*

*There came a time when Helen, one of the three in the triumvirate of Heather, Eric and Helen, had to withdraw from the group. She had already told Heather, months before, 'We will never lose what we are sharing now, but there will come a time when we have to part.' That time came.*

*As Helen described it, 'It was October 1992. I was drawing my curtains one night – and I'm not a religious person, I'm not a spooky person – I'm a practically minded person, have been all my life – but I heard a voice that said to me "If you don't get out now, you won't get another chance".'*

*Betty said, of Helen's withdrawal: 'Heather was terribly hurt. We tried to get her over it. Heather was very upset and was really devastated because they had been so close.'*

*And Helen understood the pain that her decision had given Heather, but she felt she had to follow the guidance she had been given.*

*Reflecting on these events in interview with us, Helen was drawn back to her memories of that year:*

*'I was beginning to get a bit worried about myself. I always think it was a bit strange that I chose a place like Lincoln to buy a business. I have no connections with Lincoln myself, and I was always a little mystified how we three all got together. Then Eric died and with all the other things that happened that year I began to think am I going to be all right? I have a lot of sleepless nights about that. I don't feel it's over yet. I don't believe it's all happened for nothing.'*

## Heather's own interpretation of the phenomena

I think that the reason I was chosen was because of all the traumas, trials, heartache and pain I'd endured through my childhood, through my teenage life, my marriage and up till now with my illness. Because I have endured it.

I have met so many people through my illnesses and the other things that have happened to me. I would not have met them if I had been healthy. Hundreds of lives have been touched by the visible signs of the stigmata; many have been able to see and touch the marks.

I think I am also an example; an ordinary person who has kept her humour through a lot of suffering. I think the message is that if I can do it, anyone can. It is a message of modern day living. I had a life and I wanted to get on with it; anything that knocked me to the ground didn't keep me down. Instead of staying down I would get up and brush off the dust, straighten up and carry on. The purpose of it all is that I am a blessing to others, to people that are in need spiritually. The marks, the writings, everything, are there to offer hope and reassurance. I am cutting a pathway for their spiritual growth, their hope for themselves and mankind and the future itself.

This is a visible blessing, with physical signs and evidence, not so much for unbelievers who ask for signs, but for believers who have sometimes been in doubt. It is to draw those in doubt closer to God, and for unbelievers to begin to know Jesus as a friend and as a Saviour. It is a sign that there is life ever after, life eternal, and that miracles themselves are not a thing of the past, they do still happen. It is to teach people to open themselves up and let themselves accept Christ. The stigmata and the writings were given to show that God is a living God, working now in our midst.

We are destroying our own home. Mother Earth is a living planet. We are living on this planet, she is providing rain and sun for heat and water. Mother Nature has provided everything for us. Yet we are abusing her, not just by taking the oil and the coal and everything but with pollution in the air and in the seas. And Mother Earth is dying; we are killing the living planet that has supported us over the years and there is no way that we can continue like this. If Mother Earth is dying she is not going to be able to sustain us. We can't live on a dead planet.

You might ask why God lets it happen. But God is like our parent; we are all his children. And there is a time when children grow up, leave home and get married. They become adults in their own right. And even as parents we know that we must not interfere with our children when they are adults. This is how it is with God; he can't interfere.

But I know that my real calling is the healing ministry. Father Eric, when he was in the hospice, told me, 'Don't worry if you are not strong enough to continue with the church. It won't bother me if the church finishes. But you know that the healing is important, don't you?'

I told him, 'Yes, I do Father Eric. I know that that really is the calling.'

*Heather had been a healer before the stigmata. If the stigmata was God's way of showing that Heather was special, then she thought it was perhaps because of her healing ministry, which she saw as continuing the real work of Christ.*

To me the healing is more of a miracle than the stigmata, although I know the marks are absolutely miraculous.

*Perhaps the most revealing part of Heather's beliefs is reflected in her spelling of stigmata. She spells it STIGMARTYR.*

# CHAPTER FOUR

# The Stigmata and the Paranormal in Context: An analysis

H EATHER'S STIGMATA, *and the other aspects of her life, are extraordinary, but not unique. There have been other claimants to these phenomena over the centuries, and those claimants have many common features, as well as unique features. So that we might fully understand the events that have driven Heather, this chapter examines the stigmata and these other paranormal effects in context.*

## The history and scope of the stigmata: an overview

*In 1224, two years before his death, St Francis of Assisi received on his body marks representing the wounds of the suffering of Jesus Christ. It is estimated that, in the 770 years since that time, some three hundred people have reported this phenomenon. It is thought that there may be more, that some recipients of the marks might have kept them 'secret', believing them to be for the eyes of the devout only. In Heather's case, she only made her marks public when she was 'told' in a message from the Lord that they could be made public. The vast majority of the claimants have been female; one estimation indicated a figure as high as 85 per cent.*

*In the case of St Francis, the stigmata was described as the appearance of the nails themselves; the points and the nail heads showing through the skin on both sides of his hands. They were alleged to have existed after his death, with many pilgrims filing past his body witnessing 'not the prints of the nails, but the nails themselves formed out of his flesh and retaining the blackness of iron...'*

*Other stigmatics have reported similar marks, for example, Giovanna Bonomi in 1670 and Domenica Lazzari in 1848.*

The marks are not, however, consistent. Some reports are of red patches that do not bleed, deep holes that in some cases are alleged to go right through the limb, circles, ovals, oblongs and so on. The marks can include a representation of the spear-mark in the side and marks representing the crown of thorns on the forehead. Heather displayed most of these marks, and others, in the two periods of her stigmata.

Georgette Faniel of Montreal has recently reported, in addition to the 'usual' marks, a pain that she believes represents the wound caused by Christ carrying the cross on his shoulder as he walked to Golgotha.

Some stigmatics have wept blood in addition to their marks; Therese Neumann is probably the most famous of those reports. In the case of St Teresa of Avila, her heart, which is preserved as a sacred relic, bears marks that are believed by some to represent the piercing of her heart by a spear. There have been other cases of post-mortem marks seen on the heart and attributed to the stigmata; for example, Caterina Savelli in 1691, and Charles of Sezze in 1671. The most extreme form of 'heart-markings' arose in the case of Blessed Clare of the Cross: after her death her heart was cut open and nuns believed they could see there representations of the whip with which Christ was beaten, the pillar, the crown of thorns, the nails, the spear, the pole with the sponge used to moisten Jesus' lips, and of course the image of the Cross itself.

One slightly different form of stigmata are the 'rings of the spouse'; some people 'marry' Christ and get a ring-like mark on their finger. This is suggestive of the action taken by some nuns when they take their vows; there is a 'wedding ceremony' and they are given a ring bonding them to Christ.

One very special feature of stigmata marks is that they never go septic. Heather pointed this out to us, and her doctors confirmed that hers did not.

The most famous stigmatic is the late Padre Pio. After eight years of pains he received the stigmata at the age of 31, on 20th September 1918; his wounds opened up and released a great deal of blood. For him, as for many stigmatics, his marks were painful. He wrote: 'I saw before me a mysterious person ... his hands and feet and side were dripping with blood. The vision disappeared and I became aware that my hands, feet and side were dripping blood. Imagine the agony I experienced and continue to experience almost every day ... I am dying of pain because of the wounds and resulting embarrassment...' He was a stigmatic for fifty years; even his shoes were specially made to accommodate the bandages that were a normal part of his life.

There were those who believed they could put their fingers right through his wounds; others claimed he was a fraud. Such extremes of views are 'normal' in paranormal subjects, usually reflecting the viewpoints of the 'investigators' more than those of the subject.

Padre Pio and St Francis of Assisi have many close parallels. From an early age Padre Pio – born Francesco Forgione – wanted to be a Franciscan priest – of the order started by St Francis. St Francis received his stigmata after a pilgrimage to the shrine of St Michael at Gargano in Italy; Padre Pio lived in a monastery in the small town of San Giovanni Rotondo, just a few miles from that shrine. Padre Pio's stigmata appeared just three days after he had celebrated the Feast of the Stigmata of St Francis.

However, when Padre Pio died, on 23rd September 1968, there were no signs of the wounds on his body as there had been with St Francis.

Generally speaking, those displaying the signs of the stigmata indicate that they believe them to represent a 'sign' from Jesus. As far as is known all stigmatics are religious, with a belief in Christ as a centrepiece of their conviction. There are no reliable claims of the stigmata in non-Christian religions. Heather indicated that she believed they were given to her at a time when a suffering world needed a symbol of faith.

However, analysis of the phenomenon indicates that internal beliefs and imagery may engender the markings. (This is examined later in this chapter.) This verges on suggesting that claimants actually want to display these signs; in fact we can be sure that this occasionally happens. Two years before St Francis of Assisi reported his stigmata, one man allowed himself to be crucified and therefore bore the marks, and in recent times a court prosecuted two men for crucifying a third on Hampstead Heath, even though the 'victim' admitted he had requested the crucifixion.

Apart from those who will have faked the marks – most paranormal phenomena have their fraudulent claimants – the majority seem to be displaying a psychosomatic response to their religious fervour. That the body can will itself to produce such marks has evidence outside of the realm of stigmata claims, and has even been put to the test. A Swedish girl known as Maria was badly beaten up when she was 23; after that time she would, every few weeks, produce bleeding from head, ear and eyelids. A doctor examining her concluded that she could produce bleeding at will, from no visible wounds, when she picked arguments with other patients and reached a certain emotional state.

This ability, known as hysterical conversion, is a close cousin to a form of extreme hypochondria as exhibited by 'Elizabeth K.'. Her story is explained later in this chapter.

Whether the stigmata is God-given is, of course, a matter for conviction rather than research. Research seems, however, to have identified a mechanism by which the body can – in certain extreme emotions – manifest strange markings, producing a truly extraordinary, and highly visible, mystery phenomenon.

## An association with visions

*Heather's stigmata first appeared when she was also having other
paranormal experiences; she was receiving channelled drawings and
writings, and experiencing visions. All of these experiences were of a
religious nature: channelled messages that read like sermons, drawings and
visions of Christ baptized and crucified. The visions were very clear and had
a feeling of great reality to them. Of her vision of the baptism Heather said:
'It was as if I was there. I could see the water dripping from him, sparkling
in the sunlight.'*

*The appearance of the stigmata on other stigmatics is almost invariably
associated with some form of vision. The first stigmatic, St Francis, received
the marks shortly before he died, when he had undergone a very intense
period of self-deprivation and suffering. The marks appeared when he
perceived a vision of a six-winged seraph crucified like a man. Religious
illustrations depicting this show a seraph standing before him with lines
similar to laser beams shining from its wounds onto St Francis.*

*Ethel Chapman, who in her fifties exhibited the stigmata, recalled a vivid
vision, received when she was in bed, of being crucified. She felt the pain, she
said she saw people there who were jeering at her. The next morning she
found blood on her hands and her hands were marked.*

*Like Heather, Ethel Chapman also produced writings, though with no
claim to channelling. As Ted Harrison described: 'She did say that it just
flowed when she started writing. She wrote a lot of it. It's not particularly
high standard poetry but it all concentrates on various religious themes and
sometimes on her own suffering.'*

*Visions of this nature carry with them a feeling of reality and conviction
that may be just the degree of passion needed to produce stigmata. In other
fields of research we have spoken to three people who were 'driven' by the
power of their revelations: 'Sarah' in Scotland was waiting for the results of
a biopsy following an examination of a lump on her breast. She hadn't heard
from the doctor, and was laying in bed, and had more or less decided 'my
days were numbered'. She held an orange in her hand, and then had this
extraordinary spiritual feeling. She felt completely at ease with the world,
thinking 'I have the gold of the world in my hands.' A feeling of complete
tranquillity came over her. Her perspective totally shifted; it no longer
mattered what happened to her, or however bad the results of her test might
be. That all became insignificant because of this feeling that the world was
wonderful, perfect.*

*She told us 'I can face anything now because of the feeling from holding
this simple object, grown from the earth. It just took a second or so to pass
through my mind but it was like a revelation, it summed up our place in the*

*universe. It was a signal of life's strength and continuity. I felt nourished and strengthened by the whole experience. I have never felt anxious about life since then, except minor little things day to day, of course. But the totality of existence is not now a concern to me.'* There are obvious parallels in this story to the way in which religiously driven people can accept on faith that which cannot be proven. 'Bertil' had revelations that he believed made him 'ecologically aware'. For Bertil much of his life is a mission to spread that message to others; it is as powerful a religious passion as any Christian belief. In fact, at one time Bertil and others made moves towards starting a radical church in their country.

*'I came to a bed of flowers. I knelt down and I got in touch with one of the roses: I was actually part of its system of juices running through the stem up to the rose buds and it was such a magnificent feeling. I was really enlightened. Afterwards I started becoming more and more conscious of the inner living nature of plants and trees and so forth. Animals seem to be animated beings, of course, like human beings, but I came to realize that plants also are animated in a way. I started trying to get in touch with trees and plants and I succeeded. Now whenever I like I am able to be in touch with plants and listen to them.'* 'Peter' was in bed, sleeping. He woke up, got out of bed and pulled the curtains open. This followed a feeling that he was compelled to do it; that he knew something was there. Outside was a very round, very bright light with swirling colours in it. The centre was like a ball turning on an axis. Peter described the inner core as if turning independently; the light swamped out everything and totally filled Peter's field of vision. Since that time Peter's artistic talents have developed (there were none in evidence previously) in both painting and photography; he has sold examples of both for large sums of money and for publication. And there is considerable emphasis on the swirling coloured patterns that were part of his experience. Peter was certain that the event was a 'turning point' in his life. His interest in all things paranormal started at that time. To some extent Peter said his experience was 'religious' and he recognized that his artworks were a deliberate expression of this, albeit a subconscious one. Many of his paintings and photographs are overlaid with crosses and standard religious shapes.

*These experiences are different to stigmata of course; but the visions – and the passion of conviction – easily bear comparison to those of stigmatics. The certainty of the reality and the change of perspective of 'Bertil' and 'Sarah' are similar to religious conversion. The resultant expressions bear comparison also; Peter's artistry, Ethel Chapman's poetry and Heather's channelled writings and drawings could all be coming from unlocked facets of their minds, for example.*

## Mechanisms of the stigmata, and of channelling

*It is generally thought that there are four possible mechanisms to account for the appearance of the marks. a) The first has little support within research circles, but is of course totally supported by stigmatics; that the marks are God-given. They are a sign from God, pointing at the subject, and saying 'watch this space'. Certainly Heather believed they were given to her as a message for the world. b) The second mechanism, and the first of three generally maintained by researchers, is that the marks are physically produced in some way. One subject, Elizabeth of Herkenrode, possibly created and certainly maintained the marks by banging her finger into her hand, re-living the passion and the pain of the crucifixion every twenty-four hours. It would be easy to regard such a mechanism as 'cheating' or 'faking', and against the possibility of divine intervention it probably is, but from the stigmatic's point of view it is not; the stigmata is a part of a religious experience for its subjects and physical pain and suffering are a real part of the devotion. They are doing what they believe is right. c) The third mechanism is created by people that exhibit multiple personality syndrome; in other words those people who seem to have 'other' personalities within them. While there are those who maintain this is literally real – people possessed by other spirits – it is generally thought that these people's own personality is sub-divided in a way that prevents them 'contacting' their 'other selves'.*

*Researchers have observed that when such people are in one personality they cannot recall what they did in the other personality. Usually the 'main' personality knows about the 'others', and vice-versa, but the 'other' personalities do not know of each other. If it is a 'sub-personality' that is religiously driven, then the marks may appear on that person and yet be a complete surprise or shock to the 'main' personality.*

*Some evidence of multiple personality syndrome is thought to be reflected in such areas as channelling messages. Heather, for example, receives a variety of messages in various handwritings and one theory would suggest that these are all her other personalities 'communicating' with the main one.*

*While there are signs in Heather that this may be part of the explanation, it does not fully or easily explain all of the channelled messages, for example from Father Eric shortly after his death. Here, the handwriting and the content was so like Eric's that his wife, Betty, was convinced that it was a message from Eric.*

*Ted Harrison believes there is a flaw in this theory. As he said, 'I can find no evidence of anybody ever having witnessed a person in another personality making the marks on themselves. Therese Neumann had a* number of personalities, and they were witnessed. She spoke in a different way. She had one very childlike personality, she had a very profound personality where she spoke in high German, another one where she re-enacted things of a religious nature. But no-one ever saw her making the marks.' d) The fourth mechanism is that the marks appear naturally, as a psychosomatic response to religious fervour. Most researchers put most emphasis on this theory, and it has been tested. Furthermore, it has comparisons outside of the claims of the stigmata.

It is described medically as psychogenic purpura (spontaneous haemorrhaging with no obvious cause). It is rare, but there are several cases of people who produce on themselves the evidence of some previous trauma. One case, of a woman who had been abused during childhood, involved the spontaneous appearance of her bruise marks during psychotherapy.

Dr Robert Moody, a British psychiatrist, reported the case in 1946 of an army officer whom he had treated for stress disorders, and sleepwalking. During these times the officer produced the marks on his body of ropes where he had been tied up earlier. Moody photographed these wounds, and saw them bleed. It is highly likely that, just as religious fervour is thought to cause the stigmata, so the officer's psychiatric problems related to his captivity; hence both the sleepwalking and the shape and form of his marks.

In a far stranger field, that of UFO and Close Encounter research, there is the well-documented case of Barney Hill, who believed that he was kidnapped by aliens and subjected to a medical examination. Reliving the experience years later under hypnosis, he produced a ring of warts around his genitals, corresponding to where he believed devices had been attached during the 'abduction'. In fact many people who claim to have undergone 'alien abductions' display marks on their bodies, and bleeding, from wounds they believe were inflicted by medical examination by aliens.

The belief, therefore, seems to produce marks in a shape and form that match the experience or vision as perceived by the subject. However, these types of marks appear on the subjects themselves; the army officer had once been a captive, Barney Hill believed he had been abducted by aliens. The stigmata is unique in that the subject receives the marks of somebody else's suffering, that is, Jesus's.

Ted Harrison's investigations revealed 'only one case that I have identified of a person having any form of empathetic psychosomatic experience, in other words, getting on themselves the wounds of somebody else. That case is of a woman who witnessed a neighbour being shot and got the supposed wounds of the bullets on herself.'

It is, however, important to note that Heather might constitute something of an exception to that point. Of one of her visions she said, 'I found myself on the cross with our Lord. I wasn't with him as if it were the two of us; I felt myself within him, looking out.' In that case, perhaps the marks are not, in her own mind, the suffering of another person, but marks of her own suffering. She never claimed to be Jesus, of course, but for a time she seemed to think she shared his experiences with him.

Perhaps the visions of other stigmatics have given that closeness and sharing, allowing for what appears to be empathetic psychosomatic experience.

The phenomenon known as possession has produced examples of skin markings that match the beliefs, and they have a similarity to stigmata. For example, 'Robbie', a famous American possession case, produced lines of suffering and even words, in blood on his skin. One witness said that scratches were emerging as if something was clawing from within his body.

Psychogenic purpura appears to require a traumatic experience. In addition, for the stigmata, there appears to be a need for passionate religious belief. The profound religious experiences these people undergo, taking the very vivid forms that they do, particularly in the form of visions, probably provide for that 'trauma'.

As to the stigmatics' own belief, that the stigmata is a God-given sign, Ted Harrison was clear: 'I wouldn't say that one is talking about some form of divine party trick, no. [I don't think] God looks down and says, "I'm going to zap so and so with it."'

Of Heather, Ted believes that 'What Heather is doing is reacting to her religious experience psychosomatically. Some people have a profound religious experience and their immediate reaction might be to throw their arms in the air and shout "hallelujah". They want to respond to the religious experience in some way, and she does it psychosomatically.'

## The historical mechanisms

The historical perspective is complex. Why should a psychosomatic expression start at a certain time, for the first time in the thirteenth century? Why should it cluster in time and location, as it does? Why did the number of women who have had the marks outnumber men up until the end of the last century by about seven or eight to one, but change this century to a ratio of about three to one. Why do the marks – and the variations in the marks – appear as they do?

What seems to be a very important ingredient is the religious imagery. Up until the thirteenth century you did not get graphic religious imagery of the wounds and suffering of crucifixion. Before then, the artworks had been a very stylized form of image: very tender, very beautiful, no sign of blood injury. The stigmata started when artists had the freedom, and the climate of acceptability, to depict the suffering. For the first time they showed the nail-wounds, and the blood.

There is 'control' evidence which supports this theory. Some of the Byzantine and Orthodox images of Christ on the Cross maintain this stylized form to this day. These images do not depict the blood and the mutilation; and followers of these religious groups do not produce stigmatics. The Orthodox Church concentrated then, as they do today, more on the beauty and glory of God. In medieval times there arose a fashion to concentrate on the penance and the pain of Christ's suffering for our sins. That is what instituted the feast of Corpus Christi which was introduced at the same time, to concentrate the mind of the devoted on the body of Christ.

This came about less from the established Church and more from the pressure of lay people; it was a reaction to the corruption of the church at the time. St Francis himself was reacting against such corruption. He wasn't a priest, he was a lay person who set up his own monastic order. Many other unofficial religious orders were set up at this time.

These unofficial orders were often made up of women, and they sought out these orders so that they might concentrate their passion on the pain and suffering of Christ. They were turning their backs on the Church, which many at that time believed to be corrupt. So those in the Church, mainly men, were focused on stylized images of Christ's death, while these women were focused on his pain and suffering. That may explain why the original ratio of stigmatics was strongly biased in favour of women. As the Church re-established its credibility and people were drawn back to it, and as it led people to contemplate Christ's crucifixion for the sins of the world, so the ratio seems to have begun to level off. Even priests, who were now focused on the pain and suffering, were displaying the stigmata.

The continuing bias in favour of women may arise because women are traditionally more able to display their hysteria, and express their passions, than men. As the 'sexual revolution' allows men to 'come out' with their own passions and emotions, so the numbers may one day virtually equal out.

Religious imagery seems to play an important part in the style of the stigmata. Heather's stigmata closely matched her own beliefs about the crucifixion, and images she was familiar with. Similarly, Ethel Chapman got her marks in the form of a vision which closely related to the illustrated Bible she had been reading the night before. It is only since the public appearance of the Turin Shroud – whatever the authenticity of that item, which in any case matters less than people's beliefs in its authenticity – that marks were seen on the wrists of stigmatics. The Shroud created a theory that Jesus's crucifixion consisted of nails through the wrists rather than the palms of the hands.

*Geographically, the stigmata arises in clusters. It clusters around certain towns and certain periods in history. It seems to have been spread around the world largely by European emigrants. What seems to happen is that there are forms of religious revival among a lot of people in a given area. If that religious revival is of the type that is to do with the passion of Christ then it increases the chances of including people who have that psychosomatic propensity to manifest the stigmata.*

*Stigmatics are predominantly Catholic, with a bias towards Italian origin, but there have been Anglicans this century. It is usually Caucasian peoples who exhibit the marks, probably because Caucasians make up the majority of the followers of Christ. There is only one case of a black person displaying stigmata that we know of, that of Cloretta Robinson in California, when she was a young girl. She was a Baptist, which is also rare for stigmatics. (However, it is worth noting that Heather once briefly embraced the Baptist faith and was, on the 31st March 1991, baptized in a ceremony of full immersion.)*

*No other religion exhibits the stigmata or even equivalents. This is probably because in other religions, like the Muslim faith, there is not the same idea of suffering and redemption – of sin being redeemed through suffering. That is a uniquely Christian belief. There is some suggestion of members of one or two Muslim sects displaying whip-like marks, but it is thought that they arrange to be physically whipped as part of their belief in the suffering of their Prophet.*

## The overlay of the paranormal

*One thing that often combines with the appearance of stigmata is an association with experiences generally labelled 'paranormal'.*

*Heather believed she had ESP, could tell the history of people she met, had premonitions, saw ghosts and spirits, channelled images and writing, had out-of-body experiences and gave healing in the form of 'laying on of hands'.*

*Ted Harrison confirmed this from his own cases: 'George in Scotland said that at the time he got his marks he experienced the strange effect of seeing a cigarette case pass in front of his eyes across to the other side of the room. There are stories of people who have received communion and they say that the wafer flew from the priest's hand into their mouth. You have got reports of levitation; that a person at a point of religious ecstasy will levitate. Not many stigmatics have done that; St Francis was the most famous who did.'*

*Another claim, made by Padre Pio for example, is of bi-location; that he was witnessed in two places at the same time.*

*There is also the association with a perfume smell, the odour of sanctity. There is a clear, sweet smell of roses that has been associated with many*

171

stigmatics. It is alleged that Padre Pio can be detected by his devotees by the smell suddenly turning up, even today, many years after his death.

Betty Eades, wife of Father Eric, whose perceived association with Padre Pio is mentioned in the book, confirmed that she smelt that scent even recently, after both Eric's and Heather's death. Ted Harrison had similar cases: 'I was speaking to a person on Saturday who smelt him twice that day. Ethel Chapman has talked about her smelling the sweet smell of roses. Christina Gallagher in Ireland, whom I saw recently, was saying how the smell was now becoming a more important feature and that she actually perspired a sort of perfume.'

Another paranormal aspect is the incorruptibility of the body. A number of the stigmatics have been dug up after death; it has been found that the bodies have remained uncorrupted. A similar phenomenon has been reported with others, most notably Bernadette of Lourdes. Before placing too much significance on this claim, it is worth considering that the 'sample' may be biased. Many religions, particularly in the East, cremate their dead rather than bury them, and few religions are predisposed to digging people up again. The Catholic religion has used such examinations in the case of notable people, or would-be saints. There may be 'normal' explanations: unless somebody is in some way special they are not normally dug up, perhaps those people were buried in more protective, perhaps airtight, coffins. The stigmatics who have been dug up have usually been somebody special, normally having been made a saint by the church after a suitable time and the usual processes. Possibly there are many bodies in a state of good preservation that have never been discovered simply because there has been no motivation to dig them up.

## The stigmata and healing

Although the stigmata, the channelling and the visions were very important to Heather she – and apparently Father Eric – believed that it was her healing that was her 'mission' to be fulfilled. This form of healing is itself regarded by many as a form of the paranormal. Generally, the mechanism is described by its practitioners as similar to channelling, except that rather than receiving images or messages the healer becomes a conduit through which 'healing energy' is transmitted to the patient.

The stigmata and healing do not always go together, though it is interesting that both Heather and Padre Pio were stigmatic healers. It must be remembered that Heather's stigmata arose at a time when she was involved with Father Eric Eades. He was not only a healer but, according to his wife, believed that he channelled from the late Padre Pio.

Betty explained: 'Eric always thought that he was channelling his healing energy from Padre Pio, because we used to have perfume [smells]. I have had it once here since Eric died, but we have had people here – when Eric was giving healing – and they have told me afterwards that the perfume smells have even been with them even after they got home.

As Eric was healing this perfume smell would come; he thought that Padre Pio was with him.'

Other stigmatics who have been healers include Jane Hunt, and Berthe Mrazek of Belgium. Jane Hunt was developed into healing by the support of Reverends Hill and Wyatt, vicars of her local church. At certain times she donned nun-like clothing and performed 'laying on of hands' at church services. Some of her results seem to have been spectacular.

'A lady came to church in a wheelchair,' she described, 'she'd never been able to walk, and I just told her to stand up, and she walked down the aisle fine.'

One stigmatic, Georgette Faniel of Montreal, had a friend who wanted an abortion because she feared the pains of childbirth. Faniel offered to take on for herself all of the discomforts of the pregnancy if the other woman would not abort the child. From that time onwards Faniel displayed all the symptoms of being pregnant. At the time of delivery, it was Faniel who suffered the pains of childbirth; the mother had no discomforts whatsoever.

It appears that the form of healing adopted by Hunt, Mrazek and Faniel was to take on the suffering of others, reminiscent of the origins of the stigmata itself. Mrazek in particular had to stay in bed afterwards on occasion, to recover from the effects.

Heather did not, in fact, respond in that way. She, like Father Eric and the many thousands of (non-stigmatic) psychic healers, believed that nothing was given or taken from her; she was just a channel. She was never exhausted by the work, though naturally she was often spiritually uplifted by it.

Psychic healers traditionally believe that they are channelling a natural, as yet unknown energy. Heather and members of Christian healing groups generally do not like being thought of as psychic healers, but as spiritual healers, channelling the Holy Spirit. It could be argued that these are different labels for the same energy.

As to the mechanism of healing, belief in the healer may be a factor. If the patient believes that the healer can heal, then perhaps it is all the more effective. Heather declared that this was not strictly true; the Holy Spirit could do its work whether the recipient believed or not. She did acknowledge, however, that lack of belief, and resistance, could impede the patient's progress. Heather even related the story of healing someone who had no belief in her abilities but was 'grasping at a last straw'.

*Two psychic healers we have interviewed also emphasized that belief was not, in their eyes, a factor. One had done a great deal of absent healing with people who did not even know she was praying for them, and claimed they were cured of their ills.*

*The other healer, Graham, had done work on animals, 'busting' cancers in one dog in particular. As Graham described it: 'The dog was brought to me by a very sceptical owner. He had a golf-ball size growth on the inside of his groin and he was in secondary cancer. His tummy area, normally pink, was black. I did thirteen healing sessions. At first the dog had to be carried up the stairs to my healing room. After the third or fourth healing session, instead of this seven or eight stone dog being carried from the car up the stairs, it was actually slowly walking out of the car and climbing up the stairs unaided. After around eight or nine healing sessions it walked fairly normally, but with a limp, up the stairs. On the twelfth healing session I had this enormous build up of energy. The following day I had a phone call from the owner of the dog saying, 'I don't know what's happened here but this growth has completely disappeared'. He brought the dog back to me; its tummy had returned to a normal colour of pink, the golf-ball growth had completely gone. But it wasn't faith healing; a dog couldn't have faith could it?'*

*Whatever explanations are offered, there is some scientific evidence for something real passing from the healer to the recipient, and it may directly relate to two people's descriptions of Heather's stigmata, as we shall describe shortly.*

*The most impressive experiments concerned the work of Oskar Estebany, working with animals and plants.*

*The experiments were conducted with Dr Bernard Grad of McGill University, Montreal, Canada. Grad eliminated human subjects from the experiment, recognizing that there would always be arguments as to whether telepathy, faith, the power of suggestion or any number of other aspects would interfere with analysis of the results.*

*The first experiment conducted was to remove small pieces of skin from forty-eight mice. The mice were then weighed and measured and divided into three groups. Each group was placed in separate cages in which they stayed; throughout the experiment Estebany never made physical contact with the animals. The conditions of the experiment were that one group would be healed by Estebany, one group would be ignored, and a third group would be warmed to a temperature comparable to that generated by the healer's hands just in case heat alone was the answer. It had been recognized that heat could be a part of the healing process. All groups were equally cared for in terms of feeding and other routines.*

*Over a period of twenty days the healing of their wounds was measured; the mice that had been warmed to a temperature showed no particular variation from the group that had been ignored, but there was a fast increase in the rate of recovery in respect of Estebany's 'healed' group.*

*The second experiment used barley seeds. Plants of identical barley seeds were separated into two groups, the only difference between them being that one group was watered with a solution that had been held by Estebany, who made no other contact with the plants. Those watered by the solution he had handled grew much faster.*

*As Dr Grad stated: 'Something must have passed from his hand to the solution which was then delivered to the seeds. And since the treatment in most of the experiments was through the barrier of a sealed glass container, it cannot be a material substance in the sense that it is a chemical of any kind. I know of no other way to explain these experiments, and so I am inclined to feel that there was something from the hand that was being radiated and this penetrated the glass bottle and altered the water. There is some evidence now that properties of water themselves are changed by this process.' When asked whether he believed this to be a paranormal effect, Grad made the same point that most researchers into the paranormal have made for years.*

*'People call it paranormal, but in my view it's no more paranormal than magnetism was paranormal 500 years ago. It's simply that we have not paid any attention to this kind of phenomenon.'*

*Perhaps recipients of healing energy do not need faith, but sceptical analysis of healing, doubted as it is by many scientists and doctors, suggests that what might be happening is that the patient feels special because of the attention being given to him or her, and starts to take a more internally positive outlook towards their own health. In effect, they heal themselves. Presumably this explanation could just about be stretched to take in the dog and the mice.*

*An alternative, but similar, explanation, might be that people are given 'permission' to heal themselves. There is a belief that we all have within us the mechanisms to heal our own ills but that we lack the ability to turn them on. When someone else gives us a 'command' or 'permission' we change our attitude and become healed.*

*However, these experiments have also suggested that something 'real' passes to the recipient during healing. This something that passes is often recognized by experimenters, patients and healers as feeling like heat, and that is directly related to Heather's stigmata. Her Aunt May described Heather's stigmata: 'You could feel the heat coming from it. Even the one on her tummy, you could feel the heat there.'*

May demonstrated to us how she reacted when she put her hand over the marks; she jerked it backwards suddenly, screwing up her face. It was a gesture she could have made if she had put her hand into the flame of a candle. Heather's father, George, was at the interview and confirmed that impression. He described the heat from inches above the wounds as 'hot as a match flame. Hot. Hot.' He too made this same jerking, withdrawing, gesture.

May told us that Heather's body always generated heat: 'Many a time I used to give her a hug; I'd throw my arms around her and the heat that would come from her body was unbelievable.'

Heat – Stigmata – Healing. Perhaps the connections are there for researchers into many paranormal fields.

## The Holy Spirit

There was one incident that arose in the last few months of Heather's life, just before the second time we interviewed her. She believed that the Holy Spirit she was in contact with, and which she channelled, became visible as a further proof of her ministry.

She described the Holy Spirit, as she saw it, as 'a curving beam of white light, with a spiral inside it'.

She was 'given' that she should invite a friend to take a photograph of her house church. The friend came, and took the photograph. Heather hoped that the Holy Spirit would be visible to the photographer and was disappointed when it was not.

However, when the photographer got her pictures back from the chemist, one of the images were clearly overlaid with this beam of light, exactly as Heather always described it. On the original, and some reproductions, the spiralling within the light is clear. Heather gave us a copy of the photograph for the book; it is included in the photo-set.

After we received the photograph it happened that we were having dinner with Maurice Gross, the head of the Spontaneous Phenomena Committee of the Society for Psychical Research (SPR). He was to show us some photographs he had been examining; we showed him the 'Holy Spirit' photograph. He smiled, and handed us two photos that he had been going to show us; the exact same beam of light was on two photographs taken during a christening ceremony. In one photograph the light comes down into the font, in the other it comes down directly onto the baby's head. The family concerned replied to our enquiries, confirming that they hadn't seen any lighting effects when the ceremony was underway, and that it had been quite a surprise to them when they saw it.

*Maurice told us that many such pictures had been sent to him in recent months. As yet the several photographers and analysts who have examined the photographs at our behest have yet to come up with an explanation. Maurice also confirmed that the SPR had not yet found an explanation.*

## Predictability of the marks

*Marks go into remission and then 'flair' up again; it is often very predictable. Heather claimed that the arrival of the marks was foretold to her through her channelling, fulfilling an uncertain prophecy she believed she was 'given'. Ethel Chapman, for example, relived the vision of being crucified every Good Friday for seven years, resulting in the marks.*

*A number of people have claimed that they go through long periods of time without eating anything but the wafer-bread of Communion. Louise Lateau and Therese Neumann made such claims, as did a lot of others. Padre Pio ate very little. Louise Lateau and Therese Neumann in particular were kept under very strict observation; urine was analysed and so on. In the case of Neumann there is some evidence that she sneaked bits of food in. However, even then she must have survived on very little. She didn't lose weight, either. Louise Lateau lost weight and put it on; there might have been periods when she was eating. Ted Harrison includes in his cases George in Scotland; he apparently just cannot eat. 'He cannot put food down and is maintained now by a tube down his nose and into the stomach. Liquid food is put in every two days or so.'*

*Heather was noted by everyone who knew her as eating very little; Betty Eades expressed her surprise at how Heather survived on the small amount of food she ate. We were able to verify that for ourselves; Heather stayed with us for three days on one occasion and hardly ate anything offered to her in that time.*

## A radical research approach

*There appears to be a role for hypnosis in research into the stigmata. Such an experiment has already been undertaken. In the late 1920s/early 1930s a German doctor, Alfred Lechler, was dealing with a patient, Elizabeth K. She was highly suggestible; she would bring about almost any symptoms that she heard about, or read about. One Good Friday she saw an illustrated exhibition of the Crucifixion and subsequently complained of pains in her hands and feet. Lechler decided to use this, and to try to develop in her the stigmata by hypnotic suggestion. When brought out of the hypnotic trance she remembered nothing of his instructions to her while she was 'under'; however, within the next day or so she produced bleeding stigmata –*

*apparently at some surprise to herself. She was also able to manifest tears of blood. Using suggestion, he could also heal the wounds. It is the most significant case of experimental stigmata on record.*

## Medical history of the stigmatics

*The stigmata seems to be a very rare but consistently repeated experience over time. A French doctor in the latter part of the nineteenth century compiled a list of 322, for example. There appears to be a pattern of suffering of one sort or another in the subjects.*

*Many stigmatics, when young, seem to have gone through a period of unidentified, but serious, illness; people like Therese Neumann or Dorothy Kerin. That is a consistent thing; that stigmatics have had some illness, followed by some sort of recovery from that illness. And that is often when the marks have appeared. Sometimes the illness has then recurred and the marks have continued. Where this hasn't happened there have been cases where a person has had a history of suffering, either physical or psychological, over a period of time. Heather is an obvious example as described in this book.*

*Another thing to consider is that Heather was on morphine at the time. Ethel Chapman was on substantial painkillers when she got her marks. George Hamilton, from Scotland, has taken painkillers, though he wasn't taking them when he got the marks; he has taken morphine since then, medically prescribed.*

*Such drugs are known to create or enhance hallucinations; but whether it can be argued that the drugs had something to do with the marks is debatable. We live in a modern age where people take painkillers when they have pain. In history there were no such painkillers, but there may have been natural herbs and medications that had the same effect. For example, in the seventeenth century in Italy, many alternatives were used for the production of bread, and one type of brown bread led to the description of its users being called 'bread crazies'. Of course, there are plenty of people who have taken painkillers and have not manifested the marks. The connection, therefore, while worth noting, is not likely to be very valid.*

*What is perhaps important is that medical history seems to play a part in experiencing the 'wider' range of paranormal areas. For example, in the claims of those who believe they have been abducted by aliens there are many, prominent, claimants whose history of illness is extensive and whose family relationship problems bear comparison to Heather's.*

*This is a good comparison because those who perceive UFO and Close Encounter experiences are also the closest to religious fervour when* compared to those reporting other forms of paranormal experience. Their beliefs are usually those of passionate conviction rather than reasoned analysis. In many ways, those who believe in visitors from other worlds are creating for themselves a new religion, a high-tech version of the Bible; one that is acceptable to them in their technological environment. In fact the most popular interest in UFOs is often what is known as 'Ancient Astronaut Theory' as depicted by Erich von Daniken – that the Gods were spacemen who came to Earth and created the human race.

God and the Aliens are often both seen as Saviours; and the witnesses often see themselves as The Chosen Ones, the Messengers and instruments of those Saviours. Even 'frightening' alien encounters are usually seen as part of an overall 'good' work being done. With regard to alien encounters and state of health, there are the following case in current research files: 'Rohan' has a hormone imbalance requiring hormone replacement therapy (HRT). Her mother also claims similar experiences, and has a long history of illness. Rohan also suffered the separation of her parents. She has claimed ESP, clairvoyance, alien abduction and bedroom visitation and, arguably, visions. 'Kathie' has suffered hypoglycaemia, hyperadrenalism, high blood pressure, various allergic reactions and kidney failure. She has had operations for various problems, and complications during the birth of one of her children resulted in caesarian section. Her family has a history of divorce and separations. She has a life-time history of perceived alien intervention, even forced pregnancies and a belief she gave birth to hybrid alien/human babies. 'Jane' suffers fevers and migraines. She had a stroke around the age of thirty, which left one leg limp. Describing her early life, she has said, 'I was beaten by my father every single day of my life.' Jane claims communication with entities through channelling, and has experienced several complex visions.

There are fascinating parallels with Heather in the history and paranormal claims of 'Ruth'. Ruth could produce hallucinations at will. At first they had bothered her; particularly hallucinations of her father, who had sexually interfered with her. However, she found ways to control these hallucinations, to dispense with them when she wanted to, and to hallucinate other people when she wanted to.

Most extraordinarily, on two occasions the hallucinations she produced were seen by someone else!

Heather may or may not have hallucinated, but certainly she outwardly manifested signs that others could see. Both Heather and Ruth produced major paranormal effects. Their upbringings were so similar the comparisons cannot be ignored:

| RUTH | HEATHER |
|---|---|
| *Born 1951* | *Born 1949* |

| | |
|---|---|
| *Third child of four (later discovered she had a half-sister), so brought up as one of four children* | *Third child of five (one died before Heather's birth), so brought up as one of four children* |
| *Father forged cheques* | *Believed her father might have engaged in illegal financial activities* |
| *Father spent some time in prison* | *Mother spent some time in prison* |
| *Father was in a mental hospital (schizophrenic?)* | *Mother was in a mental hospital (had leucotomy)* |
| *Father took drugs* | *Mother took drugs* |
| *Father drank too much* | *Mother drank too much* |
| *Sexually abused, raped, by her father (age 10)* | *Sexually abused, raped, by 'someone known to her' (age 7)* |
| *Witnessed her father sexually abusing a young girl* | *Heather believed she witnessed her sister being abused by a neighbour* |
| *Stayed with friends, then moved to a children's Home* | *Fostered out, told it was 'to stay with friends', then went to a childrens' Home* |
| *Brought up in children's Homes, interspersed with time at home* | *Brought up in children's Homes, interspersed with time at home* |
| *Father attempted suicide* | *Mother committed suicide* |
| *After marriage had difficulty with sex; two years before she enjoyed it* | *After marriage had difficulty with sex; around two years before she enjoyed it* |
| *Reported seeing ghosts and spirits* | *Reported seeing ghosts and spirits* |

| | |
|---|---|
| *Believed a relative was psychic* | *Believed a relative was psychic (her Uncle Tom)* |
| *Father and Grandmother were Catholic; children's Homes were Methodist* | *Heather was a Methodist, then joined a church similar to catholicism* |

It is tempting to consider that such people crave attention, and their exotic claims and manifestations are a way of achieving their needs. However, that would not detract from the stigmata since clearly it does physically exist and cannot be written off as 'just a story'.

Since stigmata has, in the case of Elizabeth K. and others, been 'tested' it cannot be written off as simple fraud, i.e. wounds dug out with an instrument to create the effect, although that might have happened once or twice.

What we might be seeing is a combination of psychosomatic response to passion with subconscious mechanical maintenance. One or two stigmatics have been seen to finger and 'worry' their wounds, no doubt maintaining them for longer than otherwise.

The sensitivity of skin to marking is a subject that has to be considered. Researchers must consider the skin condition known as 'dermatographism'. Some children discover that they can 'write' quite legibly on their own skin by scratching it gently with a fingernail. After a few seconds the skin produces a white/yellow weal-like marking surrounded by a reddened flair. It usually lasts around an hour unless reinforced, or maintained. It is a form of urticaria (nettle rash), an inflammation caused by oversensitivity to friction. Ted Harrison noted that Heather often ran her fingers round the edge of her marks when showing them, or even when passively sitting watching television. She also apparently ran her finger down the lines on her forehead that formed the cross that appeared there. Although almost certainly a subconscious action, these movements might maintain wounds already present.

In extreme cases some stigmatics might be prone to Munchausen Syndrome. This illness relates to those who want to be ill, or more specifically, to those who want to get the care and attention that illness generates; some go to the extent of seeking operations they don't need in order to fulfil their needs. Some seem to have been able to make themselves ill subconsciously, to use the 'power of the mind' to create situations where they need medical attention. Such people are usually identified as having low self-esteem, usually because of sexual or physical abuse, or by being oppressed and rejected.

*Jane, mentioned above, suffered considerable oppression and beating by her father in her youth. She believes that she was visited by aliens who educated her; a classic case of multiple personality and self-development. But she also suffered a stroke that left her leg limp. But there was an interesting occurrence during one session with her when she was being hypnotized – at her request – so that one of us (John) could speak with one of her 'aliens' (or sub-personalities, depending on your point of view). The hypnotist was careful to 'make her whole' and not leave her personalities even further divided. He gave the command that she should 'come back together again, whole and healthy' along with other reinforcing suggestions. When she came out of the trance her leg was healed. It appeared that perhaps some element of her limpness was in her mind, rather than her leg, a suggestion of Munchausen Syndrome. (Her own interpretation was even more interesting; she believed the aliens had healed her leg as a reward for allowing them to speak to John.)*

*Given that she had a classic background for it, there is some evidence of Munchausen Syndrome in Heather, but much more evidence that she sought her higher self-worth through giving to others through her SCOPE work, her work as a Samaritan and so on. However, despite her obviously genuine history of illnesses, which took her doctor a considerable time to list at her inquest, it was a surprise to hear that, contrary to her own beliefs, she was free of cancer at the time she died. It does seem that she thought herself much more unwell than she was.*

## The highest hierarchy

People seek personal development and attainment in different ways, and according to different circumstances. It is important to understand how those driven by religious fervour, including stigmatics, seek to achieve their best personal development.

There is a motivational, and self-motivational, theory known as the 'hierarchy of needs'. Put simply, it insists that there is a ladder of needs all human beings seek to satisfy, as follows:

| | | |
|---|---|---|
| 5. | Self-actualization | *becoming the person you know you are capable of becoming* |
| 4. | Ego needs | *Being recognized as of value* |
| 3. | Social needs | *Friendships and love* |
| 2. | Safety needs | *Job security, for example* |
| 1. | Physiological needs | *Food and shelter, for example* |

*The rule of this ladder is that the lowest level needs must be largely satisfied before the person 'moves on' to the next level. Food and shelter must be attained and secured before the person considers their longer-term safety needs. These needs in turn must be met before worrying about friendships, recognition and so on.*

*For those who have, in their minds, satisfied their lower level needs, the path is open for satisfying the higher level ones. Deeply religious people often have satisfied the lower needs because those needs are not strong in them. Monks, nuns, many priests, for example, live very austere lives from choice: food, a bed, a roof over their heads and a Bible have been the only possessions of some such people, with no evidence of craving for more material possessions. As such, therefore, these people can be ready to seek out level four or five on the ladder. And for some deeply religious people, perhaps 'oneness' with Christ is 'the person they know they are capable of becoming', and for a few that oneness might be displayed through the stigmata.*

*Faced with stresses caused by illness, rejection, abuse and so on, people generally respond in one of two ways; they take control of their lives by 're-creating' themselves through assertiveness training, stress management, psychotherapy and so on, or they 'give up' and fall victim to their inner illnesses. Perhaps stigmatics – and other religious converts – have found a compromise: Christ is perhaps a person who can be trusted with control over your life, and those who surrender control to Him and become his instrument might be regarded as neither 'giving up' nor 'taking control'.*

*In Heather's case, she lived a fairly simple life but never seemed to need more. She secured a home for herself and her son, basic but sufficient, and seemed to seek nothing else. The latter part of her life was mostly one of giving to others; probably her way of dealing with levels three and four. Her passion for the Lord was evident, and her desire to be the instrument of her Lord very obvious. The stigmata, to Heather, in this context, could be regarded as either a sign that the Lord had recognized that desire, or an outward sign of it to the rest of the world.*

*Clearly the stigmata was, for Heather, a sign that she was 'becoming the person she knew she was capable of becoming'.*

# Epilogue:
# But Mysteries Remain...

## Heather's death

SADLY, HEATHER was not able to see the publication of this story of her life. She passed from this world during the night of 21st-22nd November 1993.

She was strongly committed to this manuscript and helped enormously in composing it. Despite her illness and her pain she worked hard – at her insistence – through interviews with us from June onwards, and a three-day interviewing session on video-tape at our home in September. We spoke many times at her home, at our home, and on the telephone. She was able to see only a little of the style of the final manuscript but we were delighted at her one-word endorsement – 'Brilliant.'

She helped in compiling the photo-set, and allowed us to borrow all of her channelled writings and drawings, only a sample of which can be included here for reasons of space.

Heather's last days had been troubled by her illnesses. She had travelled from her Lincoln home to the south coast to spend some time with her sister, Hazel, during early October 1993. She was keen for us to speak with Hazel, and agreed with our wish to interview as many people involved with her life as practical. She arranged for us to telephone Hazel on Sunday, 10th October. When we called, Heather was quite ill; Hazel was worried, and so were we. Heather told us on the telephone that she felt 'without purpose', a phrase we were astonished to hear from her, so purpose-filled was she. But she was of course very ill; anything could have upset the delicate balance in her chemistry. We spoke for some time, and she was much more positive when the call ended; if nothing else she was looking forward to the reading, and publication launch, of this book.

She returned to Lincoln within the following week but spent a few weeks in hospital 'resting'. She came out for a short visit to her home one weekend;

when Lindsay spoke to us he was pleased with her progress, though she was obviously tired. We spoke several times and, in early November, found Heather had returned home. She told us she wanted to see us, and we wanted to see her. We fixed a time for us to go to Lincoln to visit her on Tuesday, 23rd November.

On Friday, 19th November, John (Spencer) was with Ted Harrison at Ted's home. Ted had assisted in a TV documentary of Heather and other people displaying the stigmata, and has written a book about the subject featuring Heather. John was interviewing Ted about both Heather and the stigmata generally. Ted and John telephoned Heather to confirm one or two matters; she was in fine fettle: buoyant, enthusiastic, and full of her familiar spirit. She confirmed that she was looking forward to meeting with us on the following Tuesday.

'Don't bother ringing,' she said, 'because I'm really well now.' As usual she asked after the health of our two children, and ourselves, and we exchanged good wishes. She was looking forward to the outline of the publicity for this book which she was keen to be involved in. On Monday, 22nd November we telephoned only to confirm that we might be later arriving than expected due to the sudden onset of snow and ice over that weekend, and the probable effect on traffic on the two-to-three-hour journey from our home to Lincoln. Lindsay answered the phone and told us of Heather's death the previous night.

Her death needs to be put into context because, unexpected and shocking as it is for us both to consider, Heather may have taken her own life.

The facts appear to be: Heather suffered a loss of faith and wrote a note for her son. The note asks for forgiveness, but says 'there is pain both physical and mentally'. The note was found after she was discovered to be missing, but as the coroner at the subsequent inquest pointed out, the note was undated, its time of origin uncertain. It is probable that during the night of 21st-22nd her loss of faith came to a head. She left the house, and went to the riverside near where her late husband used to work.

Her son found the note later that morning of the 22nd. Her body was found in the river later that day.

What really went through Heather's mind we shall almost certainly never know. Her confused thinking may well have arisen from her illness, or some effect of her medication. In the note that was discovered, she stated that 'they have stopped the morphine' though the doctors at the inquest denied this, stating that medication was available to her on request.

If she did take her own life, then there were a variety of ways available to her; the method she either took, or at least considered, was drowning. This is interesting; a high number of suicides by religiously driven people are by drowning. It would appear to be a form of total immersion baptism, a last way of reaching out for the Lord.

The circumstances are poignant, however. At some time during that night, probably in the early hours of the morning, she must have arranged her bed, and the note, and stolen out of the house. She would probably have visited the church in her house, and perhaps said some final prayers. Her thoughts – and her prayers – would probably have turned to Ray, to Pop, to Father Eric, to her friends in the healing ministry and, of course, to her family.

Pottering about in the kitchen, knowing Heather, she would have had a few gentle thoughts for her two cats. They had just come into the house as tiny kittens when we first met her in June and she always fussed over them; they had had to be sent to a new home just weeks before when she was hospitalized, but almost certainly her thoughts would have turned to them before she left the house.

The cold was bitter, and Heather was wearing only a light blouse and other thin clothing. No coat. The first winter snow and ice had settled over the country that weekend. The thought of her tiny, six-stone figure plodding through the darkened streets of Lincoln is a troubling one for us both. Was she alone, as her earliest vision had promised she would never again be? Or was she – even if only in her own mind – walking with Ray, or Father Eric? Did she walk around her neighbourhood, perhaps even visiting some of the local areas of her youth, many of which were just in the nearby streets, or did she go straight to the riverside?

The location at the riverside where her body was found was significant. It was on the River Witham at Smith-Clayton forge where her beloved husband Ray had worked. In some way she had gone to be with him.

On 13th December 1993 an inquest into Heather's death was held in Lincoln. Hazel Spencer (Heather's sister, and no relation to us) was there with one of the authors (John). Heather's daughter Barbara and her foster mother were present.

Hazel had stayed overnight with the authors prior to the inquest and, during the drive to Lincoln, John and she had discussed certain points that they felt ought to be taken into account. Hazel requested a pre-meeting with Dr Nigel Chapman, the coroner, and invited John to join her. The three sat together in an ante-room discussing procedures. Dr Chapman was, then and throughout, most considerate of the family's feelings and needs but, of course, was quite clear that he would discharge his duties fully and properly. Hazel could ask questions of the witnesses called, John could not as he was not a relative and had no official 'interest'. It was not, however, an *accusatorial hearing; Hazel could not make statements or make accusations, she could only ask questions. Hazel wanted John's help with framing questions but Dr Chapman made it clear he could not. With only the slightest smile he pointed out, however, that he would allow pauses during which John could 'remind' Hazel of any questions she wanted to ask and might have forgotten.*

*At the hearing Hazel was composed and logical; she questioned the witnesses on certain points that needed clarification: the availability of drugs for Heather, the results of the post-mortem.*

*The psychiatrist called to give evidence, Gillian Garden, confirmed that Heather had no suicidal tendencies. Hazel's questions to her established for the coroner that her previous suicidal 'attempts' had probably been cries for help.*

*The question of whether Heather had deliberately put herself in the river was, of course, central to the inquest. As the coroner had already pointed out, he had what might be a suicide note and a body pulled from the river. He acknowledged that a suicide verdict was probable.*

*The pathologist confirmed to the inquest that death was 'by drowning'. The police officer who was called to the scene to recover her body, PC David Wilson, confirmed that it was freezing on that river bank even during the afternoon when her body was located; it would have been more so during the night of her death. The coroner asked if a person could slip into the river from the bank by accident; the officer confirmed that it was highly possible. Through questions to the officer, Hazel was able to establish for the record what the family knew: that Heather had many times visited that spot for peaceful contemplation, and not with suicide on her mind.*

*In the end the coroner asked Hazel if she had further questions, and in a gesture that was very considerate to both Hazel and John he caught John's eye and briefly nodded to see if he had any further 'reminders' for Hazel.*

*He summed up: 'I have a note that suggests a suicidal intent, but it is undated. I have heard that there was no evidence that she was suicidal in the past, but she had been depressed for many years. She had cried for help before, but as is often the case when this sort of thing happens it is not clear that she intended to take her own life. I have heard that she had frequently visited the spot where her body was found for peaceful contemplation, and that it was a dangerous spot that night, where she could have slipped into the river. As to whether or not she committed suicide, I think it quite likely that she did, but I have to be certain beyond all reasonable doubt. I cannot be, and I shall record an open verdict on Mrs Woods' death.'*

*And an open verdict was, we are sure, the right one. Certainly it seems likely that she had a crisis of faith, reflected on her various pains, wrote a* 'goodbye' note and left the house that night, probably with intent to take her own life. But did she carry it through?

The pathologist, Dr John Harvey, reported bruising on her knees. Did she go to that spot where she had gone so often before, to be near Ray, and – on her knees – to pray to her Lord? Did her prayers tell the Lord that she was suffering a loss of faith? There is a precedent for that at least – on the cross Jesus cried to his Father 'Why have you forsaken me?' But did Heather recover her faith, return to her optimistic, fulfilled self? It had happened before during her illnesses. Did she pray, find her faith, stand up, and turn to return home? And did she slip and fall in the river? No-one will ever know for sure. It would have been easy for Dr Chapman to arrive at a simplistic verdict of suicide, given the note and other factors. It is good that he took the trouble to seek out the information that let him discharge his duties thoughtfully and properly.

## And of Heather?

She believed in the afterlife of course. The Lord's work had dominated the latter part of her life, and given her purpose. The stigmata she held to be so important was the Lord's sign, she believed, of his presence here on Earth.

If there is an afterlife, then Heather must surely be there now, at peace and free of pain. Perhaps for the first time since childhood.

If there is a world beyond this one, then perhaps she is there now; reunited with her beloved husband Ray, and safe in the arms of her Lord.

## But mysteries remain...

Heather's death has left many questions unanswered, many enigmas.

Her priest, Father Eric, believed that her stigmata would appear when she was laid out in her coffin. We passed that thought on to Heather's sister, Hazel. She was, of course, fully interested in, and supportive of, Heather's experiences, and resolved to find out if Father Eric's belief came to pass.

When Hazel went to pay her last respects to Heather in the Chapel of Rest, she determined that the stigmata had not reappeared. On one of Heather's hands she found a patch of gauze, and enquired of the coroner what it was there for. Skin had been removed, and the family was quite upset by the shock of this discovery.

What had happened related directly to the stigmata. The autopsy had been performed, and Heather's body sent to the undertakers to be laid out in the Chapel of Rest. Then the coroner had discovered that Heather was the local woman who had reported the stigmata; he recalled the body, and ordered that a patch of skin be removed for 'research' purposes. The patch of skin represented an area where the stigmata had appeared.

We spoke to the coroner about this, and he confirmed that X-ray and other tests concluded that there was no evidence of fraud on Heather's part. There were no obvious signs of fraudulent tissue damage, and no dyes or inks had been used to discolour the skin.

The coroner apologized to the family for any distress that the tissue removal caused, confirming that he had the authority for it.

The coroner's office has therefore confirmed that it has undertaken research into a phenomenon generally regarded as paranormal. Indeed, Dr Chapman showed some enthusiasm for this research. He was keen to point out that while he could not prove what the stigmata was, he was giving some confirmation of Heather's honesty.

Another question raised relates to the medication Heather received. The note found after her death, which may have been intended as a suicide note, indicates that her medication had been withdrawn. On oath, at the inquest, her doctors denied this and confirmed that painkilling drugs were available to her. It appears that, for some reason, her medication was changed from being on 'routine renewal of prescription' to 'supply on specific demand'.

More than anything, Heather's tortured plea in her note, 'they have stopped the morphine, and wouldn't even give me DF118' upset even quite senior members of her church. (DF118 was another of her painkillers.) The most extreme question raised to us was to ask whether anyone offended by Heather's stigmata could have organized circumstances to lead to her death. If that question had reflected the truth it would have been all but an accusation of murder. Almost certainly it was only the emotion of the moment, and a reflection of the mixed responses the stigmata has produced.

Less extreme suggestions were raised at the funeral, though all seem to be ruled out by the doctor's statements at the inquest: a bad, but honest, medical decision; a manipulative medical decision to do with cost savings; her doctors trying to wean her off her drugs, and so on.

Why Heather believed what she did is not resolved.

A further mystery remains. At an extreme stretch it is even suggestive of the stigmata.

When Hazel paid her last respects to Heather in the Chapel of Rest she, and her husband Warwick, saw many prominent, some deep, scars on the right side of her face. They also commented that her neck and cheek on the right side were bloated, swollen. One other person who saw the body described Heather as looking 'as if she had been mugged'. Hazel asked the pathologist where the marks had originated. On oath, categorically, and in *response to Hazel's questions and direct questions by the coroner, the pathologist stated that when he had undertaken the autopsy there had been no such marks on her.*

*We confirmed with Mr Lupton, the undertaker, that indeed Heather's face had been unmarked when her body had arrived from the pathologist. The marks had appeared while she was laying in her coffin, some six days after her death. Mr Lupton explained, 'there certainly were marks on her face, like bruise-marks ... they appeared over the weekend, between the Friday night and the Monday, between her coming back and before we had the funeral.'*

*It is apparently unusual – though not impossible – for such marks to arise several days after death. We confirmed with Heather's doctor, Dr Bhanja, that marks caused prior to death can appear after death. The time they appear depends on the thinning of the blood, and whether or not preservative chemicals are used which further thin the blood. Usually such marks would appear within forty-eight hours, but later is conceivable.*

*It seems unlikely that it is the stigmata. Certainly neither Ted Harrison, who we discussed this with, nor a senior member of Heather's church, believed it was connected to her stigmata. Both of them hold the view that the stigmata is produced in a form dependent on the way the stigmatic believes the crucifixion to have happened; these marks match no known stigmata, nor the known wounds of the suffering of Christ. Most theories of the stigmata suggest that it relates to the person's mind; marks might remain after death, but they could hardly form then.*

*But Father Eric had predicted that the marks would appear 'when she was laid out in her coffin'; if nothing else it was a near-miss...*

*Slightly closer to the classic stigmata, the pathologist indicated that Heather's knees were bruised. Quite possibly, they were bruised on her entry into the river, or by her praying prior to that. However, such marks are a recognized form of stigmata that has been manifested by others – Therese Neumann, for example. The reason for that type of mark is that Jesus is believed to have stumbled onto his knees while carrying the cross to his crucifixion. Some crucifixes have bleeding wounds in the knees of their depictions of Christ. Heather had never exhibited that form of stigmata in her life, but again it is, if nothing else, a thought-provoking near-miss on Father Eric's part.*

*The last mystery is Heather's own fate of course. It is the Great Mystery of Death that we all have to face. For her journey into death we conclude our book with a passage from Heather's own channelled writings.*

*If death should beckon me with outstretched hand,*
*And whisper softly of 'an unknown land',*
*I shall not be afraid to go,*
*For though the path I do not know,*
*I take death's hand without a fear,*
*For He who safely bought me here,*
*Will also take me back.*
*And though in many ways I lack,*
*He will not let me go alone,*
*Into the 'valley that's unknown',*
*So I reach out and take death's hand,*
*And journey to the Promised Land.*

# THE EVERYDAY MEDITATOR

## Osho

East comes to West in this fully illustrated
book filled with meditation techniques
refined over thousands of years. Meditation
is no longer a pastime but a way of life.

1–85283–504–4                               £9.99 pb


# DAVID CARRADINE'S
# TAI CHI WORKOUT

## David Carradine and David Nakahara

With photographs, diagrams and the
enlightening poetry of Lao Tsu, this book
takes you through all the stages and
elements that combine to form the ancient
and invigorating art of Tai Chi.

1–85283–475–7                               £9.99 pb

# JUST JULIA

## Julia Grant

In 1980 George Roberts took the biggest step of his life. He became Julia Grant. The operation was broadcast on television, but that was only half the story. Now, Julia tells the whole truth about life before and after surgery.

1–85283–481–1 £6.99 pb

# ANGELS

## Malcolm Godwin

An illustrated study of angels from ancient times to the present, this is a glorious celebration and comprehensive survey which will fascinate all of us who sense an angelic presence in our lives.

1–85283–506–0 £16.99 hb

# A CAT'S GUIDE TO ENGLAND

Pat Albeck

A very proper English cat takes the reader on a journey round England. With Pat Albeck's glorious watercolours this is an irresistible treat for everyone who loves cats and England.

1–85283–526–5                    £8.99 hb


# THE TRUE NATURE OF THE CAT

Dr John Bradshaw

Britain's foremost expert on pet behaviour separates the facts from popular myths and misconceptions, allowing the dedicated cat lover to understand what it is really like to be a cat.

1–85283–513–3                    £14.99 hb

## OTHER TITLES AVAILABLE FROM BOXTREE